COST OF CLOSURE

The Cost Series, Book 1

A debut novel by
Amanda Purser

D1247660

Contact publisher for more information:

www.queensbriarpress.com

queensbriarpress@gmail.com

ISBN: 979-8-9866658-0-1

Cover Design by: Nikolas Bicknell (Nik Designs)

A *trigger warning* is in effect for those who may be sensitive to graphic content about sexual assault/rape, abuse, suicide, traumatic events, and murder. Please be advised and proceed with discretion.

Resources and information for those experiencing personal traumas, in a mental health crisis, or recovering survivors are available in the back of this book for your consideration. No one should struggle in silence or alone.

66

This book is dedicated to my father, who taught me how to tell a good story. I'm forever grateful for his guidance over the years. Here's to being more than ordinary, I love you.

99

1

Nightmares

Her scream pierced through the silence like a tornado siren in the dead of night. Ray's eyes flutter open with a pounding heart and sweaty palms. He releases his tight grip on the steering wheel, and the blood returns to his white knuckles. Ray hates awakening from these nightmares. The eerie faceless woman has revisited his subconscious. Once more, she has left him shaken and disoriented.

He squirms in place, unable to reposition himself. His legs are bound by khaki pants and boxers, bunched around his ankles near the brake pedal. His overworked manhood tries desperately to escape the brisk morning air yet finds nowhere to hide in Ray's bare lap. He looks at the passenger seat where an empty whisky bottle sits alone. Wiping the condensation from the windshield reveals the sign for Taft Liquor. Ray didn't make it very far after picking up that second bottle last night.

With a throbbing head, he glances at his watch through squinted eyes. Abruptly pulling up his pants, as Ray noticed it's already past seven, and the church crowd will be out soon. He slides off the ripped-up leather seat of his old pickup, unable to wait any longer, with his bladder ready to burst. Stepping out into the crisp October morning, he glances over each shoulder. Ray grunts through the pain as he stretches and yawns while relieving himself onto the back tire. His body regrets the sleeping arrangements from last night.

In the truck, Ray searches through the glovebox, then around the floorboard of his passenger side. Finally recovering a small orange bottle, only to discover it's empty. "Shit," he utters aloud while tossing the container back onto the pile of debris. He needs more medication, and a refill isn't likely until tomorrow when the pharmacy reopens. Ray decides to record a message for his psychiatrist before he forgets. While the line trills in his ear, he starts driving the few miles back to his trailer. After a couple more rings, the doctor herself picked up, to Ray's surprise.

"Good morning. This is Dr. Pfeiffer; how can I help you?"

"Oh, hey doc, I didn't expect to catch you in person. On a Sunday? That's dedication! Oh, sorry, it's umm, Townes, uh, Ray, I mean…sorry," he fumbles through his words.

"Mr. Townes, thank you. I am rather dedicated to my patients, but you should know it's Monday morning. Are you okay? Do you need an emergency appointment?" she asks with concern.

"Oh no, ma'am, I do not. I apologize; I was mistaken. I'm not sleeping well, and I've had several of those migraine headaches lately. And the meds are working, but I'm all out again."

"I see. Well, Mr. Townes, I'd love to call that in for you, and I'm glad the medicine is working. But, as I mentioned at our last visit three weeks ago, you need to be consistent if you want therapy to work. We can have a quick chat right now. I don't have an appointment for thirty minutes and I already have you on the phone," Dr. Pfeiffer insists.

Ray truly feels desperate now. He knows he needs to be straightforward with her yet is unsure if he can trust her. After all, it was the department that required this evaluation. Dr. Pfeiffer will be giving them updates. He must consider everything he shares with her and be cautious moving forward. Ray needs to play their game if retirement with benefits is still an option. He agrees to proceed with the impromptu session.

"Have you been abstaining from sex and alcohol according to our plan? It's important to be honest, Townes, your health depends on it."

"My health isn't the concern here, ma'am, but yes. No sex. No drinking. I'm doing what I need to. I just feel like—I'm running out of time. These last few months have been a nightmare," he admits.

"Well, administrative leave is usually difficult, even though you went through this a couple of years ago. Accepting when you need a break or stepping away from the badge and responsibility never gets easier. Especially for you, Townes, with your career completely encompassing your life."

Dr. Pfeiffer tries to be reassuring but only reminds Ray how lonely his life has become. A distant and bitter ex-wife, no kids, and not even a dog to share his trailer with. If he wasn't an alcoholic sex addict, he might have all the qualities of a great detective. Yet he's been unable to manage his addictions for years, and his career has borne the burden. His perverse thoughts darkened, and his desires became harder to alleviate, even with masturbation and the occasional hookup from local dive bars. His cravings are becoming so insatiable that not even porn can help at times.

Dr. Pfeiffer continues, "Listen, Ray, you should know that the 31st has reached out. Your lieutenant from Special Crimes went to bat for you with the chief and your commander. I got an email on Friday asking my opinion on your return."

Ray begins to listen intently as he parks his truck in the grassless patch that is his driveway. He observes the morning sun reflecting off his rusted tin roof and focuses on what Dr. Pfeiffer adds. "The captain wanted to know about your progress and any updates on your treatment. I don't think it's my place, and it isn't official, but I believe they want you back, Ray." She continues after a brief thought. "I know you don't trust me. And I don't think you're being completely honest. But I know that we can get back on track! You should continue to adhere to our abstinence plan and make your treatment a priority. Then I can recommend you back to duty. Sooner than you might think," she confidently states.

"Well, I have to say, doc, that's better news than I planned to hear this morning. I didn't think I made much of an impression on Lieutenant Zimmer before my admin leave. Especially for him to defend me and request my return. But I'm glad he did because I need to get back to duty! Being a cop is all I have, and I'm running out of time to retire with respect. I'll do whatever it takes to get that recommendation. *Please*, I can't wait much longer." Ray admits.

"Okay, let's do this. You come in this Friday; I can do nine a.m. We'll resume our weekly meetings from there. In-person, no excuses. You must do the work, Ray. It will be worth it." Dr. Pfeiffer concludes.

"You got it, Dr. P., I will be there at nine sharp. I'm committed to this doc. You will see. You can let the brass know I'm ready!"

"I look forward to giving them that message, Ray. We discussed your healthy outlets, and you remember the mantra, right?"

Her question catches Ray off guard. "Oh yes, I recite it every morning in the mirror, like you advised. And I have to say, I feel more—at ease," he innately lies.

Now inside, Ray's frantically searching his desk drawers for the envelope on which the mantra was scribbled six weeks ago. Yet the doctor doesn't ask more about it and takes him at his word. This minor manipulation brings some temporary satisfaction, which Townes has missed. Not having any control or power without his badge is taking a more significant toll than he expected this time.

"That's good to hear, I thought you would enjoy that positive reinforcement. I'm so glad you made the call this morning, Mr. Townes. I will get your prescription called in and respond to your commander. He'll know the requirements I've set up for a recommendation back to duty. I'll keep him posted on your progress as well. I hope you see this as a fresh start. Let's get your badge back, *detective*!" Her excitement is almost contagious. Ray thanks Dr. P. for her time before ending their call.

Gazing into the bathroom mirror, Ray hardly recognizes the face staring back. His beard is thick, with highlights of silver sprouting like wildflowers. The bags under his eyes are darker and puffier than he has ever noticed. Undressing completely, he finds large purple and green bruises on his legs and right hip. Pressing into them to ensure he still feels pain, Ray doesn't recall acquiring these contusions. A failing memory may be the worst side effect, after being tethered to the bottle for so long.

His trembling hand reminds him how long it's been since his last drink. "Get a fucking grip, Ray," he says aloud to his unfamiliar reflection. He hates feeling weak and dependent on the bottle. He gets in the shower and masturbates to regain some control.

Raymond Townes chooses to focus on the only healthy outlet he does have. He puts a bottle of water and two beef jerky sticks into an old tackle box. Gathering his net and fishing poles he heads outside. Ray loads the gear into his pickup truck and hitches his little bass boat, the *Cayenne Cruiser*. Headed for Lake Gerbeau, he considers Dr. P.'s advice of "positive affirmations and focal breathing." Ray laughs to himself, recalling her initial "Yoga and meditation" recommendation. He imagines himself in a small, stuffy studio, surrounded by women in tight pants, bending and contorting in various positions. Him trying to control his impulses and an erection, while simultaneously clearing his mind and relaxing—*what a joke.*

He only further convinces himself that Dr. Pfeiffer doesn't understand him. How could she? For so long, Ray has been hiding the truth about his devious depths from everyone around him. He doesn't know how to be open about his addictions. He fears the repercussions of his behavior, and the consequences of his actions having long-term effects. He can't confide in anyone—they couldn't handle it, nor trust him after. It was too risky and almost torturous even to ponder.

Arriving at Lake Gerbeau, Ray unloads the old bass boat. Hopping into the *Cayenne Cruiser,* he slowly trolls into the calm waters. For now, he gets to let all the thoughts fade away and concentrate on his favorite hobby.

Approaching a familiar spot to anchor, Ray considers *this* could be his therapy. With a quick cast, the line swings away, and the lure plops into the cool, murky water surrounding him. He follows the ripples as they fade from his line in a hypnotizing pattern.

Ray cherishes the temporary solace he finds on the lake. Knowing the ominous thoughts will soon return, since the peace never lasts too long.

2

Reinstatement

Three weeks after the agreement with Dr. Pfeiffer, Ray is back on the *Cayenne Cruiser*. Heading towards the dock from an early morning excursion, his cell buzzes. Ray quickly answers, hoping it's the news he's needed.

"Hey, Lieutenant Zimmer, how are you this lovely morning?" Ray asks lightheartedly.

"Good morning, Townes. I don't think I've ever heard you so excited to hear from me," the perky young lieutenant joked.

"Well, sir, I've had a lot of time to reflect. I'm doing many things differently as of late. I've thought about what you said when I signed my admin papers in June. And you were right, I was being selfish. To the entire department and especially the team. I uh, I apologize. There's a lot I should be sorry for, and I'm ready to take some responsibility," Ray says, without wasting any time.

"That's great to hear, Townes. And all the updates the commander has been getting are looking good too. He's confident that your drinking is under control. Captain Thompson also explained that you've done a lot of work in therapy, especially over the last few weeks. He believes we're ready to have you back, *detective*."

Hearing that title roll off the L.T.'s tongue gave Ray some pride. The anticipation of having his badge and gun back was stimulating his excitement. He suddenly considers the additional responsibility and stress attached to new cases. Concern sets in for the first time since he proclaimed to his therapist that he undoubtedly wanted this. Ray remembers that Lt Zimmer pleaded with the brass for his reinstatement, and he dredges up some confidence.

"Hearing that word 'detective' does something to me, sir. And I have to say, also, that Dr. P. told me about you standing up for me. While it's unexpected, I must admit I'm relieved. So, thank you, sir."

"Detective Townes, you're more than welcome. I know how much of an asset you've been to our unit, especially the Special Crimes Team. Hell, you practically started this task force, Townes. This team is why our parish didn't have a significant rape backlog for years. Or a stack of cold cases a mile long. If you could've found some better resources and outlets—" Zimmer cuts himself off, taking a second to analyze his advice before he continues. "This isn't easy work, Ray. And we understand your sacrifices for this team and the Beau Ridge PD. And while there was some apprehension, because let's face it, none of us know what you're capable of. We all agree it would be in the best interest of our precinct and the town of Beau Ridge to have you back in action!" Zimmer concludes.

Townes agrees that starting the Special Crimes Team in 1991, was partly his idea. Only a year into their inauguration is when his urges began to intensify. Ray started drinking on duty in an unsuccessful attempt to suppress his hormones and emotions. He was a few years removed from an affair with his superior officer, Lieutenant Ele Miles. Ray became convinced that throwing himself into his work would allow him to forget her, but he was wrong.

Ray's obsession with Lt Miles consumed him. His intense sexual appetite and desires became overwhelming. He loved becoming numb—initially. But he was usually too weak to stop himself once he started drinking. Townes knows needs the watchful eye of the force but is scared to have them back in his life. He won't remain in therapy nor follow the abstinence plan without accountability. What's worse, Ray can't think of anything other than that badge, which might stop him from drinking himself to death.

"Sir, you have my word and that of my psychiatrist. I assure you we're doing everything possible to find better coping mechanisms. I didn't realize what a toll this job taking on me for so many years. I've never taken my sobriety seriously until now, and for that, I'm sorry. I'm also sorry for the colossal shits I've taken on this unit over my 19-year tenure with BRPD. Most men don't get to return; they don't always get to clean up their messes and right their wrongs. But I want this, sir, and I'm ready to finish my career the right way."

"I believe you, Townes, and I know that you deserve another chance to depart the right way. The SCT is under contract for a complete overhaul. We have some federal funding coming through next spring. They want to bring on more investigators, and we should have a few new detectives promoted soon. This is what we were discussing before you took off in June. It's the revamp you've wanted for years. So, you should return and help project us into the next phase." Zimmer concludes.

"Well, that's good to know," Ray states warily, knowing more money and eyes mean more opportunities to get caught slipping. Suddenly, Townes is nervous and already doubting the claims he just made.

"Indeed, Townes, it's certainly good for Beau Ridge! We're ready to continue fulfilling the original purpose of this team. To find answers, piece together the tough crimes, and get these victims justice. Like you explained to me in 2002 when I got here," Zimmer tries to reassure Ray before a quick segue. "Oh, and the Natalie Ruiz case is going to trial, as we knew was coming. Arturo Ruiz was arraigned last week. They finally set trial proceedings to begin this coming Monday. And Townes, you should know that you're on the prosecution's list to testify."

Those words fall onto the stoic detective with concern. "Um, okay. But are you sure, sir? I mean, there are other investigators involved. I don't know if my testimony is one of uh, *value*." Ray questions, trying not to sound condescending.

Zimmer assures Townes that he is ready and more prepared than anyone else. Although, he admits that Townes' competency from the investigation will be in question. He explains that Mr. Ruiz's attorney intends to bring up Townes' tumultuous career. He will try to slander the 31st and reduce their credibility for allowing Townes to work so many cases while clearly under duress.

After talking in circles for a minute, Ray decides Zimmer may be on his side, but he's still very much caught up in the political power struggles of the unit.

Townes now knows that his reinstatement is not based on merit. This isn't a final effort to let him retire with pride. This is about the precinct. This is about getting one more conviction and closing this big case. The naïve young officer may have admitted how vital Ray is to them right now. Listening to Lt Zimmer's attempted justification only angers Ray more. He keeps his cool and assures his boss that he'll be preparing for the case and will be ready for the court proceedings. The relieved lieutenant ends the call and leaves Ray to reconsider his future.

Ray drives down the country roads near the lake on his way home from fishing. He has a few miles to burn and allow his anger to subside. The rage only builds stronger, intensifying with every passing minute. Like roots into his soul, anchoring Ray to his disdain for this profession. He wants nothing more than to grab a bottle and chug it down, until every sensation is gone, and thought silenced.

It's been two weeks since Raymond Townes had a drink, and he doesn't want to backtrack on this progress. He recalls his body's intense detox during the last relapse. He refuses to endure that pain and discomfort again. Instead, he resorts to an older technique that he hasn't used in months.

Back at his trailer, Ray rummages through his bedroom closet, until he uncovers a faded brown briefcase with scratched-up bronze corners. As he opens it up, his senses heighten, and hormones rise like lava, fueling his internal passion with a warmth that takes over. He stares down at the collection of VHS pornography tapes that he's been holding onto for decades. Finally, some excitement is back. While this could be a mistake, Ray fears drinking and finding a partner could have far worse consequences.

He chooses a title and inserts it into his bedroom VCR. Grabbing the bottle of lube from the side table drawer, he goes to work on himself until he finds relief. Short-lived, but worth it, he decides.

3

Ruiz Review

Townes is inside the Special Crimes trailer on Monday morning, about 45 minutes before anyone else would arrive at work. Wanting to take a moment alone to appreciate being back. Ray begins reacquainting himself with the Natalie Ruiz case. He could be called upon to testify at any moment and must be prepared. Staring at Arturo Ruiz's mugshot and then back at the crime scene photos, he thinks about how angry this man must've been with his wife. The woman who birthed his two babies. The woman he gave his last name to and promised to love and cherish in front of a judge, their family, and God. Since Arturo is a self-proclaimed, 'devout Catholic' marriage had to mean something.

Arturo Ruiz's entire alibi was that he was with his grandmother, praying on her rosary beads and reading from his late grandfather's bible. You might think that was solid coming from Catholics, yet no one believed him. How could you when you knew their history and saw her body? Her face was unrecognizable. The fractures around her eyes left them swollen shut and bruised so deeply that they appeared black. She had four front teeth knocked out, and one was still in her throat during the autopsy. Two more were found inside her stomach. She was still alive at that point. As the coroner concluded from the blood and saliva she swallowed when choking on her teeth. Natalie's bottom lip was lacerated so significantly that it was hanging there, exposing her shattered gum line. *This poor woman,* Ray thought. *How could Arturo look at that face and do so much damage?*

Ray closed the manila folder and sat there wondering whether this man was capable of this atrocity, or innocent after all. He pulls out two more folders from a Cold Cases box and opens each file on his desk. The two unsolved murder cases were from a couple of years ago, in 2001. They belonged to Tina Richard and Roxanne "Roxy" Williams. Townes takes some time to compare the cases. He remembers his thoughts from months ago, before his administrative separation. He still sees several similarities between these three cases and believes the Special Crimes Team may need to take another look at the possible connections.

Townes recalls how all three women were dumped in various places, separate from where the murders occurred. All three had been beaten and likely raped. Unfortunately, no viable DNA was recovered from the bodies. He knew that Roxy's case was different from the other two. She was 52 years old, while Tina and Natalie were in their twenties. Roxy died from a heart attack, thought to have occurred from extensive torture. Based on her family and coworkers' statements, it could have been up to 24 hours with her attacker. There was evidence of sexual trauma and electrocution, which Roxy sustained during her abduction.

Although all three women had similar beatings, no solid connections were ever made. Ray believes Roxy's case wasn't taken seriously from the start. Roxy Williams was profiled based on old habits, and their prejudice didn't allow for a proper investigation. Due to her past drug usage and being a known prostitute, she had a history in the West Beau Ridge industrial area for nearly twenty years.

However, Roxy's family insisted otherwise to Townes when the 31st took over her cold case last year, in 2002. Just as they had insisted to West Beau Ridge PD when they first opened the case, in 2001. The statements claimed that Roxy had been clean for years, and she was holding down a job at a local convenience store for months before her murder. The investigators' bias didn't sway. Townes even pointed out to Cpt Thompson that Roxy's toxicology report was clean, so he didn't suspect this to be drug-related and the evidence didn't support the theory either. The superiors still attributed it to her previous prostitution connections. They told Townes to place the case back into a "cold status" until they had anything solid. He still doesn't have much to go on now, outside of his instincts. But something is telling Ray that these cases all need a closer look.

He sits back in his old office chair. Gripping the cracked leather armrests, Ray looks around the cold, empty trailer. There's still a familiarity in this workspace, even though it's been nearly four months since he was last in here. The dust and clutter he spent years collecting have vanished. This trailer no longer had the same appeal it once did. *Have I come back in vain?* Ray thinks to himself.

Just then, Lt Zimmer walks through the door and captures his attention. "Detective Townes, in early I see. Impressive." The chipper lieutenant states with a big grin. "I snagged breakfast from the work-call-briefing. Still a glazed fan, I hope?" Zimmer asks while setting down a coffee and a small paper bowl with two glossy donuts inside.

"Thank you, sir. The flavor isn't important if the coffee is strong." Townes smirks.

Ray gets briefed by his superior officer and caught up with any pertinent information circulating through the unit. Zimmer is suddenly distracted by the three open files sprawled across Townes' desk. "You already jumping into the cold cases? I thought you were going to focus on the Ruiz case. For now, at least?" Zimmer asks with confusion.

"Oh, yes sir, I am. Um. I can refresh your memory if you need on these other two here, Tina Richard and Ms. Roxy Williams. I don't know if you recall my *theory,* if you will, that we threw around back in June before I took off?" Ray asks.

The lieutenant interjects, "I do recall, and I'm quite familiar with both cases. But I'm unsure what they have to do with the Ruiz trial. Detective, I will be clear here, we won't jump to conclusions or make wild accusations. Our precinct, especially the SCT, is under a fucking microscope right now!" Zimmer snaps while growing agitated.

Ray sits up straight, somewhat embarrassed. He's still learning to respect his superior, despite being 10 years his senior. Ray doesn't want to overstep his boundaries further, which he's already miscalculated.

"You just got your badge back, for Christ's sake, Townes. I'll leave it at that. I spoke with Chief Diehl and the District Attorney this morning. They intend to see a smooth and quick trial for Mr. Ruiz. This has been a shit show from the start, and we're barely back on track. Please don't derail us again! I, uh, I need more coffee," Zimmer stammers as he darts outside, letting the thin metal door slam behind him.

Ray understands Lt Zimmer's outburst. He doesn't need a reminder of the public outcry after Natalie's body was identified. Arturo's weak alibi, plus the rumors of them having marital issues were more than enough for him to be the prime suspect. The outrage intensified when the news broke—three former domestic violence charges between the couple. Arturo's recent arrest was only nine months before her death. On those charges, Natalie claimed Arturo fractured her forearm in another violent dispute. Arturo plead not guilty and stuck to his story that "She was drunk and fell down the stairs," and that he "never touched her."

Natalie, however, unexpectedly refused to testify during the trial. The charges were dropped after the prosecution's case fell apart. The assistant D.A. at the time, Robert Lange, took this loss personally. He's convinced Arturo was responsible for Natalie's re-cant. He's now the acting District Attorney, and Lange intends to, "… finally serve justice to Mrs. Natalie Ruiz and her two beautiful children. They never should've gone back into the arms of that monster, Arturo Ruiz."

Townes understands the city's position and why they felt it was necessary to prosecute this man. Yet, Raymond Townes also understands that Mr. Ruiz will not have a fair trial. There are already people surrounding the courthouse with signs and chants. They call him a "woman beater" and suggest he will "burn in Hell." Some blame the police and the city for allowing Arturo out the first time. Others were there to pray and pay their respects to Natalie Ruiz.

A group of her family and close friends set up a vigil with an altar on the sidewalk nearby. Candles were lit, and tears were shed, as they knelt and said their goodbyes. Pictures of Natalie's beautiful face were on display—before it took the brunt end of a merciless beating. Her lips and facial features were all intact, her hair was long and perfectly curled. A high school graduation picture was on display in her cap and gown. Natalie held their daughter Iliana, who was only nine months old then. She was six when her mother was murdered. Iliana sheltered her younger brother Israel from most of their parents' struggles and hardships over the years. She is used to the chaos, sadly. But even Iliana was shocked and confused to learn of her mother's outcome, especially at her father's hands.

Townes recalls seeing the siblings back in August of 2000—sitting on a bench in the station's waiting room. They were scared and confused, their eyes shifting from each passing adult while they held each other tight. The siblings waited for their aunt Nikki to pick them up the night Arturo was arrested. This was following Natalie's identification finally being confirmed, four months after her body was discovered. Ray knows their lives must've been shattered since then. Losing both parents and learning about the dark and unsightly skeletons in their closets, must be devastating at their ages. Their childhood was stolen, and the Ruiz kids will never be the same.

Ray accepts that there's only one conceivable way to get Iliana and Israel's father back. The Special Crimes Team would have to prove that Arturo did not kill their mother. Unfortunately, the only viable option was in Natalie's rape kit, which Townes was solely responsible for destroying. He knew her rape kit was positive for sexual activity. The semen found inside Natalie could have been evaluated, but it never made it to the lab. Instead, it burned to ash inside the trunk of the patrol car Townes wrecked in a drunken accident. Ray has made many mistakes while drinking, but the evidence lost during that incident affected the Ruiz family significantly. Townes will never forgive himself for that egregious error.

The rape kit was the primary evidence that Natalie had sex with someone before her murder. Arturo reported that they argued late the night before, which prompted him to stay at his grandmother's house—wanting to avoid confrontation with his estranged wife. Natalie's sister, Nikki, came to pick up their kids. Claiming that Natalie told her she "needs to get away from Arturo," and that "the kids should be safe in the meantime."

Arturo swears that Natalie must have left their home on foot, after the kids were picked up, since he had their only vehicle all night at his grandmother's. He claims to have called their landline several times that night, in April of 2000. When Natalie still didn't respond by the following evening, Arturo asked Nikki to go by and check on her sister. Mr. Ruiz added in his statement that Natalie "would often go for walks." She almost always ended up at a neighborhood bar, The Parish Pub, about ten blocks away from the Ruiz home. There, Natalie would drink in excess until she was cut off in one way or another. Arturo was called on multiple occasions by various bartenders to take her home. By then, Natalie was unable to walk and often passed out cold.

Despite Natalie's reputation and history, no one believed Arturo. Least of all, Natalie's little sister, Nikki. She called the police to report Natalie missing that evening in April of 2000 after she went to check the house. She told them instantly that she believed Arturo was responsible. After the police heard

Nikki's statement, they dug into the Ruiz family's past. The investigator's started to imply that Arturo had planned an elaborate scheme to get the kids away and have an alibi intact. So that he could finally get rid of his wife, whom he couldn't seem to get along with or handle any longer.

Nikki's statement implied that when the couple fought, things would get violent. She admitted that her older sister did instigate most arguments that Nikki was around to witness. While Natalie was a beautiful woman to everyone around her, she reportedly had low self-esteem and regretted being a young mother. She would consume alcohol to feel better but always took it too far. When Natalie drank in excess, she would get physical with anyone in her way. Nikki insinuated that her sister had a problem with alcohol, but admits, "I don't know the full extent. Natalie rarely burdens our family with personal matters, especially incidents that arise from partying."

The statements also implied that Arturo didn't drink at all and hated that his wife had a dependency on alcohol. He was also bothered by how "angry and violent Natalie gets while intoxicated."

Reading back over the statements from Natalie's file is alarming. Townes remembers how Arturo got this all pinned on him so quickly. He reaffirms that this trial will not end in Arturo Ruiz's favor. Most of all, Ray feels bad for their kids Iliana and Israel. Raymond Townes knows he will never forget this case. Like so many tragedies he's worked with the Special Crimes Team. These mementos are etched into his mind forever.

4

Perjury

The following day is a chilly November morning at the Beau Ridge Federal Courthouse. Newly reinstated Det Townes takes the stand in the murder trial of Arturo Ruiz. He carefully answers strategic questions from District Attorney, Robert Lange. Townes repeatedly lies on the stand. Especially when asked about a rape kit or if there was any evidence of sexual activity. Townes says a test was, "run through the lab," yet he claims the results to provide a DNA match were "inconclusive" and that the report had been "misplaced." Ray admits this was his wrongdoing, although nothing of the drunken car accident that engulfed his patrol car and obliterated the evidence. Townes implied that it was simply, "a clerical error," but that he had "personally reviewed the report before it disappeared."

The judge appeared to be on the side of the prosecution. She made it difficult for Mr. Ruiz's inexperienced attorney to object or call into question the reputation of Det Townes or the wrongdoings of the Beau Ridge Police Department. Judge Burns wouldn't allow the defense to "*slander* the police force." Despite the claims all being true. The D.A. went as far as explaining away Det Townes' previous leave of absence in 2000. Claiming it was, "a psychological evaluation period, which was both necessary and required by the precinct, following a traumatic case within his line of duty. And this case—" D.A. Lange continued. "…finding Mrs. Ruiz in that horrific condition. Investigating the inner workings of this reprehensible and very personal crime, was nothing short of traumatic! Even for a seasoned detective like Mr. Townes." This caused Ray to bow his head into his hands in apparent disbelief. To Townes' amazement, the jury responds sympathetically to his gesture, furthering the prosecution's agenda.

When questioned on the most recent admin leave Townes just returned from, Judge Burns sustains DA Lange's objection, and had that remark stricken from the record, as they deemed it irrelevant to the Ruiz trial. The prosecution wouldn't admit that Townes was required to seek therapy and get help with his substance abuse issues, all mandated by the precinct this past June.

Mr. Ruiz's amateur lawyer attempted some defense for him, questioning why Natalie didn't have an order of protection in place. Or why she hadn't filed any additional charges since the last accusation against her husband?

This is spun as "victim-blaming a battered wife." Then delivered to the jury with another accusatory blow. "Perhaps the fear Arturo put into his beautiful, young wife was deeper than any of us could ever know." Chilling, coming from the Cajun draw and convincing demeanor of Robert Lange.

The jury was affected. They're eating up every spoon-fed lie, precisely as the prosecution intended. Mr. Ruiz's ill-equipped counsel is outmatched against D.A. Lange. Yet the green attorney boldly attempts to call Arturo and Natalie's oldest child Iliana to the stand. A close family friend who is also a social worker testifies instead. Claiming that the children were both traumatized by this entire situation. "Putting Iliana through a trial could do further, possibly irreparable damage," she claimed. Judge Burns sided with this woman and doesn't allow them to put Iliana Ruiz on the stand.

The defense was out of options and lacked any support. Although Judge Burns and D.A. Lange made it easy for Townes to lie, he couldn't help but feel responsible for railroading Arturo. The graphic pictures of Natalie's unrecognizable face and body are on display in the courtroom. The past charges Arturo faced from years of a tumultuous relationship were aired. Compiled with his lack of a credible alibi, or any witnesses to what happened to Natalie. Most of that courtroom was convinced that Arturo Ruiz should pay for this tragedy.

After the closing arguments, the jury deliberated for only 95 minutes. They find Arturo Ruiz guilty of first-degree murder in the death of his wife, Natalie Marie Ruiz.

Townes was done for the day after the trial and needed a break, so he wastes no time heading out. He is deeply bothered by his lies and the stress of this job flooding back over him. He drives around aimlessly with a heavy heart and clouded mind. Ray Townes considers calling for a therapy session, but truly wants good sex. He doesn't want to make the mistake of coming on to his doctor and jeopardizing everything they have already established.

Unfortunately, Ray no longer has contacts or anyone around for a casual hookup. And he isn't in the mood to talk or get acquainted with someone new. He sits in the parking lot of Taft Liquor for a while, contemplating the results of another relapse. He doesn't want to give in to his craving so soon, yet he can't summon any self-control at this moment.

Becoming weaker and in need of a quick release from this negativity, Ray hops out of his truck and instinctively walks right into the liquor store. Inside, he places a small bottle of whiskey on the counter along with a pack of chewing gum from the display next to him.

Before pulling off, he unwraps a piece of the gum and takes in the strong cinnamon aroma, inhaling deeply with closed eyes. An effortless smile comes over Ray's face as his mind travels back in time to Ele Miles and her gum vice. She was constantly chewing on a piece and preferred this spicy cinnamon kind during their affair. He remembers the flavor lingering on his tongue long after she was gone. For a while, he could still feel her body on his. He remembered how his hands felt running through her long brown hair—grabbing and rubbing all over her as they made love. Their passionate encounters have left an impression on Ray. He longs for another opportunity to have his way with Ele Miles. Ray feels things could be different for them now. He sneers while accepting that they won't ever get a redo at this point.

Arriving home, Raymond chugs the entire bottle of whisky to drown the loneliness and suppress the sexual urges, which have resurfaced intensely. He's ashamed of his lack of willpower. Stark reminders of his failed relationships linger, and Ray agonizes over his impulsivity. He must dig deeper and find the strength if he will survive this reinstatement.

He knows this bottle won't help him for long, but for tonight his choice is made. He'll deal with the consequences of this decision tomorrow. As usual, putting off responsibility until it's more convenient.

5

New Day, New Body

Ray awakes the following day to his phone ringing from under his pillow. He peeks at the screen with a throbbing head to view the missed call. Seeing it was Lt Zimmer, instant confusion sets in. Sitting up in his bed, Ray looks around his trailer to determine what happened last night. His eyes fix on the empty whisky bottle lying on the floor at his bedside. He remembers stopping at Taft, but this was a different brand, and much bigger than his original buy.

Ray suddenly realizes that he had a guest. The other pillow and blankets were slept on, yet she is nowhere in sight. He hates that he can't remember a single thing after that first bottle. Ray knows he must have been blackout drunk *again*.

He picks up the phone on the second ring this time, trying to convince the L.T. that he had a bad signal on the *Cayenne Cruiser* and has been out on the lake since dawn. Zimmer buys Ray's improvised lie but is more concerned with their new case.

Zimmer's tone is authoritative yet concerned. Townes assures his superior that he's ready and can manage this.

Ray quickly gets dressed and heads out for his first full day of real police work since reinstatement. Eager to start a new case, yet nervous at the same time. Ray glances at the red gum wrappers discarded onto the bench seat, as he climbs into his truck. Another smile naturally comes over his face. Somehow the thought of Ele Miles and her memory is calming. Which is a welcomed change of pace, considering she used to leave a pit in his stomach and the impression of eternal emptiness when she first moved away.

After he arrives to work, Lt Zimmer briefs Townes on the body found four days ago near a nature preserve on the outskirts of their parish. The body was already decomposing and had considerable damage from violent physical assaults and sexual torture. The words hang there while Townes makes eye contact with Zimmer. They share a mutual understanding that the similarities are striking.

Their victim is Justine Nichols, a 24-year-old Beau Ridge native. She dropped out of school at Beau Ridge University (BRU) last semester, in the spring of 2003. According to statements, Justine began bartending at various local places for money. She was likely abducted sometime in September, and its now mid-November. For more than 45 days, she was held and tortured in an unknown location.

Zimmer reads from the Autopsy report and explains, "Justine was experimented on with amateur medical treatments. She had several lacerations stitched with odd patterns. Other wounds were affixed with super glue. Ms. Nichols suffered compound fractures of the tibia and fibula on her right leg. As well as a minor fracture in her right femur. The trauma to cause these injuries would have occurred from what the examiner described as a 'fall from high above.' Off a tall ladder or scaffold-like structure, perhaps. Those fractures weren't treated and caused an infection inside Justine, which spread to her blood. Dr. Cox hypothesizes in his notes. '*Ms. Nichols suffered severe compound fractures, which should have resulted in an amputation of her leg, to save her life. Since treatment was not sought, it created staphylococcus and eventually osteomyelitis (infection in her bones). The infections caused severe sepsis, which shut down her organs.*' There were no antibiotics or pain relievers present in her bloodwork. They did discover rabies immune globin in her labs." Zimmer concludes.

"Jesus, the poor girl had rabies too?" Townes blurts out with concern.

"No, I'm told this is from getting the shot to prevent the rabies virus, if exposed. They assume she was being *treated* with it for the infections. Which obviously wasn't effective." Zimmer explains.

"Okay, got it. That's interesting," Townes says.

The two men exchange some ideas and try to understand what the evidence highlights. Townes grabs the other three case files from his desk for Tina Richard and Roxy Williams, then includes Natalie Ruiz's file. He lays them out on the conference table the pair were sitting across. He watches the lieutenant slide Natalie's folder away from the others.

"Detective, regardless of what theories we cook up in here. Regardless even if we are on the right track, the Ruiz case is *closed.* Unless we have concrete evidence. Got it? I'm talking written in fucking stone, smoking-gun, definitive proof. Before we even *glance* at that folder again. For both our sakes. Okay?"

"Sir, yes, sir!" Ray responds militantly. Understanding the lieutenant's position and not wanting to overstep again.

The pair agree that while there are many similarities, there are also several inconsistencies. Neither are experts in serial murders, but for the first time since Ray theorized, they finally agreed. They could be looking at the same killer for each murder, and all four cases. Zimmer points out that the women are of different ages, races, and appearances, with various socioeconomic backgrounds too. Townes agrees that finding a pattern among their victims will be difficult.

Both men decide to continue investigating for Justine Nichols, as she is their priority. They can't help but focus on how Justine was treated. This person was abusing her, torturing, and experimenting on her young body. Yet her wounds were dressed in bandages and medical tape. Showing she was cared for in some way. They consider a veterinarian not in current practice, or one who dropped out of their medical training. Especially with the rabies vaccine, they knew this was intentional and might be important.

Townes agrees to get with the medical examiner's office to get more information from the autopsy they conducted. He jokes about them needing those new detectives soon. Zimmer assures Townes that he will check on their new transfers and see what else he can do about getting some expertise on their team.

Before Ray knew it, hours have passed, and the lieutenant mentioned he was going home for dinner. Zimmer needs to let his dog out since they worked through lunch. Townes agrees, since he should be famished too. Even though he hasn't eaten all day, the rush of the investigation keeps fueling him further. At this point, Ray's running on pure adrenaline but admits to himself a break is for the best.

Zimmer jokes lightheartedly as they are walking out, that if Townes was still a sergeant, he could train up new detectives with much quicker results. Townes nods with a forced grin as he hops into his pickup. He's departing with a stark reminder of his demotion three years ago, and tries to suppress his yearning to drink, which slithers in effortlessly. The memory of returning to duty without his stripes is still a dark point. Ray cranks the volume up on the radio with a shaky hand before it crackles out of the speakers. He's never heard this song but attempts to concentrate and get lost in the bass until his urge is gone. He is becoming more balanced with each passing mile.

Raymond believes for the first time since his reinstatement that he's maintaining some stability and sharpening his mental aptitude. He begins to create the smallest amount of pride, and only hopes he can keep this progress going.

6

Stag-Giving

Another week wraps with tireless research taking them in circles, and investigating dead ends. Det Townes was leaving the Special Crimes trailer for the day, defeated again. Lt Zimmer stops him in the parking lot with an update that grabs Ray's attention.

"Sorry, this isn't about Justine Nichols' case, detective. Arturo Ruiz got sentenced today. I thought I would let you know before you heard it anywhere else." Zimmer continues, "He did get life without parole, as we expected. His lawyer claims they will attempt an appeal, but Judge Burns didn't seem affected by that. Before sentencing, she allowed his grandmother to speak—giving an impact statement in Arturo's defense. Mrs. Ruiz brought damn near the entire courtroom to tears. It affected us all, I'll be honest. She prayed for him in Spanish and Arturo lost it. Judge Burns appeared unbothered, though. That stoic woman sat right through it, then reminded everyone of the "heinous nature of this crime" and proceeded with sentencing. It was impressive." Zimmer admits.

"Right, well, case closed then I guess?" Ray states with a shoulder shrug while turning towards his pickup.

"Yes, and just in time for the holidays," Zimmer continues while following behind him. "Let's not forget there are two children still recovering from this tragedy, Townes. Maybe now they can move on. Bond with the family they have left, and try to find closure, perhaps?"

"Closure?" Ray contests. "*Perhaps,*" he replies sarcastically.

"I get it, Ray. Let's just take this one step at a time, okay? Listen, I shouldn't assume, but I must ask. Do you have plans for Thanksgiving?"

Townes checks his wristwatch, "Shit, is that this week?"

"It's tomorrow, yes. And I knew you wouldn't have plans, which is fine! Because I am hosting my second annual Stag-Giving."

Ray raises an eyebrow.

Zimmer explains quickly— "It was between that and 'Guys Giving' we settled on Stag. Look, it's just some single guys from around the department and a few other friends of mine. Maybe fifteen guys or so. We will have lots of food, and it will be a good time. You should come. *Please.*" Zimmer requests humbly.

"Do I have to bring anything?" Ray asks, already annoyed at the thought of socializing.

"How about Cool Whip?" Zimmer adds.

Ray shoots him another raised brow, assuming he must be testing him at this point.

"For the pies!" Zimmer quickly clarifies.

"This better not be some weird shit you youngins' are into, sir. But yes, I guess I'll be there."

Zimmer laughs and sends his address via text message, which Townes hates. But he accepts it, knowing he will likely forget otherwise.

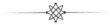

Townes awakes on Thanksgiving morning, proud for the first time in a while. Although he hasn't made much progress on the Justine Nichols' case, he is managing his drinking well. He's abstained from sex since that random hookup with the mystery woman, who was gone before he woke up. That night was also his last relapse in weeks. While his therapist advised against masturbation, Ray believes he can handle it. He has refrained from watching porn for a few days. *Actual progress*, he thinks to himself while showering.

The Stag-Giving was early, set to start at two p.m. Despite being ready for hours, Townes was late, as usual for social events. Arriving during dessert and without the cool-whip, Zimmer tried not to seem upset. However, he does find it mildly offensive.

Ray is hoping for a chance to bond with his boss and get to know him better during this impromptu event. Yet he doesn't want to interrupt the current atmosphere and has little desire to take part in the festivities and conversations. So, Townes was careful to avoid any private interactions.

While making his plate, Ray compliments the group on their pot-luck-style dishes. They had a huge spread of potatoes with gravy, collard greens, stuffing, green beans, turkey, ham, corn, salad, and at least three different dinner roll options. He jokes that some of these guys must have had a woman's help cooking. "A few mothers might have contributed to this meal,"

Townes remarks to the small crowd before leaving with the reciprocated laughs of the unfamiliar men behind him. Ray makes his way outside with a hefty serving of everything they had available. Settling into a wooden rocker on the large porch, Ray digs right in. It has been a while since he's had decent, home-cooked food, and he appreciates every bite.

After making his rounds and socializing with most of his guests, Zimmer heads to his front porch to join Ray as he finished his satisfying holiday dinner. Zimmer tosses a tennis ball into his yard for his dog to retrieve. He thanks Ray for coming and facetiously adds that he isn't mad about him being late *or* forgetting the only thing he was asked to bring. Ray chuckles but is slightly embarrassed, although he does enjoy his boss' sense of humor.

Their work dynamic was already complicated by age. Ray is 44 years old, while his superior only turned 34 this past summer. Professional experience differed, with Zimmer in about 13 years and was already promoted to lieutenant. While Townes has 19 years in service, lost rank, and only narrowly regained his detective privileges. Townes wondered if his boss was gay at first but was convinced otherwise when he overheard him describing a woman he was dating—concluding that Zimmer was a boob-man after eavesdropping that day.

Still unsure how to relate to the lieutenant, Ray knew it was crucial to do so if he was to keep someone in his corner. Ray has little trust and support from his fellow officers and superiors at this point. These revelations are disheartening and begin to diminish his mood.

Zimmer breaks the silence with an update for their team, discussing a new criminologist he has reached out to and finally heard back from. Dr. E.V. Gaston responded to the

Lieutenant's email and agreed to assist Special Crimes. The men must be careful with who they query for information, and how they research going forward. Concluding they need an outside source—someone without affiliations to the FBI or any local, federal, or government agencies. Zimmer explains the up-and-coming criminologist, who is a retired police officer, and a former Louisiana resident.

"Dr. Gaston was responsible for recently solving a notable case in Alaska. They discovered an active serial killer there late last year, in 2002. The criminologist discerned they had a female killer and was instrumental in making the arrest." Zimmer explains that "not many profilers are working independently, yet Dr. Gaston has reportedly turned down an offer to work with the bureau already." With limited resources and few options, they both agree to move forward with the consultation.

Townes asks, "So, when do we get to meet him? You said he's from Louisiana, right?"

"Well, we'll start on a conference call for now. Dr. Gaston currently lives and works out of Washington state. And Townes, don't be so presumptuous—it's a female criminologist. So, let's not offend her too quickly," his boss remarks with a half-smile.

"Oh, sorry. Uh, my bad. You're right, and I'll be more considerate. But you said she was a cop, right? She should be able to take some, uh... banter," Ray states, somewhat flustered.

"I know we don't work with too many females in the SCT, Townes. And while I realize you have way more experience than me, I still feel I should ask. Before we start sharing information with this woman, are you ready? Are you sure you can handle this investigation?" Zimmer asks with a concerned tone.

The lieutenant may be thinking back to Ray's unfiltered mouth, or the generally reckless way he operates. Townes assures his boss that he's making considerable progress in therapy and is managing all aspects of his life better. Ray claims to have had plenty of female coworkers over the years with no problems. "It's the men I usually take issue with," he tries to divert. Then further explains that drinking played a huge role in those past mistakes, admitting that liquor changes his behavior. Ray clarifies that "those incidents don't reflect my true nature or professionalism. More importantly, it won't be an issue, as I no longer consume alcohol."

Zimmer seems to believe Townes and now appears more comfortable and ready to get into the next phase of their investigation. "I have a good feeling about this, Townes! Dr. Gaston can help us find some answers and make sense of what we have here. This could be big. But we also need to prepare for being wrong. In fact, I'm almost hoping we are." Zimmer laughs nervously. "I'm confident that she can help, but I guess—well, you know what, we'll take it one step at a time and go from there."

Townes feels his boss is now sugar-coating their reality. Afraid of where his career will go from here, perhaps? Worried he might self-sabotage his future promotions if he befriends Townes? Zimmer is certainly more caught up in the unit's bureaucracy than Townes ever was. Ray's inquisitive nature made him reluctant to comply and posed a significant issue to his career. He was always too rebellious to conform as much as they required. The lieutenant, however, was well into the rat race now. He appears to adhere to their every demand. *Too far gone, perhaps?* Ray ponders. Knowing he's on his way out the door, while Zimmer still has at least another decade of duty to prepare for. *We're not on the same page*, Ray concludes.

Townes attempts to uplift his boss and allow him to enjoy the rest of his holiday. They share a bit of small talk, off-topic from the department. After a few minutes, Ray feels Zimmer is in a better place and sees the opportunity to make a quick exit.

"Alright, sir, I have to get out of here before any of your other friends want to talk," he says with a wink. "I'll probably spend the rest of my evening on the lake since it's still early. Thanks for the invite. This wasn't as weird or uncomfortable as I thought it would be." Ray remarks while tossing his empty foam plate into a trash can nearby and making his way down the porch steps.

Zimmer appreciates Ray's authenticity. They walk towards the vehicles parked across the yard and Zimmer's Labrador, Rex, follows close by his side. The lieutenant suggests he might need to join Townes on a fishing excursion sometime soon. Ray welcomes the idea and admits that he would enjoy the company. Adding, "The one other seat on the *Cayenne Cruiser* has your name on it, whenever you're ready."

The men share a firm handshake. Townes climbs into his old pickup, noticing the brand-new super-duty parked beside him. As he heads down Zimmer's lengthy paved driveway, he smirks, considering the contrasts of their lives. The differences were clear when comparing their neighborhoods, vehicles, and general interests. Raymond Townes prides himself on being a simple man and having what he *needs* in life, without much more. The large houses and well-manicured lawns of Zimmer's environment are rigid and high maintenance. They present with too much structure and more boundaries than Ray is willing to commit. He's baffled by how much money and time these people invest into material belongings. *Ridiculous*, Ray concludes while searching the radio for a clear station. He twists the knob in one direction until the static clears. Settling on a good blues song, he allows his mind to wander the next few miles home.

Ray contemplates Zimmer's questions earlier. About his ability to sustain a working environment with a woman. He hasn't shared the depths of his complicated sentiments about women with his boss. Yet Zimmer still understands this to be a sensitive area. Ray wonders if he has given other indicators of his past indiscretions. Suppose Zimmer knew that the relationship with his only other female boss was a steamy affair. One that lasted until her husband (also an officer) found out. Zimmer would likely be more concerned about Townes' professionalism, if so.

Ray recalls sharing some details with his therapist about Lt Miles. The doctor may see red flags with their team's impending expansion. Townes must be careful when mentioning work stresses at his appointment tomorrow. Being so selective with his truth is challenging. Blurring the lines was common for Ray, though. He finds comfort in the chaos and should be able to execute the mission. After all, deceit gives him power and ignites his passion like a wildfire.

7

Cold Case
Connections

Monday morning following Thanksgiving, Townes walks into the Special Crimes trailer, beaming with awareness. Today is their first call with Dr. Gaston, and Ray has anticipated this all weekend. He sits down across from his lieutenant at their brown rectangular conference table, which is riddled with cracks and worn around the edges.

"Morning, sir." Ray says while jotting '*1 December*' on his legal pad.

"Good morning, Townes. I…almost…got us going here. Let's see—" Zimmer mumbles, as he fidgets with the cords coming from the back of the conference phone in front of them. He dials a long number and after a couple of rings, they had a connection to Washington state.

"Good morning, Dr. Gaston, this is Lieutenant Zimmer, and I also have Detective Townes here with me. We are with the Special Crimes Team in the 31st precinct of the Beau Ridge bayou, Louisiana. We thank you for taking our call today. We won't take too much of your time. And, as per my email, we don't know if you can help us. We just need some guidance and fresh eyes."

"Good morning, gentlemen." Gaston's voice echoed through the speaker. Her tone was softer than Ray expected. "Ms. Gaston is fine too. I'm happy to be on the line with your team today. Start with what you know, explain the facts and the possible victims you may have connected. Please, take all the time you need. I don't have much else scheduled for today. And if you're right about this, we have a lot of work to do!" she asserts.

"Right, well, let's get into it." The lieutenant continues and takes the lead in explaining the details of each crime. "We have three cases we're looking at—two are cold. First, is Tina Richard, she was a 25-year-old Caucasian female. Her remains were discovered in March of 2001. She had her face beaten-in postmortem. Her skull was crushed, and the damage to her skeletal structure was significant. Dental records were eventually run against state DHS records in Louisiana and Texas. That has been a common practice with any Jane Doe over the last few years. The cause of death for Ms. Richard was difficult to pinpoint. Most likely from strangulation, the coroner suggested. She was discovered completely naked, covered in fallen leaves and branches. Found off a remote path in the dense Gerbeau Forrest, on the outskirts of our parish.

"She was likely dumped in December of 2000, not found until the following spring. Her decomposition through the winter was significant, with temperatures varying as they do here, from below freezing to the mid-70s on any given day.

There was no evidence at the scene other than the small rock used to crush her face, which offered no forensics. Once we made an I.D., we gathered some basic intel. Tina had only moved to Louisiana in the late fall of 2000. She was homeless and bar hopping to find company most nights. We had a few recognize her at the local women's shelters when we canvased, after getting her DMV photo printed out from Texas. However, the photo was from several years before and we later realized her appearance had changed a lot since then. The shelters pointed us towards the bars she had frequented. Acquaintances informed us that she had dyed her hair several times and was no longer wearing glasses as in her Texas DMV photo. In December, she allegedly left with various men over the last few weekends leading up to her disappearance. That was the last time any witnesses saw her around, and most thought she moved back to Texas. To date, that's all we've compiled on Tina Richard. Her case has been cold since." Zimmer continues, shuffling through the paperwork.

"Next is Roxanne Williams, she was a 52-year-old African American female. Reportedly a former drug addict and prostitute for two decades, in West Beau Ridge. Primarily known near the industrial-freight area, by the river and docks. That is the same location her corpse was found in April of 2001. According to timelines compiled from witness statements, Ms. Roxy Williams was held captive for more than 24 hours. Before that incident, she worked at a convenience store and was supposedly clean for years. Her family claimed she was 'doing great' and insisted that something terrible had happened to Roxy from the start.

"Based on the statements, Ms. Williams didn't show for an early shift on Friday morning, April 13th. Her manager called her home phone a few times, believing she had overslept. Roxy's 23 -year-old son Darius, finally answered around zero six. After speaking with her boss and realizing Roxy wasn't home, Darius contacted their neighbor and close friend, Miss Hattie Jones. They determined Roxy had left for the corner store the night before, Thursday, April 12th. Miss Hattie said that Roxy headed on foot to the store like she often did, as it was only about six blocks away from their apartment complex. She planned to get a gallon of milk and some cigarettes, then return home since she had to open the following day at work. It was about 20:30 when she left Miss Hattie's porch. No one saw her alive after that.

"They didn't seem to get much support from West Beau Ridge PD, after reporting her missing. Darius said his family spent that entire Friday calling around. They were checking hospitals and other police stations to no avail. The following morning, Saturday, April 14th, Darius got an early call from the police in West Beau Ridge. Stating they found a body at the docks around midnight and that he should come to verify if it was his mother. Miss Hattie drove Darius to the morgue. There he identified his mother, Roxanne Williams. Despite the swelling and bruising on her body and two broken orbital sockets. Her distorted face still resembled his mother.

"She died from cardiac arrest. Likely a result of the sexual torture she endured. There was evidence she was bound by her wrists and ankles. She had small, symmetrical wounds consistent with cigarette burns. They ran up and down her left arm and chest area. The examiner also annotated *'signs of electrocution, via a powerful stun-gun or possible cow prod.'* With burn marks on her inner thighs, rib cage, and under her chin. There was no viable DNA found inside any of her orifices. A spermicidal contraceptive was apparently used. Some of her wounds were cleaned with alcohol. As a forensic countermeasure, perhaps? They didn't appear bandaged or treated otherwise. We confirmed with the convenience store in her neighborhood and several others nearby, that Roxy never made it in for her purchases Thursday night. We gather she was likely picked up along the way to the store while on foot, Thursday evening, April 12th, 2001. West Beau Ridge PD claimed there was evidence that she was still working in prostitution. Possibly keeping it from her family they considered. Assuming it was a job gone wrong, and Roxy was dumped after an unexpected cardiac arrest during the encounter. That is about all we have on Ms. Williams. We took over the cold case from West BRPD last spring and haven't made much progress since, unfortunately."

Zimmer pauses. Closing Roxanne's folder and shifting the next file on top of the stack. He immediately proceeds.

"Then our most recent victim is Ms. Justine Nichols. She was 24 years old, Caucasian, and abducted in September of this year, 2003. She remained for about 45 days in an unknown location, until her death in early November. She died from *'septicemia'* or massive infections, triggered from compound fractures in her right leg, and other untreated injuries. We know the sexual abuse and torture continued as the infection ravaged her young body. She had many facial fractures, and her left orbital socket was so damaged it could not hold her eyeball in place. As with our other victims, their faces seem to take most of their beatings. Justine Nichols suffered extreme pain and repeated trauma, resulting in a brutal and agonizing death." Zimmer clears his throat before wrapping up. "That's about all we have, which we realize may not be much of anything. Um…what do you think, ma'am?" the lieutenant asks humbly.

Both men focus on the small black speaker awaiting a response from Dr. Gaston. After a few seconds of silence, she responds.

"Well, I have to say, I'm glad that you reached out, lieutenant. You gentlemen are on to something here, and I see several possible connections, as well as a pattern. I know this might not be what you expected to hear, but I must inform you. There is a strong probability that the same offender committed each of these crimes. I would even say you could have an active serial predator on your hands."

Townes and Zimmer make eye contact. They begin to undergo mutual anxiety and fear. The confirmation they just received is jarring. Gaston proceeds, clarifying that this perpetrator would have earlier victims. Those *fortunate* ones would have been only raped and possibly beaten at the time. "His anger likely increased with each new victim taking on more punishment from his violent wrath." Dr. Gaston instructs the team to search for earlier, open rape cases. Or anyone assaulted by unknown perpetrators. She also mentions the pause in crimes between Roxanne in 2001, and Justine (now) in 2003. Gaston explains "this break could have been from working on his technique. He was correcting the errors he could have made with his earlier victims." She also feels this assailant is escalating and fears he may have been working on acquiring a better location to carry out his sadistic plans uninterrupted.

Gaston says, "If he is abducting women and having longer periods with them, he may want to prolong the torture. Getting off on their pain and what the women can endure."

Zimmer asks about the women all being different ages and races.

Gaston explains, "They're victims of opportunity and or convenience. Low risk to the perpetrator getting caught. They're chosen due to their accessibility or size, and ability to overpower, rather than based on his specific sexual preferences."

Now armed with fresh information and professional insight, the team is more prepared to accept their reality. They must move forward solving the actual crime at hand here. Yet they still must tread lightly. Unsure if they can trust Dr. Gaston at this point. They acknowledge that there's no more time to waste.

The duo gets right to work going through cold cases and past sexual assault and battery reports. Carefully looking for any DNA recovered or even untested rape kits, which could have provided an early piece of overlooked evidence, or a link to their perpetrator.

The Special Crimes Team knows that they must explain these connections to the brass. First, getting them to accept the possibility of an active serial killer. One they had no idea was even operating in their jurisdiction. Then, approving personnel and funding for investigating this massive project.

The men face a daunting task, but now with more purpose than ever. Townes hopes staying busy will be a healthy distraction and not another trigger.

8

A Breakthrough

His Friday session with Dr. Pfeiffer has come around once more—weeks later. This time Ray was ready for it. He wants to confide more in his therapist. Willing to finally break down some walls and be honest with her. To an extent, of course. Ray wasn't naïve enough to believe he could share too much of the darkness he felt mounting inside. Not without condemnation or consequences. Ray is hesitant to share the truth about his shortcomings and the few relapses he has had.

Townes is certain the management of his psyche and urges, are better now than ever before. He finally feels more control, and some growing confidence in his abilities. It's a small indication that *therapy could be helping.*

Arriving at Dr. Pfeiffer's office, she instantly comments on Ray's appearance and demeanor, noticing a difference as he walks through the door. She asks if his Christmas holiday was in good spirits? Townes informs her he worked right through it, trying to stay busy and make some progress with their case. As well as operating the phones for the precinct. Not wanting others who have a family to be there when their time could be better spent at home with loved ones.

Dr. Pfeiffer reassures Ray that he is strong enough to handle this job and he should feel confident moving forward with this big case. She only hopes he finds healthy ways to spend his free time and reminds him that "balance is necessary." She then returns the conversation to his team expansion, to learn how this change of events is affecting Ray.

Townes is careful not to mention too many details, only that the entire investigation has recently taken a turn. Admitting that it's already been taxing and emotionally draining at times. He decides to divulge some information about his past indiscretion. To determine if the new stress from working with Dr. Gaston will be an issue for him.

Townes discusses how he became involved with Lieutenant Miles, and that he still has a hard time working with women because of their relationship. Even though he has never seen her and doesn't interact with Dr. Gaston, he admits her voice sounds attractive to him. Ray discusses some of his weaknesses and sexual impulses becoming overwhelming at times.

After a moment, Ray realizes this is the true nature of what he needs guidance with. Ray shares more intimate secrets about his past affair, believing it's the next logical step in therapy. Explaining how he seduced Lt Miles while intoxicated at a company New Year's Eve party in 1985. Assuming he had crossed the line, he panicked at first. He believed their quick and steamy hookup in the basement evidence room was a one-time event. Yet Ele Miles surprised him by continuing it. Ray knew she was a married woman. Her husband, Stewart Miles, was a Louisiana State Trooper. When Ele chose to continue the affair, Ray felt they had something genuine. He trusted and opened to Ele, and she was doing the same with Ray.

He explains them having mind-blowing sex and that their intimacy was unmatched. Ray admits he hasn't reached orgasm like the ones she gave him in almost fifteen years—as far as he can remember. Ele Miles had an interest in exploring erotic practices, telling Ray, she wanted to experiment with BDSM and see how he felt about trying some things with her. Ele Miles admitted that she had hinted at it with her husband, Stewart, first. He was not into it at all, leaving her rejected and embarrassed. Ray tried to console her and make her feel less self-conscious. He wanted Ele to be more comfortable with herself. He sat there holding her naked body for hours. Ray thought they shared a bond that would last a lifetime.

His body language shifts as he becomes agitated and uneasy. Reflecting on his past and how their relationship unfolded, it becomes clear. Raymond Townes is still affected by this woman. Ray hates that Ele chose Stewart when he discovered the affair. She wanted to "stay faithful to her vows," she claimed. Such a choice that not only did Ele end the affair, but she then followed Stewart to Texas. An abrupt move that ripped her out of Ray's life quicker than he was ready for or able to process.

"That rejection, that loss... nearly broke me," Townes admits through a shaky voice.

Dr. Pfeiffer listens to Raymond go on for almost fifteen minutes, describing the intimate details of his affair. And how the years they shared in secret had such an impact on him. Ray has sat in her office and discussed his ex-wife Irene many times over the last few months. Not once did Dr. P. feel the passion or earnestness from Townes like she has today.

Ray admits that marrying Irene was a mistake. He was facing pressure at the time from his superior officers. Told to, "settle down" and get his drinking under control. Ray explains that he and Irene had many differences. But he loved her spirit and could see the many attributes she had. He wanted to move on with his life and thought he could make the marriage work. Yet Ray knew that he could never give Irene what she deserved or needed.

"It was more than having children," he recognizes.

While he feared the idea, Ray felt that having a baby with Irene could have been an exciting next step in their life. Admitting that it was relieving when they discovered she was barren. He didn't know he was expressing this sentiment until Irene called him out on the drive home from the clinic. Heartbroken and distraught, she accused him of being "a monster." He thought Irene was reacting to the hormones or the news they received from their fertility specialist. Ray thought he would have more time to make things right, but Irene filed for separation a week later. Ray and Irene divorced in 1997, two years after they married.

Irene was a secretary at the church he attended for Alcohol Anonymous meetings. They likely would have never crossed paths if not for that chance interaction. Early on, Ray thought it might have been for a reason. "Of all the churches I could have attended. It was Trinity Baptist and that woman's big blue eyes that greeted me first. Irene's smile and friendly demeanor welcomed me every Tuesday and Thursday." Ray admits. Irene was proud of Ray; showing up consistently was impressive to her. Although he didn't mention that he was required to be there by his precinct. "Before I knew it, Irene was my only support system. I realized early on that she needed more than I could give. Most of our relationship was built on lies and secrets." Ray admits, realizing it was never fair to Irene, but it was his norm for so long, he did it with ease.

Ray concludes, "I've yet to commit to any woman since the divorce. But it wasn't losing my ex-wife that was too difficult to overcome. My biggest regret, and most epic failure thus far, was when I let Ele Miles walk away. Her memory still plagues me and my nightmares." Townes admits for the first time to his therapist that he "can't get over Ele." Believing *she* is the faceless woman who haunts his subconscious most nights.

Making that connection is powerful. Finally being honest about the differences between Irene and Ele, is illuminating. Ray's sweaty palms release their grip from the red chair he is on the edge of. Sweat residue lingers on the leather armrests. Ray rubs his knees and then exhales quickly before acknowledging the physiological effects.

"Wow. I feel better. Lighter even, from finally admitting that aloud. Thanks, doc. For your patience and for sticking with me here. This has truly been eye opening." Ray concedes.

"You're quite welcome, Mr. Townes. But you're doing most of the work. So, thank you for trusting me, and choosing to share your innermost thoughts. Getting personal in this office allows me to see who you are. Your health and progress are my only priority. And we're making great strides with your recovery. You stick to the plan…do the work, see the results; it's that easy! I'll see you next Friday, detective."

He appreciates Dr. Pfeiffer's professionalism and consistency. On his way home, Ray confidently passes the liquor store. His sexual cravings are subsiding, and he feels more level-headed and in control. Finally, he is getting his shit together.

Ray contemplates their consult with Dr. Gaston, while barreling toward his home. Believing they are on the cusp of something big with their investigation. He suddenly gets a call vibrating from his pocket.

"Evening LT, what can I do for you? Have another dinner party I should be in attendance of?" Townes asks jovially.

Zimmer's tone in his greeting is serious. Ray pauses his joy, knowing what this means. "We have another body, Townes. A young, Caucasian female. She was dumped near a commercial construction site at the old Fairmount Creamery. It's not our scene, but West is processing everything and expects to have an I.D. soon. I wanted you to know, Ray…this might be *him*."

The lieutenant's words strike the veteran detective like a heavyweight punch across the jaw. Ray feels his mood transition into guilt and obligation. He feels compelled to fulfill his duty. This man is still out here, operating without repercussions. Ray knows they were right all along and refuses to wait for approval or further guidance.

Raymond Townes decides that he will not retire without finding this culprit and ending his reign of terror over Beau Ridge. He can't move on without closing this case.

9

New Year's Eve

Michaela Hardy was the young woman found at the old creamery. Her case only brought more questions for Ray, and the stress is weighing on him. Zimmer returns about twenty minutes before their scheduled phone call with Dr. Gaston. He has a greasy take-out bag in hand. Hungry and relieved, Det Townes graciously accepts the food. He hasn't had a decent meal in days, or at least one that didn't come from a microwave.

Inhaling the burger and fries, he tries not to slurp his soda down too loudly. Every sound tends to echo in the small and silent trailer they share. Ray opens his mouth, releasing a ferocious burp that smacks Zimmer in the face. The lieutenant can't help but laugh. He jokes about being glad Dr. Gaston can't see them during their briefings. The team concludes that they aren't used to working with women, and may lack the etiquette needed for such an environment.

A quick clean-up ensues. Ketchup packets and crumbled wrappers are tossed into the trash bin nearby. Followed by a few swipes of salt and fry crumbs onto the floor. The pair are ready to brief their new counterpart. The line rings twice before connecting Gaston from Washington state, to her unofficial team in the bayou. Informed via email that they have a new victim; Gaston is ready to get into the briefing. Her tone is more powerful than ever before. Townes is stricken by the familiarity he feels as she takes charge.

Zimmer takes his time explain what they know about Michaela Hardy. "A 19-year-old, Caucasian female who stayed in a small tent community near the river in West Beau Ridge for the past year. She was reported missing by her girlfriend Jazz, whom she lived with in Tent City. Jazz is twenty years old and claimed that while Michael is only nineteen, she appears older. Especially when she wears her long blonde wig, which she had on the day she went missing.

"Michaela was to finish panhandling near the mall and then use a fake I.D. to buy a bottle on her way back to their tent. When she never returned, Jazz was frantic. Jazz began searching all the known locations they frequent and asking if anyone had seen Ms. Hardy. Showing a grainy polaroid to whoever would pay attention, she began to gather some intel. Jazz determined that Michaela made it to a liquor store with her collected funds in hand.

"The store clerk claimed Ms. Hardy bought two 40-ounce malt liquors. She drank one on the bench out front, while still collecting money from any willing donor who passed by. The clerk said a man in a white pickup truck approached Michaela. The clerk noticed the man came back at least two separate times, despite blatant rejection. This man appeared to make the uninterested Michaela quite upset. She came back inside almost an hour later, more intoxicated by then and working on the second bottle she had purchased earlier. Ms. Hardy attempted to buy more alcohol, but the clerk thought she might become a problem, so he kicked her out before conducting the second sale. Claiming, 'she took her half-full bottle and disappeared.'

"Jazz took what she had to the West Beau Ridge police, before Thanksgiving. She was confident the love of her life had fallen prey to a terrible fate. Weeks passed of calls and questions, followed by 'random interrogations' of Jazz at their tent. Investigators assumed that Michaela had left Jazz and their tent life, or even run away with a man. Jazz was furious at their implications. She made several statements about how Michaela was 'still a virgin and was proud to have never been with a man.' She claimed, 'Michaela vowed never to give up her body for any amount of money.' Jazz admitted to being a recovering addict, but insists Michaela only drank alcohol. She reportedly 'feared trying anything harder than marijuana, after finding her father dead—from an overdose—when she was nine. Michaela was never the same and hated anyone who used,' according to Jazz. Further disproving the officer's accusations that this was 'drug-related.'

"The 31st finally opened the missing person's case due to Jazz's persistence. It was about thirty days after her initial statement to West Beau Ridge PD. The case went into a stack of files for transfer to us at Special Crimes. We would've taken over the investigation, yet it never made it through the process. The file was found three days ago, still on Cpt Thompson's desk awaiting approval. This was upon my search for cases that could be related to the Jane Doe they found at the creamery site. So, Michaela was never even investigated as a missing person." Zimmer concludes despondently.

Gaston does the daunting task of explaining what her counterparts feared most but need to hear to grasp the entirety of their circumstances. "Ms. Hardy was likely held captive from late November, after Justine Nichols' body was discovered. Until this December, when Michaela Hardy was dumped at the creamery, five days ago."

The team understands that Michaela took a beating. She endured extreme torture during her tenure with their psychopath. As with the former victims, she had broken orbital sockets and sustained significant damage to her face. She had extensive vaginal and anal tearing with evidence of penetration by a large foreign object. Michaela had internal bleeding from a ruptured spleen, which ultimately caused her death, the autopsy proved. The perpetrator cleaned and bandaged some of her wounds, as with previous victims. Michaela was treated with painkillers and antibiotics, based on her toxicology screenings. Which also showed she was clean from any narcotics and other substances. Michaela was discovered wearing a dress that her girlfriend Jazz didn't recognize. The dress is the only evidence they may have from their suspect, and it's still under analysis.

"So, he was again prolonging the torture. Attempting to keep her alive, and even to maintain a level of comfort. That would prevent her from becoming unconscious or going into shock." Dr. Gaston explains. Believing their suspect to have, "Control issues. Damaging relationships with family, especially his mother. This would have started early on. He may have significant unresolved childhood trauma. Depending on how much he talks to his victims, he might get angry with their responses. Their reactions to his ideas or requests have an effect."

Gaston continues, "He wants total domination and control. He's a sexual sadist but may lack the skills or resources to articulate his intentions or expectations. That, in turn, could enrage him. Ms. Hardy was not only a lesbian but completely celibate to penetration, which could have been another unforeseen complication. He likely thought he was getting a blonde prostitute. When the wig came off, a stark contrast would have presented. Causing him to question himself, his instincts, and what he's getting from any of this."

Gaston goes on to explain that "this limited theory is a working profile." She needs more time and information to complete her assessment. Even then, her work isn't an exact science. She is careful not to make too many assumptions. Still, the team is impressed with her insight. This is the most they've had to go on, ever.

With no time to waste, they end their call and proceed with their investigation. The pair search for more information on their victims until well into the evening. For any details they may have missed, or for answers to make sense of this puzzle. Knowing they will need to present their findings to their captain and chief soon. The team fears the reactions they will receive. Both men are on edge and stressed.

Before they head out for the night, they realize it's New Year's Eve, and laugh together since they've forgotten completely. Zimmer explains he has no plans and little time to find anything to do now. Townes goes out on a limb and extends an offer to his boss, to ring in the new year with him while fishing. Ray mentions the marina on the other side of Lake Gerbeau sets off a large firework display at midnight. He claims it's a must-see, especially from his favorite spot in the *Cayenne Cruiser*. His exhausted boss was not expecting anything fun to arise today. He is happy to accept Townes' impromptu invitation. But Zimmer admits "I haven't been fishing since I was a kid. I'm out of practice and might need a refresher."

Zimmer is told to meet Ray, "At the last boat ramp on the east side of the lake, around 2230," which is in about an hour. Before the men depart, Zimmer asks Townes if it was okay to bring some beers, then immediately backpedals. He respects his subordinate's commitment to sobriety and apologizes for the inconsideration. Townes assures him that it's completely okay and he will be fine with a little celebration. Especially since he's not a big beer drinker; only the whiskey proves to be an issue for his self-control. Zimmer is relieved to hear this. They part ways to prepare for their meeting at the lake momentarily.

Zimmer arrives a few minutes after Townes. He's instantly clowned for the brand-new boots he decided to wear and informed that this was an amateur move, especially for the bayou. He assists Ray in unloading the small boat. Zimmer returns a joke about his beer cooler taking up any extra space they had on the vessel. Then asks if the tiny *Cayenne Cruiser* will leave them stranded.

Townes confirms that his boss can swim, then informs him of the life vest under his seat. He assures Zimmer that most of his spare time is spent tinkering with this boat and his pickup. "Which are each quite mechanically sound, despite the rust and age they present with. No worries, sir." Ray concludes with a wink.

Zimmer never expected their banter and working relationship to progress this far. Yet he has grown to enjoy it and is thankful that Ray has taken a chance on him. Townes admits that their working relationship has been good for him too. While also unexpected at times, claiming that Zimmer is, "pretty cool for an L.T."

The pair get the boat in the water and troll towards the lake's center. "I thought there would be more people out. I don't see very many boats on the water. Are you sure they'll do the fireworks this year?" Zimmer asks as they bounce along.

"There are plenty on the other side of the lake. This area is more remote; it's known for fishing. The other side has a shallow swimming hole and a little pier with activities for families to enjoy. That's where most of the audience is. I don't care much for people, so I stick to the lesser-known spots. Plus, it's much darker on this side, so we'll have the best view when they light up the sky in a bit. Don't worry, sir. Try to relax and enjoy the night. Hell, crack open a beer and look around. Have you ever seen that many stars in town?" Ray asks while pointing his chin towards the sky.

The lieutenant takes a second to do as instructed and stares straight up at the twinkling abyss.

"Holy shit, you're right. I can see every star in the galaxy. Look there's Sirius shining bright. And the moon, that waxing gibbous is beautiful too." Zimmer states enthusiastically with wide eyes.

"Wow, okay, so you're a space nerd then? I didn't see that coming." Townes says.

"I became a little obsessed with Astronomy in college. A good friend introduced me, and it's fascinated me ever since. It's calming for me." Zimmer states, trying to hide his fervor.

Townes feels he may have stifled Zimmer's interests and apologizes. He wants this outing to be pleasant for them both. Ray has a strong desire to connect more with Zimmer, since he doesn't have many adult friends. Even throughout his entire career on the force, Ray never acted like most police officers. He never joined a softball team or went out drinking with the guys. He was ridiculed early on for sleeping with Lt Miles. Despite them keeping it a secret, many had their suspicions. After she moved away with her husband, coworkers spread more rumors. They called Townes a "homewrecker" and commented about their wives not being "safe" around him. This usually didn't bother Ray and he thought eventually things would change.

After a decade, Townes realized he had built no significant friendships that he could rely on. He stopped trying altogether, became more reclusive, and fell into a solo routine. He kept his gloomy secrets and thoughts to himself as they intensified. Townes felt it was less stressful than trying to entertain people and pretend. Until he faced several downward spirals and had no one to provide any help or support. Ray remembers the viewpoint of drowning in life and having no one to reach out a hand or throw him a preserver. No relief from the murky waters that were pulling him under. This strengthened him and his character, but it also nearly cost his life.

Unsure if his politically correct and stern lieutenant would understand. He likely can't relate to Ray's true character. But Zimmer is about the last viable option for a friend at this point. Ray doesn't have much to lose. They spend the next few minutes in a fishing crash course. After some help getting his lure set up, Zimmer was finally ready to cast his line.

"I think we can both admit you needed more than a *refresher*, L.T. But it looks like you're finally ready. Now hold the button as I showed you. Don't release it until you have swung the pole overhead." Townes explains. Then oversees his boss handling his instructions. They both do a little cheer when the shiny plastic worm splashes into the cold water.

About fifteen minutes have passed and both men are still sitting in silence. Townes is unsure how to proceed. Communication is not usually a problem for him, but he's putting too much pressure on this friendship. Ray begins to fear this was a misstep. Shuffling through his thoughts a few minutes longer, Townes feels embarrassed now. He is drawing a complete blank on any conversation starter or small talk. *Great*, Ray thinks to himself. He brought his boss into his only spot of solace on this planet. He's now sharing it with a near stranger and an awkward silence.

Ray needs to take the edge off. Without giving it too much thought, he reaches his hand into the icy cooler and grabs a can. He pops the top and takes a big drink.

"Whoa, I thought you didn't drink beer, Townes?" his boss questions. The concern grows as Ray proceeds to gulp half the beverage down without stopping for air.

"Sorry, sir, but if we're both going to enjoy this night, I need to relax. This case, well, all of our cases, and this entire year, have been draining. You know that! And I promise, I'm okay." Townes states with some hesitancy, hoping this doesn't turn into an issue.

To Ray's surprise, Zimmer grabs another beer for himself. After cracking the top, he clinks his can against Ray's. "Cheers —to a crazy year. I can only imagine what 2004 will have in store for us. I know we can handle it. And I want you to know that I've learned a lot from you, Townes. I look forward to closing this case with you as well." Zimmer affirms with their cans pressed together above them.

Townes nods in approval before stating, "Cheers to that, sir." Then guzzles down the rest of his beer.

It's about a half-hour to midnight and the two have shared some insignificant small talk. Townes senses the lieutenant getting tipsier and realizes going in for a second beer, that Zimmer was already working on his fifth. Ray begins to fear this night may take a turn. He is worried that his boss might be a different person while intoxicated, as most men are. Ray proceeds with caution.

"You, good, sir? You seem a little quiet, and you're smashing those Heineken like they're water. It seems like something is on your mind. Uhm, if you want to talk...I'm listening."

Zimmer agrees that he is trying to find the right words because he does have something to share. Realizing LT's attempting to intake some liquid courage; Ray gets nervous about what he might hear. Yet he knows that this could be necessary for their friendship to advance. Townes tries to make Zimmer feel safe to speak.

"You should know that no topic is off-limits on the *Cayenne*. You can share anything out here, and the lake keeps all the secrets. So, whatever it is, no worries."

Zimmer smiles. "Thank you, Townes, I appreciate that! And you know, I've wanted to discuss this for so long, but can never find the right time or place. I'm relieved, I suppose, that you invited me here tonight. It wasn't until I began to drink and loosen up, that it started to feel like the perfect opportunity to share this. *Finally*."

Ray feels Zimmer might be leading to something big yet is lost on which direction they're headed.

"Do you have secrets, Ray? Some things you are unsure if you can share with anyone else in this world? Something that you know once expressed, will change everything moving forward?"

Unsure where Zimmer is going with this, Ray starts to panic. Contemplating whether he let something nefarious slip that his boss noticed. Has Dr. Pfeiffer shared parts of their intimate therapy sessions? "Umm, of course. I mean, don't we all have secrets, sir?" He retorts ambiguously.

"Right, of course. We all do, you're right! I know we all have our paths to walk in this world. While most go in similar directions, every individual has different obstacles. We are all similar, yet still so different. I'm different, Ray." Zimmer states. With a shaky hand gripping his green can, the lieutenant musters up more courage. He extends his long skinny arm out and raises his beer into the air, proclaiming, "I am different!" Then proceeds to chug the rest of his drink.

Townes considers his boss may need to let off some steam or release some pent-up stress from their intense investigation. He tells him that being different is not a bad thing. That he should embrace it. Zimmer stops him right there, asking if he is serious and believes that?

Townes nods his head and claims, "Of course! Why not? Being different sets you apart. It can give you the edge you need, especially in this job. Hell, I say be proud of whatever makes you unique and use it. This world moves quickly, sir; you never know what the latest craze or trend will be. You can't spend too much time trying to be like everyone else, to fit in and assimilate. You might be selling yourself short or worse, losing yourself in the process. Don't deprive the world of the real you because you think that people won't understand or accept you. Hell, be a nerd, study every speckle in our galaxy and all the zodiac stuff. Whatever your thing is, you should stand by it, proudly." Ray tries to relate and believes he got his point across.

Zimmer attempts to stand up in the small boat. He shuffles around, losing his balance, before abruptly sitting back down. He plants his hands firmly on each of his narrow armrests and closes his eyes while the boat rocks back to a steady position.

"Whoa, sorry about that. I won't fall in, I promise. But I want to shout from the rooftops. I want to yell my truth, Townes. I'm ready!"

Confused and not nearly intoxicated enough, Ray gives his drunk friend the platform he needs and allows him to continue with his declaration. "Please don't fall in, it's pretty fucking nippy in there. But it's only us and the fish out here. We're all ears... let 'er rip."

Zimmer clears his throat, then begins, "Raymond Townes, for the first time since I left college, I'm ready to say this aloud. To another person, a friend as of tonight. That I, Christopher Zimmer...am gay. I'm gay!" he asserts, with a puffed-up chest and his chin held high.

Ray waits in silence for him to continue, assuming there is more to learn here. Yet they only hear the faint murmurs from the crowd on the other side of the lake—energy buzzing as alcohol consumption and anticipation increase. The light show they were all about to witness is moments away.

"Umm, is that it?" Ray asks after a few more seconds of silence.

"Is that it? Of course, that's *it*! I've been hiding that for over a decade, Raymond. Is my secret not good enough? Is it…oh God, did you already know?"

"No! Sorry, I didn't mean to downplay you there. And I assure you I had no idea. Well, I had some questions at times, if I'm honest. But I will say you did a decent job concealing it. I don't think anyone around the department knows. Not that I hear much of the gossip these days. Even if they did, sir, do you think it would matter? I mean, I know we aren't the most evolved group at the 31st, but I'm sure the majority can handle it. Of course, it's up to you to share whenever you're ready. I hope it eventually goes beyond the *Cayenne* and Lake Gerbeau. Secrets get harder to keep—their burdens heavier with each passing life phase. You don't want to carry that extra weight around. Everyone has their shit, sir, trust me. I have seen it all throughout my career. If you're ready to be open and honest, then do it completely. For you and no one else. Your terms, your life, your truth." Ray even impresses himself with his sound advice and considerate support.

Zimmer breathes in deep and slowly exhales while nodding his head. "Wow, I would never have thought I would be coming out like this. On a boat, in the middle of a lake, on New Year's Eve. To Raymond Townes, of all people." Ray shrugs with a smirk. Zimmer continues, "But I have to say, this night feels special. And I can't thank you enough. I didn't know you were so *progressive*?! I should have gone out drinking with you a while ago! But I'm glad I waited until tonight... this is perfect. Thank you."

Ray responds quickly to lighten the mood. "Don't make it weird, but you're welcome. More secrets for the *Cayenne,* and she's heard plenty. But you can come back anytime, sir," he states with a pat on the LT's shoulder.

Just then, the fireworks begin to erupt into the sky above them. Townes watches Zimmer staring up at the vast canvas overhead. A childlike smile plastered on his face. His eyes lit up with bright reds, whites, and blues. The lake water sparkled around them. With colors dancing like a kaleidoscope from each burst of light above. All while the thunderous roars drummed across the night sky. Each explosion sounded closer and louder than the last.

Ray can't help but laugh, considering tonight will likely be stamped in his boss' memories for life. How significant it will sound in the future when he retells it to others. The two of them alone, intoxicated, and sharing secrets. The water, the fireworks, it's almost romantic—he chuckles again. Zimmer notices the big grin Townes dawns. The two men enjoy this expedition for different reasons. Their mutual energy in the small boat is powerful.

Townes is ready for a fresh start. He ponders the upcoming challenges he will face next year. Per tradition on his New Year's Eve-lake excursions, as this is his favorite time for reflection. Ray has rung in the last ten New Year's right here on this boat. In the same dark, frigid waters. He is thankful now to provide this shared experience. Despite the chaos he finds in life, the lake and his *Cayenne Cruiser* always seem to provide refuge. He might not have much in life, but Raymond Townes believes he has everything he needs. Right now, he is content and appreciative.

After loading up the boat, Ray walks Zimmer to his blue hatchback. He thanks him again for joining in on tonight's adventure. "When you wake up in the morning, it might be with a hangover and regret from spilling your guts. Remember, I won't tell a soul, even if you still want to shout it from the rooftops tomorrow. Although, I might share that you're a terrible angler if anyone asks."

Zimmer grins, still buzzed and seemingly elated from his confession. "Thanks, Townes. But I don't plan to digress here. I'm ready to move forward, and I hope to wake up with the same intentions and confidence. Thanks again for this, I needed it more than you know. And I appreciate you, Ray. Next time I'll catch something big, you'll see."

"You're welcome, anytime, sir! I look forward to seeing that, next time." Townes jokes, then with a firm handshake and a tap on the roof, he sends Zimmer on his way.

On the few miles back to his trailer, Ray considers the gravity of tonight. The enormous weight lifted from Zimmer and Ray's minor role in assisting. He knows what it's like to hide parts of your identity and keep people on the outside. It's exhausting at times. The lies, and cover-ups, trying to keep up with each little fabricated detail. In most situations you seem to go against your strongest instincts. Portraying the façade everyone around you is expecting can be so taxing and stringent.

While Townes can't imagine what it's like to be a gay man working in their environment, he does understand concealing the private aspects of one's life. After all, who cares about their coworker's sex life or choice of partners, right? Ray has never wanted details about the boring sex from all the married men he knows. Neither should they, he imagines, care with who or how he gets his rocks off. Ray knows that his grim sexual desires are not comparable to homosexuality. Believing that gay men shouldn't face judgment or be demeaned for their lifestyle and sexual preferences. Yet this is quite different from the reality they face. Growing uneasy as he approaches his driveway, pondering the condemnation he knows his boss may be subjected to. Ray realizes he gave Zimmer a direct pass to rejection. Along with possible ramifications that even he can't fathom, worry sets in.

Shit, Ray thinks to himself, *did I set L.T. up for failure? Holy shit, I made him believe they're civil and able to handle this news. Have I convinced him that the department will embrace him with a rainbow flag?* Ray continues internally. *I gave him a chance to speak his truth. That doesn't mean I'm liable for the outcome. Right?*

He starts to become torn and off balance. Wishing it weren't after one in the morning so he could consult with his therapist. Townes can't help but feel overwhelmed. This new friendship was already proving too tricky to navigate. *Damn, this is exactly why I don't do this*, he concludes—while laying down on his lumpy old mattress, searching for a comfortable position.

As Ray finds his way into a deep slumber, the faceless woman re-visits his subconscious. This time without the help of alcohol. He takes the time to study her body and the foggy abyss where her facial features should be. She is still a mystery he can't place. Ray knows now that this is an ominous visit and not a pleasant one from his unfinished past.

He awakes around two, shaken and distraught with fear from this cryptic encounter. *Why is she here, again? Why can't I shake this nightmare?* Ray wonders while pulling his sweaty t-shirt over his head. He flips his pillow over to the dry and cool side. Then watches the clock tick by.

One hundred minutes pass. Growing more restless, Ray attempts to masturbate for some relief. What felt like an hour of tugging and stroking was only frustrating him more. He fears he'll once more need to drown in alcohol to find some reprieve. Unsure why he's a prisoner to his torturous thought process or how he might escape this maddening cycle.

Growing more agitated and impatient, Ray grabs a little orange bottle from the kitchen. It's his prescription sleeping medication that he hasn't taken in weeks. Ray chases a small handful of pills with the remnants in an orange juice jug from his fridge.

Ray plops down in his lazy boy chair and switches on a western movie to drown out his thoughts. He covers himself with the old, knitted blanket draped across the back of his recliner. He pokes and twirls his fingers through the small holes until his eyes fall shut. Ray slips away into a near comatose state. Finally, some peace.

10

A Rude Awakening

It turned out to be about 30 hours of peace. When Ray awoke Friday morning, he felt rested and rejuvenated. Aside from his bladder so saturated that it's causing pain as he stumbles to the bathroom. After taking the longest piss in history, he checks his phone.

Ray is first struck by the *26 missed calls* from his boss over the past workday, followed by the *13 SMS* next to the small envelope icon. Ray fears he missed something significant and then notices the date. *Friday, January 2nd,* displayed in tiny font on the corner of his screen.

"Shit." he exclaims aloud, as his heart sinks. In a panic, Ray searches his room and then his entire trailer for the empty bottles. Assuming he drank himself into oblivion and did something terrible. He hastily explores his truck and outside shed. Not finding any obvious signs of destruction, he takes a second to catch his breath outside. Ray rests on a rusty metal bench under a giant oak tree in his front yard. Shaded from the morning sun, until the light pierces through like laser beams. Warming his face in patches as the boughs sway above him in the brisk winter breeze.

Raymond Townes has feared the worst and is troubled with how quickly he accepted this fate. Not a simple mistake, but he felt in his bones that the error would have been a life-altering tragedy. He was sure of it. So much so that he frantically searched his entire property. *To find what?* He thinks to himself. *Was I looking for a woman? Someone I hurt or felt compelled to help?* His mind is rapidly shuffling through emotions, and he has so many questions.

With his head in hand, Ray reviews the last recollections he has, before drifting into the tranquil abyss where he remained for too long. He needs to make sense of things before he returns Zimmer's call. He reenters his home and tries to recall each step after arriving on New Year's, which is his last clear memory.

Unable to focus for long with his mouth as dry as the Sahara, he advances to the kitchen for some water. There he finds the sleeping pill bottle still opened, next to the empty OJ jug sitting on the counter. Ray feels foolish and awkward since he must now explain this to his boss. Feeling his cell vibrating, he apprehensively checks the screen. Instant relief sets in as 'Dr. Pfeiffer' flashes.

"Hey doc, morning, uh, Happy New Year." Ray's husky voice addresses his therapist.

"Townes, good morning. I'm so glad you took my call. I wanted to reach out after reading your lieutenant's email."

Great, Ray thinks to himself, *he already got to her.*

"Oh, and what did he have to say?" Ray questions. Anticipation builds—contributing to the pit in his stomach, beyond the hunger pangs now raiding his empty abdomen.

"He has concerns. He wanted to see if you made contact or if there was something urgent going on. He mentioned your absence from work and ignoring his calls yesterday. He sounded afraid that he may have pushed you away, or offended you with some big news he shared? He told me you invited him onto your boat. That's huge, Ray! We'll discuss that more this afternoon if you can make your appointment. But I had to check in."

Ray assures Dr. Pfeiffer that his boss is misinterpreting the situation. He admits the truth, explaining that he overmedicated and slept through the entire previous day. Which was the only reason he missed work and all communication with Zimmer. Ray admits that while he had two beers during their outing, he was able to end it there. This is a foreign concept for him, simply telling the truth. No embellishments or excuses.

She is understanding and tells Ray this isn't uncommon. But sternly warns him to be more careful. If he takes that many pills again, especially mixed with alcohol, "it could prove fatal." Her words are a stark awakening, and he is thankful to be here still. Ray might not have ever woken up if he did drink more that night. She informs him that while Lt Zimmer took Ray's absence personally, he hasn't gone to Cpt Thompson yet. So, there is still time for Ray to make things right. Dr. Pfeiffer advises him to tell the truth, but the decision is left up to Ray.

Raymond is thankful for Dr. P.'s support and quickly reads Zimmer's texts after ending their call. The messages start with concern about Townes being late; then not showing up to work at all or answering any calls. The texts get harder for Ray to read, knowing his friend was experiencing so much anxiety, confusion, and possible embarrassment. Zimmer was left to drown in his worst fears all day. Assuming Ray wasn't as receptive to his confession as he claimed on the lake. The lieutenant went on to apologize if he made Townes uncomfortable. Then asked for any response to ensure he was okay. The last message states that Zimmer would be reaching out to Dr. Pfeiffer for guidance.

Ray wastes little time calling his boss to explain the situation. He heeds his therapist's advice despite wanting to lie and sugarcoat things a bit. Ray feels compelled to clear the air and make his new friend feel comfortable again. To his relief, it was easier than he thought. Zimmer was elated to get the call. He informs Ray that he began to give him a scare, and he was on the verge of looking up his address to make a house call if Townes didn't reach out soon. Ray thanks his boss for covering for him on his "personal day." Zimmer concedes that his confession was an unnecessary burden to put on Ray. Admitting that he has decided to hold off on *coming out* to the entire force, for now. This situation proves Zimmer isn't ready for the possible backlash or reactions that may arise.

"Well, sir, I hope it's not just because of this mess. I still feel the same way I did when we parted on New Year's Eve. This was a mistake, and it won't happen again! I assure you. I hope you reconsider, but we're still on your timeline."

Zimmer thanks Townes for his continued support and adds that he must head into a meeting with Captain Thompson and hopes to see Ray soon. "I'll hop in the shower and head right in. See you in less than an hour." Townes confirms.

Despite wanting to be a friend to Zimmer, while in the shower Ray realizes that he knows a vital secret. One that his boss isn't willing or ready to share with anyone else. He can't help but feel some power in this dynamic. Ray knows that he could use this information for extortion, but it would damage their friendship, and especially their working relationship. Unsure what could require such betrayal, Ray knows he should always be ready. He isn't proud of this shady role, the controlling and power-hungry man who's willing to take anyone down that might pose a threat. But he understands the need for a plan and to have some collateral on his side. Townes believes this strategy makes him stronger, smarter, and more prepared. He reevaluates the title 'friend' as well. He knows that Zimmer is his superior officer, above all else. While he has defended Townes and has always been fair, Zimmer is still in charge and can always put Townes in his place.

Ray has limited time, and there is too much on the line for him to contemplate an idea like this. He chooses to keep the rebellious thoughts locked away and focus on the mission. He needs to get back to work and let Zimmer off the emotional hook before he does something drastic.

As he pulls into the Special Crimes parking lot, it's now after ten in the morning. This is the latest Townes has arrived at work in almost twenty years. After missing the entire day before, he is feeling unprepared and anxious. Ray remembers that only himself, Zimmer, and Dr. P. are aware of his mistake. He tries to swallow his doubts and channel some confidence.

Zimmer intercepts Ray's focus, meeting him outside and holding the door open. Appearing relieved to see Townes, he also emits concern. Townes was ushered into the trailer by his anxious boss. Zimmer looks around before closing the door behind them.

"We have a huge problem here, Townes. I, I messed up. I should've informed the captain already about our suspect, but I didn't. And now…damn. This is so bad. I'm done! We're done, Townes. This entire unit. Oh God, my career. I'm sorry, okay?"

The frantic lieutenant is pacing around, and Ray quickly determines that this isn't about his absence. His boss appears bothered by something with the case. Ray realizes what has likely happened and his heart drops. He probes for information. "Slow down, sir, I'm here now, and we can figure this out together. Tell me what happened."

Zimmer sits at the conference table and confirms precisely what Townes feared. "A woman is missing, Raymond. Not an easy target like the others, but I think it's our guy. And if he has her, we're done! This girl, oh God." Zimmer runs his hand through his hair, his legs taking turns bouncing like a toddler is on his knees. "Okay, all I know is that she comes from a prominent family, and if our guy has her, Townes…we're done!"

Ray calms his boss down to get out all that he currently knows. The missing woman is Maddison Broussard-Turner. Cpt Thompson and Chief Diehl briefed Zimmer moments ago, making him aware of the case and their concerns. They said that her family is *connected* and wants extreme privacy during this investigation, as well as extensive cooperation and urgency. When updated on the circumstances of her disappearance, it became clear that she could be the next victim of their enigmatic suspect.

"We know nothing, Townes. We've been working behind the scenes with Dr. Gaston for weeks now. Although we have a working profile on this guy, we really have *nothing*. Not a single thing of value to present. Now, I must explain why we not only sat on this theory but that our worst fears might have just become a painful reality. This sadistic monster is still active, and raging his destruction throughout *our* parish, under *our* watch." Zimmer takes a seat and sighs while shaking his head.

Townes steps up to create a plan moving forward, realizing his experience can lead the way. Zimmer needs a push in the right direction. "Okay, listen. We'll first call Dr. Gaston and make her aware of the situation. She is the expert here, sir, and she'll help us. Then once we have a better plan, we execute our briefing to the brass. L.T., remember there was a reason we sat on this theory. Until Ms. Nichols and Michaela Hardy gave us more connections, we had nothing concrete. Still, we have no DNA or evidence at all, aside from our theories and minimal knowledge. If this is our guy and he has this woman, we'll find her, sir. Hopefully, alive. But... prepare yourself for what we both know might be the outcome here. Okay? And push comes to shove, if someone must take the blame—I'm on my way out the door. You can put it all on me, okay?" Townes works to motivate his young friend.

"Thank you, detective, but that won't be necessary. I'm the superior officer; this case and task force are my responsibility. I appreciate that offer and regardless of the outcome here, we'll still get you out the door the right way. You have earned your pension and your retirement privileges Townes. No one should take that from you. Especially not because of the massive cluster-fuck that this case has created. I'll get Dr. Gaston on the line, and we'll go from there."

"Roger that, sir."

This case was a burden of the Special Crimes Team long before the lieutenant arrived. He was a desk sergeant working patrol reports when some of this psychopath's victims turned up. Townes fears that their investigation will highlight many mistakes made during his tenure. Zimmer won't be on the line for that. Ray is too far into this to turn away or bow out. He plans to continue to have his lieutenant's back. To work this case with all that he has left and walk out the door of the 31st precinct with pride.

The team clings to a sliver of hope as they make the call. Desperate for Dr. Gaston to better guide them. The conference phone speaker trills throughout the silent trailer. Echoing off the thin metal walls around them as they fester. Each contemplating their future with this unit, both filled with guilt and discomfort. Desperate for their unofficial team member to dig them out of this hole.

11

A Fond Familiarity

As soon as Dr. Gaston answers their call, Zimmer informs her that they have a missing woman. Who they believe to currently be with their suspect and his likely next victim if they can't find her. Both men flinch as the table begins to vibrate. Zimmer's cellphone dances in a small circle in front of them. He sees that it's the chief and excuses himself outside for better reception.

For the first time since they brought Dr. Gaston on board, Townes is alone and forced to speak to her. Nervous, but trying to stay professional, he initiates. "Good morning, ma'am, uh, Happy New Year." He sticks to the same casual ruse.

"Morning, detective, and Happy New Year to you." Gaston's voice sounds different this time. Still strong and authoritative, yet there is a subtle inflection. Her tone lingers in Ray's ears like a comforting hug.

A few seconds of silence pass before she chimes back in, catching Ray off guard. "Can you describe her?"

"Um, what? Who now?" Townes' confusion was amusing to the Dr. as she exhaled an audible snicker.

"The woman, the missing one. Mrs. Turner, was it? Can you please describe her physical appearance to me? Your lieutenant didn't get far."

"Yes, of course, I'm sorry. Let me see what we have here…sorry, I'm just getting this info the same as you, ma'am." Ray shuffles through the slim file and discovers a recent picture they have.

"Okay, it looks like the family gave us a college graduation picture. According to the file, this would have been from this past June of 2003, when she graduated from BRU. She is 23 years old, Caucasian, slim build, bright blue eyes, and long blonde hair."

He looks for the missing person's report to find her exact height and weight. Ray hears Gaston utter, 'Shit," before he continues.

"She's 5 feet 8 inches, and about 120 pounds…I'm sorry, did you just say, 'shit'?" Ray asks, unable to move on.

"Yes, I'm worried about a small detail, and if I'm right, then…you guys are too," she bleakly responds.

"It's the hair, right? Long and blonde like the Hardy girl. You think that's what he's going for?" Townes surprises Dr. Gaston with his keen observation.

"Yes. Exactly. And worse, all the other victims might have been practice for *this*. He was substituting, if you will— until he found the right one. Mrs. Turner's appearance may have triggered something innate. He might not have known what he was looking for until he saw her. And he has had her for how long now?"

Ray verifies the time she went missing with a scan through the file. It was written by Cpt Thompson around six this morning. The reporter was a Mr. Broussard, who Townes assumes to be Maddison's father.

"Hard to say; the report has limited information. It claims that the family hasn't seen her since before New Year's Eve. It also says she was living with her new husband, and we're still in need of a full statement from him. L.T. should know more when he gets back. Sorry."

"It's okay; I understand we have little to go on. His timeline is consistent though, so we should've expected this. I could've been more proactive here and called in some favors. You guys didn't even present this to your superiors yet, so the FBI is a huge jump, but we must run this up the chain. Perhaps sooner than your lieutenant will be ready for. So, I may need your help, Raymond."

Her request stimulates arousal. She used his full first name, and it felt personal. Townes thinks to himself while adjusting his pants, *of all the times to do this.* Trying to hide the slight bulge, he is thankful to only be on a conference call. Ray tries to understand how a professional request from a woman he has never seen can invoke a sexual response. But he is proud at the same time to know it still works. Zimmer flings the trailer door open, intervening before Townes needs a cold shower.

"You still have her on the line? Great. You both need to hear this." Zimmer exhales as he slumps down into the cracked leather office chair. He rolls himself close to the table where Townes has the Broussard-Turner file opened.

"So, this has taken a turn, and I want you both to know that I take full responsibility here. No matter what happens. Okay? Now, there's a reason we're hearing about this case already, and it isn't sitting in a pile on the captain's desk. Mrs. Broussard-Turner is the daughter of a prominent retired Federal Judge. The Honorable Jack Broussard retired from the Fifth Circuit in New Orleans. He and his wife moved back to Beau Ridge almost two years ago. He still has a lot of pull all over the state, it appears. Mr. Broussard called Chief Diehl directly last night, to inform him that his youngest daughter Maddison has been missing since Wednesday night.

"He requested the chief investigate her new husband, Joseph Turner. He's on his way to headquarters to give a formal statement. The chief passed the case to Cpt Thompson and then onto us. Hoping our little team can work it quietly without making many aware. Mr. Broussard wants the utmost confidentiality, especially until we know more. So, here we are, and I can't say that we shouldn't have expected this. I... I don't know." Zimmer gets flushed with red cheeks, and Townes steps up to help.

"Sir, Dr. G., and I were discussing this, and we all want to take some blame here. None of us are absolved from responsibility, that's for sure. We all agree we should've done and said more but we can't change the circumstances now. So, please tell us what we need to do, and let's move forward."

Townes' assertive nature resonates with the lieutenant. He takes a moment to gather his thoughts and proceeds with instruction. "Okay, Det Townes, I want you to go over to the station and get the statement from her husband, Mr. Turner. He's coming from downtown and should be here in about an hour. Let's see where her father's doubts and concerns are coming from. Even if this is our guy, her husband might know something significant. Get as much as you can about exactly when and how she disappeared."

Zimmer continues, "Dr. Gaston, I would like to request your services—in person. This case is already out of hand, and if we're going to get a grasp here, we need every resource available. You're the biggest asset to our team right now—we need you!"

The lieutenant's request stops Townes in his tracks as he was sliding his chair away from the table. He never considered having to work face to face with this woman. Ray shuts down his selfish concerns, trying to stay focused on the task at hand.

Zimmer adds, "I'll figure out what to say to the chief. I'll explain what we're dealing with. He should see the importance of your expertise and approve you to come aboard." Zimmer's tone turns somber. "Otherwise, I'm out of options. I can't even say for sure if they'll accept the help, let alone be able to pay you. You've been so generous with your time thus far, and you only agreed to consult remotely. We never even discussed your rates. I'm sorry, I guess I didn't think this through."

Gaston chimes in to regain control and give the pair a much-needed morale boost. "Gentlemen, you don't have to worry about me. I can assist with the remainder of my consultation without requiring any financial compensation. I'll make my travel arrangements and arrive in Beau Ridge as soon as you gain approval. I've been looking for an opportunity to obtain more field experience. So, let's handle our next missions, and I'll await your call to move forward, lieutenant. If you have any trouble at all, please let me know. I'll be happy to discuss the matter with your brass and gain some resolution."

Gaston's conclusion sent the team on their way. With newfound confidence, they're now ready to gain some traction on their suspect.

12

Truck Therapy

He won't have much time later to make it to his therapy appointment. Townes calls his doctor to have a remote session, awaiting the interview for Mr. Turner, he doesn't want to travel too far. Ray worries about his ability to manage everything going on right now. Knowing how easily things can spiral, he must be vigilant. With the acceleration in their case, he's preparing for the worst.

Dr. Pfeiffer is first worried about them only having a phone conversation. But she understands his profession and this case's demands. She only wishes to ease the burden. She expresses concern about his sobriety, following the temptation he must have faced during the New Year's Eve excursion.

Ray reassures Dr. P. that their celebration was tame. To his disbelief, he never stopped at Taft Liquor or had much of a desire to drink more after that. It's time Ray let his therapist in a little more. He must better illustrate his actual trigger in life and what he has a harder time managing than alcohol.

"Okay, it's time to discuss something else. An issue that's a bigger concern than my drinking." Townes finds the phone session is providing the reassurance to explain his true affliction. Ray takes a deep breath, then continues. "I haven't been one hundred percent honest about my sexual *addiction*. I'll call it what it is. I'm ready to admit it. I told you about the blackout drinking and waking up with a random woman next to me. Or in an odd place, like half-naked in my truck, in a liquor store parking lot. I also told you that I was abstaining completely, but that wasn't true. I've still been, uh, masturbating. Regularly."

Ray knows this conversation is only going to get more complicated. Talking to a woman he's not sleeping with about all the wild shit he likes to do in the bedroom is awkward for him. But he can't continue to bear this burden alone; he swallows his pride and prepares to let it out.

First, he allows her to address this transition in their session. "Well, I'll start with thank you—for feeling safe enough to share this new information. I'll reiterate that even phone sessions fall under our confidentiality clause. Okay? So, moving right along, I'd like to address how often you notice the urge to masturbate?"

Townes is unsure how to answer at first but appreciates her undaunted progression. "Well, I guess it's many times a day. I'm unable to give in to that, obviously. So, I think the impulses have dissipated a bit. I was doing it as often as possible on leave. Being back on duty, not as much."

"And is that because it lost its appeal or you're unable to reach sexual gratification? Or more for lack of opportunity to carry out the act?"

Ray takes a second to mull over her questions. "Well, you initially advised of a no-sex plan, complete abstinence. I tried that at first, but I felt the cravings become more intense and more frequent. I thought taking care of myself would be better than finding a woman to sleep with. While it feels much better to be inside them, they come with requirements that I usually don't have the patience for. I hoped to curb the urges, but the relief was uh, wearing off. I would feel good for a few minutes, then suddenly need more. It's like I can't keep up sometimes. I can go to work on myself three or four times a night and still want more." Townes pauses to see if this is alarming to his therapist.

"When you're with a woman do you care about her needs? Do you ensure that she reaches climax as well?"

Ray retorts with a puffed-out chest, "Of course, every time. I usually do that first, then take care of myself. I'm all about pleasure and I want us each to enjoy it. Sometimes I wonder if I'll always need *more*."

Dr. P. allows Ray to continue. "Like with my ex-wife, Irene. I felt I was always taking care of her sexual needs. The effort I was getting in return was never sufficient. That's when I started to get into a routine, I guess. I was finding it harder to get off from, *regular* sex. But Irene wasn't into much else, and I didn't want to push too hard. I thought I was respecting her boundaries, but it left me unfulfilled, often. I felt selfish but knew I had to take care of my needs too. I thought that what I needed from a sexual partner was too much for her, maybe?"

"I see. And during 'regular sex,' to which I assume you mean missionary positions or the like—were you always able to finish?"

"Yes, eventually."

"And did that eventual orgasm require you to fantasize about other women or positions? Perhaps, ones your wife wasn't comfortable with or willing to do?"

"Well, yes. I had to. Almost always."

The Dr. continues, "And these fantasies, you were able to visualize the sex you wanted? Able to see yourself with another partner? Someone more willing to do the things you needed?"

"Yes."

"Did you gain this mental material from personal encounters? Or from watching others, such as pornography?"

Ray appreciates the trajectory of their conversation and her not making him play coy. "Both. I had fantasies and flashbacks I guess, to my ex. Uh, my affair with my old boss. I thought about the sex Ele Miles, and I had often. We broke things off in '88, and I spiraled for a while until my bosses noticed. I went to AA and met Irene in 1994. We got married six months later, in February of '95, at my commander's urgency and advice.

"The Special Crimes Team started in 1991. We were gaining traction and producing some heavy workloads, it was intense. I wasn't over Ele, but I tried to throw myself into the job and ignore all my own needs. That didn't work well, and it worsened after I married Irene. It put a strain on our marriage, but it wasn't because of Ele. I tried to block her out, but it didn't help much with Irene. She was a very different woman.

"I knew I made a mistake marrying Irene, and I regret that. If I'm being honest, I was never sexually satisfied with her. I thought that it might not be important. That I could handle it on my own, and if not, I was willing to settle I suppose. She was a great wife and homemaker, and she had maternal instincts without ever bearing a child. Which I found admirable and comforting." Ray takes a second to think about Irene's caring and nurturing disposition. Her memory resurfaces fondly today.

Dr. P. doesn't give Ray much time to ponder. "So, the pornography. You said you used both mental mementos and explicit content made by others? Can you tell me about that?"

This was where things took a turn for Irene and Townes. But he is ready to get this off his chest and admit the truth about his downfall. "Well, yes, it was an escape at first. I was new to it all. The internet porn, I mean. I had seen all the good magazines by then, in '96. I had plenty of old VHS tapes and I got some better-quality DVDs later. But the internet, whew. I had no idea I would find some of the crazy shit I've seen on there.

"I was introduced to it at Alcoholic Anonymous, actually. I started attending a new meeting after Easter in '96. I wanted to get away from Trinity Baptist, where Irene was still working. I found a regular meeting at the library in our town. I was enjoying the new environment and group. Many of the guys had addictions to other things, not just alcohol. This guy Bill was big into the porn scene; it's all he would talk about before the meetings. I overheard him one day going on about this new actress and her, uh, *skills*. My curiosity was piqued, and I had to know more.

"I approached him after the meeting, but he was cautious at first about me being on the force. We went to a waffle house and talked for a couple of hours. I convinced Bill that I was barely holding onto my shield and needed it strictly for personal use.

"Then he spilled it all about his freelance jobs as a video editor. He had worked for several different porn producers across Louisiana. He showed me a folder from a briefcase with twenty different women's pictures. They were still shots from the sets of X-rated movies. They were graphic too. It was all enthralling to me. Bill explained that he had thousands more at his place, saved digitally on his computers. He invited me over that night, but I waited until the next meeting, a couple of days later.

"That meeting couldn't end fast enough. We got to his place, and I felt like a high school kid about to lose his V-Card. It wasn't a dingy basement like I feared, and Bill was a decent guy. He showed me the three computers he had set up in a spare bedroom of his house. I could barely work the one I had at Irene's house, which she gifted me for Christmas in '95. He had tons of material and even video clips of various explicit scenes. Bill explained that he could put content onto a disc that I could bring home and view on my own computer. I couldn't believe it at first, and it took me a bit to understand how it all worked. He was patient, though. I felt confident soon enough, got the disc loaded up and went on my way.

"I had to get started that same night—I was so eager. I told Irene I finally had a sponsor and that I had been with him after the meeting. She was supportive and excited. I told her he gave me an 'assignment' to work on before our next meeting. Irene encouraged me to go into my office and have all the time and privacy I needed. Fortunately for me, she was more committed to my sobriety than I was." Ray smirks before continuing.

"So, I lied, and it became easier as time went on. I would sit in that office for hours analyzing the images and the positions those women were in. I tried not to pleasure myself right there. Fearing she could walk in at any time, I knew I couldn't explain that. Occasionally though, I would give in, and it doesn't take long to get used to it all: the routine, the excitement, discovering new footage and actresses. It almost became like a game.

"But it also didn't take long to get dependent on having the material there. I guess I started to need it. Not only was it more difficult to have gentle sex with Irene. Like many other habits, I felt my involvement in porn was going too far. I was getting more into the rough, S & M-type stuff. But it was finally providing relief. I was thinking about the scenes and the women in the videos all the time. I thought I was hiding my new hobby well enough."

Ray sips some coffee and then continues. "Irene had her teenage niece and nephew over every weekday after school. Her only sister was a single parent living on the other side of town, and she worked crazy hours as a nurse. She used Irene's home address for the kids to attend the high school a few miles from her neighborhood. They rode a bus that dropped them off right down the street. They had a great relationship, and I didn't mind the kids being there, not that it was my place to have an opinion. In fact, I would rarely see them. I often got home well into the evening with the workload from Special Crimes. I occasionally gave them a ride home, when their mom got stuck at the hospital because Irene hated driving at night. I would let them control the radio and most of the drive was in silence, which they seemed to prefer. I thought we all had a good thing going for a bit.

"Well, I was working late one night, and I guess her niece had a project for school. She mentioned needing to go to the library to use a computer for research. Irene remembered I had the internet hooked up to my office computer. She says she tried to call me to ask permission, but, unable to reach me, she let her niece into my office. I had no security or passwords back then; I still don't understand it all.

"Anyways, her niece was horrified. She tried to open a document to type up her report and had to sift through tons of graphic pictures that she claimed, 'kept popping up.' I had gotten so complacent I didn't even bother to close the files. We're talking violent images from amateur snuff films, torture porn, and bondage. I wasn't always into it all for arousal. Sometimes it was just intriguing. I got home to an earful about using their personal computer for all my 'perverted work stuff.'

"Irene set it up that way, so I went with it. I agreed that what they saw was all for work. Irene was gullible, but her niece was far from naïve. After that, both kids acted differently around me. Everything went downhill from there and it wasn't much later that we found out she was infertile, and we split. Sorry… wow, I'm rambling!" Ray takes a second to catch his breath. Realizing he is trying to get a lot of his past into this short session.

"It's called opening up Mr. Townes, and it's literally the point of therapy." Dr. P. laughs. "I know you don't have much more time, but this is all helpful. It gives me a better understanding of your past and how to keep us moving forward. Is there anything else you think I should know while we're still on the line?"

Ray hesitantly continues with more truth. "Well, you remember I mentioned that criminologist we began working with a few weeks back?"

"Sure, Dr. E.V. Gaston, was it?"

"Yes, that's right, Dr. Evie Gaston. I haven't had much contact with her until today, but something about her voice, uh, got to me. Now she might be coming here, and I'm worried about working with her. In case her voice has the same results when we meet. If she can tell, it might affect her. I don't want to do anything to further jeopardize this investigation. I know my time is dwindling. If I ruin this case, that illustrious career isn't in the cards. The brass will do everything possible to take my pension and ensure my name is forever tainted in Beau Ridge."

Dr. Pfeiffer can hear Ray's fear and wavering confidence. "Is your issue with this woman's voice, or more from the stress of this case and your impending retirement? That alone can spark involuntary arousal. Especially considering the victim's images you're studying regularly. Your brain may have trouble differentiating the material as work versus pleasure. I wouldn't worry about the doctor. Just focus on your case. Be there for your lieutenant and you guys come together to solve this. I want you to get out on the lake every day that you can. Get your line in the water, and work on your breathing and focal points. You can do this Detective Townes." Dr. Pfeiffer concludes with confidence.

They hang up and Ray takes a second to reflect on her advice. The arousal might not be due to any specific woman. Least of all their new team member, whom he has never even seen. This conversation has satisfied Townes, he's beginning to appreciate his time in therapy.

He heads towards the precinct's old brick and brownstone building, to interview Mr. Joseph Turner. Ray allows his focus to shift back to Maddison Broussard-Turner. She is counting on their small team. Townes is ready to find her, or at least some answers.

13

A Hopeless Husband

Townes walks into their precinct's main building, noticing the nostalgic aroma of burnt coffee and mildew still lingers in the air. He doesn't get as many looks this time. There are so many new faces and transfers, that he hardly recognizes anyone. He enters the interview room, where Mr. Turner was escorted about fifteen minutes ago.

Joseph Turner's tattered sneakers, the holes in his shirt, and the paint on his jeans spoke to Ray first. Telling him this guy might not come from the same type of family he married into. Townes introduces himself and sits in the metal-framed chair across the table.

"Hey there, we appreciate you coming in. I have this audio recorder to tape our conversation. So, I can write up the details in the report later and not miss anything. Is that okay with you, Mr. Turner?"

"Of course, no worries. But please, call me Joey," he replies calmly.

"Sure thing. So, Joey, please tell me a little about your relationship first. Whatever you can illustrate to help me better understand who your wife is. Let's start from the beginning to get me caught up."

Joey clears his throat softly and then begins. "Okay, well, Maddison and I met two years ago at BRU, while she was going to school. Shortly after we started dating, her father retired. Her parents then moved from New Orleans back here to Beau Ridge. They were a close family. But Maddi felt like she needed more independence and space than her folks allowed. We moved in together last summer after she graduated in June of 2003.

"Her dad got pissed and kept trying to lure Maddi back home. He even offered to help with her *own* place. When that failed, he tried to guilt-trip her with the bible since she's like a super-Christian. It worked, too; he made her feel like shit, telling her we were 'living in sin.' Maddison said she needed to 'talk to God' and get some guidance on how she was living her life. She stopped eating real food. Calling it 'fasting for clarity.' She lost a ton of weight and wouldn't do much outside of church events.

"Her sister Maggie is two years older than Maddison, and she has a daughter, Jillian. The three of them are very close. In her senior year of high school, Maggie got pregnant with Jillian. She was only seventeen, so their dad flipped. He practically wrote Maggie off, saying she ruined her life and shamed their family and God. Mr. Broussard made her hide the entire pregnancy. Maddison said he even tried to talk Maggie into an abortion several times. And went as far as setting up a potential family to adopt Jillian, when she was only six weeks old. He wasn't receiving any Best Dad Ever mugs, but he still provided for his family quite comfortably. Being a fancy lawyer and judge had its perks. And he's sure to remind us of that regularly.

"So, after a few months of watching Maddison dwindle away, and seeing how affected she was by her dad's opinions, I made a choice. I told Maddi that I loved her more than anything and that I want to spend my life *with* her, and there was no reason we couldn't. I proposed to her right there, with my grandmother's wedding ring. I told her I'd give her the wedding she always dreamt of someday. But for now, we just needed to make it official. Her sister helped me plan it all and was our witness, along with her boyfriend, Mark. He's not Jillian's dad, but he's a good guy; been around a year now, so I hope he'll stay. We brought Jillian as well; she held the rings and loved being a part of our little ceremony.

"We all drove down to New Orleans together a couple of weeks after the engagement. To a little chapel that officiates weddings. It wasn't like a cheesy Vegas chapel either. Maddi loved it; she thought it was 'beautiful and quaint.' And she adored the old man who officiated, Mr. Gil. He was blind but told her she was 'radiant' and that he could 'see' her 'aura glowing.' Maddison smiled so big on that day in September, when we said, 'I do.' I'll always cherish that snapshot in my mind."

Joey cracks a short smile before continuing. "Maddison waited a couple of weeks, working up the courage to tell her parents that we eloped. Her mom was happy for us, which was refreshing. Mrs. B always liked me, though. And she's a saint for putting up with her husband all these years. Of course, *he* was less than impressed with his youngest daughter's choice of husband. Jack Broussard never thought I was good enough because I couldn't make enough. I do all right, and we have everything we need. But I can't compete with his pockets, that's for sure. He always hated that Maddi and I met at the University. It's where I work as a contractor doing repairs and basic construction around campus. He made it clear he thought she could do better. She proudly told him that we were married and that it was what she wanted.

"They went into his office to chat, which lasted like two hours. I think he needed to ensure she wasn't coerced. Maddi came out of those large French doors wiping away tears, but still smiling. Jack shook my hand before we left and told me that he would like to talk with me as well, 'sometime soon,' but that has yet to happen."

Joey rolls his eyes and sighs. "I thought we were all making progress. But on Jillian's 10th birthday in December, nothing seemed to change. Mr. Broussard still acted like it was an obligation to be there for his family. He was on the phone for most of the celebration, which started at a play that Jillian had a role in for their church youth group. She was so happy to have her whole family in the audience. Maddison is the reason Jillian was so involved in the church. She loved studying the bible with her niece and sharing her favorite passages. They had a great bond. Maddi was ecstatic at the announcement after the play. Jillian had finally completed the recommended classes and was on the list for baptism, which was important to Maddi. She had the day marked on our calendar in the kitchen. Circled in red, with huge stars all over the Sunday it was to occur, January 4th."

"In two days, this Sunday!" Townes chimes in.

Joey nods his head in agreement and a lock of his long black hair slips free from his low ponytail. He brushes it behind his ear and continues. "Maddi wanted to make it a special occasion for Jillian. She told her the new year was a perfect time to make this change. And that devoting herself to Christ would be the best decision of her life."

Joey gets a little choked up and apologizes to Townes. Ray pauses the tape, allowing Mr. Turner to collect himself.

"Take your time Joe."

Joey takes a deep breath and pleads with Townes. "Anyways, I don't know if this is useful, but I know something happened to her. Something bad, I can feel it. *Please*, do you guys have anything at all? Her dad isn't telling me shit, and I'm going crazy here. I know Jack thinks I had something to do with this. But I didn't! Please, detective, is there anything at all you can tell me?"

Ray can hear the despair in Joey's voice. This man loves her and appears genuine and honest. "I wish I had more, but my team just got the case this morning. I'm working to understand the facts myself." Townes wants to tell Joey the truth. That a deranged monster has likely abducted his beautiful wife, and he will never see her alive again.

Townes presses on withholding the grim truth. "Joey, tell me about when she disappeared. What happened exactly? Based on her father's report, she's been missing since New Year's Day. Maddison was last seen by a friend around 2:30 a.m., after their party Wednesday evening."

Joey scoffs, "That asshole! I knew he would do this. Is that in the report? Jesus, this guy. Look, I don't know what this crazy old bastard has planned, but this guy is bored out of his mind, okay? Jack Broussard has not taken retirement well. I think he's realizing he has such little life experience outside of the courtroom and it's finally caught up to him. He has no skills; he hires out for every damn thing any man is proud to do. He has been itching for a new project or focus, and now, *this*. I wouldn't be shocked if that control freak arranged her kidnapping. He is always talking about these 'cartel connections' he has. From the federal cases he's presided over, down in New Orleans. He tries to control everything. Their entire lives. Maddi just wanted some space. Man, do you think he's capable of that?" Joey questions.

Townes tries to calm Mr. Turner down and keep him focused. "I don't know what he is capable of, Joe. Then again, I have only known you for about an hour now, so we aren't too acquainted yet, are we? I'm still here to listen. Let's get through this, so I can get back to my job of bringing your wife home." *Likely in a body bag, but I will get her back*, Townes callously concludes.

"Okay, this is what happened, detective, and this is *all* I know. Her father planned a huge party for New Year's Eve and invited her two days prior. Maddi still went with her original plans, made weeks ago with her friends. She was attending a reunion party with her sorority sisters from BRU. I was proud of her for getting back out there and reconnecting with them. She knew I couldn't go out to celebrate, having work early the next day, so it was a solo mission. Most of her friends are still single, so they thought a 'girl's night' was great. They planned a pub crawl near the campus, visiting their old spots from their college days. Then they were going to sober up back at their sorority house before heading home. Her *sister* Brynn was her Beverage Buddy. It's a person you're like, assigned all night to watch over your drinks and make sure you get home safe.

"So anyway, she went to pick Brynn up that night, and the two of them drove to the sorority house. I had Maggie call and she confirmed this. Brynn explained that Maddi wasn't feeling well and didn't drink much. The two of them left early as a result. Brynn was cool with it since she has a new baby at home. She arrived home just after two, and Maddison should have been back by 2:30, at the latest. Brynn only lives like ten minutes away from us."

Townes interrupts, "you said she '*should*' have been home by 2:30. But you aren't sure exactly when? How do you know she made it home at all?"

Joey continues cautiously, "I'm sure she made it home. I have proof, in fact, with the note. She left it on my bedside table, right on my alarm clock, which blared away at 6:30 like it does every morning. And her car was home too, but I didn't know that until later."

Townes was intrigued, "What did this note say? And where is it right now?"

"It said, '*Babe*,' that's me," Joey grins, '*Couldn't sleep, going for a run, will stop at Walden's, can't wait for pics. Love you, Madly.*' That last part is a play on words, she signs everything for me with it." He replies with another grin, likely thinking of his loving wife leaving this note casually.

"And where is it now? The note." Townes asks again.

"Uh, I gave it to Mr. B. He said he would file it with the report, that it was 'evidence' and was necessary for you guys to have it. He took it in a damn sandwich bag last night. He came by at like midnight, looking all over our place. He's never even been there before. I asked if Mrs. B was coming by or if she had heard from Maddi. He freaked out, saying that she hadn't and that she also had no idea Maddison was even missing yet. He insisted I only speak with him about everything and leave his wife out of this entirely. He explained Maddi's absence at their party as a lack of communication. Jack spun it like he always does, and of course his wife believed him. Man, when it comes to Mrs. Broussard, I tell you. That woman lives in a total fantasy land. He shields her from most of what goes on in the family. Jack always makes himself look like the hero, fixing everything with all his money. Mrs. B. has gotten pretty comfortable with their lifestyle it seems." Joey shakes his head in disgust.

"Mr. Broussard is hiding everything and lying as usual. Expecting we'll magically find Maddison before Sunday. Then we will all show up to Jillian's Baptism and make amends for the last decade of secrets, hate, and judgment. Ugh, this is exactly why I'm not religious. It's all complete bullshit. So, to answer your question, I guess *you* should have the note?" Joey concludes.

"Right, then it should be in evidence; I'll check for it after this. So, I get the whole 'girl's night out,' and you work early, so no partying makes sense. What I'm not understanding is how you didn't wake up when your wife got home. She says she couldn't sleep, so she likely laid down in the bed and attempted that, right next to you. Then became restless, got up, and decided to go for a run. Because she needed some pictures, in the middle of the night? She left a note, again, right next to you there, on the nightstand, was it? And still, you're asleep soundly until 0630. Only awoken by your alarm clock. Do I have that right, Joe?" Townes wants to be thorough and feels he needs to press harder to ensure he's getting the truth.

"Yes, sir, you do. But I didn't skip the celebration just because of work. I don't drink or party, *ever*, especially not at night. I don't sleep well, not since I was a kid. For the last two years, I've been on medication for it. Since I was eligible for health insurance with my job at BRU. I take a pill every night like clockwork at 9:00 p.m. I wouldn't even have made it to midnight to get a call from her saying, 'Happy New Year,' even though I wanted to. I missed the call like she knew I would, and she placed the call anyway like I knew she would.

"If it weren't for the ear-piercing siren that blares from my alarm clock, I wouldn't have been up for a few more hours. I grabbed the note and read it in the bathroom, taking a piss. Didn't think much of it, honestly. She loves to run and rarely sleeps. The pictures were of her niece and sister. Maddi planned to frame a few to gift Jillian on her baptism. She's impatient, and Walden's is like two miles away, plus she knows they're 24 hours and had already confirmed they would still be open on New Year's Eve. I jumped in the shower and got ready for work. I was there by 7:30. I assumed I would see her after work. No big deal. And now... we're here." Mr. Turner's voice gets more somber.

"Okay, so you went to work all day. 7:30 to what time? And tell me exactly what happened after work."

"I get off at 5:30 and was home 20 minutes later. I saw Maddi wasn't there and at first, I thought she had been back, but already left for church. They have a youth group meeting around seven every Thursday night. I needed a shower; we did insulation yesterday and that shit is so itchy. So, I went to put my clothes straight into the washer. Our laundry room is next to our garage. I noticed her car was in there, so I checked the hood, and it was cool to the touch. I thought it was weird for her to be out running *again* but wasn't sure what else could explain her absence.

"I went ahead with my shower and then checked the messages on our answering machine when I got out. There were four from her father—typical guilt trip. I heard one play over the speaker when he called but was asleep for the rest. His next call was around midnight. Right after Maddi called me. He wanted to record a 'Happy New Year' message. Adding that he's 'looking forward to Sunday… no hard feelings.' What a joke."

Joey scoffs while rolling his eyes. "The other two reiterated that he needed to talk. Those were after nine Thursday morning when I was at work. Then on the last one, he mentioned calling the church office and that they hadn't seen Maddi all day. He was sure she was home and ignoring his calls. Which he claimed was 'disrespectful on so many levels.' I'm telling you, detective, that man, Mr. Broussard. Well, good luck working with him on this investigation. You decide for yourself how to feel about him." Joey adds.

"Thanks, I'll keep that in mind. Please, go on."

"Okay, so my first call was at about 6:35 last night to Maggie. She was on her way out the door to drop Jillian at church. She got concerned when I mentioned the car was home and that I technically hadn't seen Maddi since the night before. She told me to call their dad and that she would keep Jill home. She was going to call around to check with Brynn and other friends.

"I called Mr. Broussard, and he was pissed of course. He wanted to know why I hadn't called sooner or done more, claiming that she could've never made it home. When I told him about the note, he realized she 'left on foot in the early morning hours,' and went into full lawyer mode. He said he had calls to make and told me to go to Walden's to verify if she made it. I asked how I would do that, and he told me to see if her pictures were picked up. Which I admit I didn't think of.

"So, I went there and confirmed she made it to the store *and* conducted a purchase with her debit card. The cashier said it was for the pictures and a couple of other items when I showed them a photo of her. The register had the sale recorded at 6:37. She should have been on her way home just before seven. It could have taken her up to fifteen minutes, depending on her pace. She usually runs through the park and the paths around Glendale Forest. I thought maybe it was there she could have been taken? It's a big park. But I don't know who would be out at 7:00 a.m. on New Year's Day, snatching up pretty-blonde joggers?" Joey Turner says.

Townes could think of someone, although it is an interesting time frame. Their guy is known to take women on foot, so it's within his M.O.

"This is all great info, Joey. I appreciate you coming in to give your statement. My team will investigate the details of everything we discussed. I hope to have more answers for you soon. And I'm sorry you're going through all this." Townes concludes with a pat on the shoulder.

Townes gathers his tape from the recorder and heads out of the interview room.

Moments later, back in the SCT trailer, Townes places a call to the evidence room of the state's crime lab. Verifying the case number, the clerk tells him one item is logged as evidence. Reportedly, 'One notecard or letter, handwritten. No date, no signature.' It was entered into the lab by Captain Thompson that morning as a 'VIP Rush status.' Ray had to call the lab technician directly to determine what analysis was being done. Before he could make that call, Lt Zimmer walks into the trailer.

His eyebrows raise when he sees Ray sitting at their conference table.

"Townes, so glad you're here; I have an update. I just left the chief's office. I've convinced him that we need to bring Dr. Gaston on board full-time for this case. He couldn't believe I had a 'colleague' who became a criminologist... and was already planning a trip to Louisiana for some field experience." Zimmer winks. "I explained it would be great to provide Ret Judge Broussard with the best resources obtainable. The chief was impressed with Dr. Gaston's credentials and immediately authorized her to consult for the remainder of the investigation. She should be in by tomorrow morning to begin formally working the Broussard case. The chief clarified the importance of this investigation, and we don't have a second to lose here!"

Zimmer's urgency starts to raise Townes' blood pressure. Along with the rapid changes that are taking place. "She'll be here tomorrow. Wow." Ray utters.

"Yep! Were you able to get Mr. Turner's statement? How did that go?" Zimmer asks.

"Uh, yes, sir, I have the tape right here for you to listen to, and then we can go over it together when I get back. I was going to go for a food run. How about tacos?" Townes needs some fresh air, and lunch can't hurt.

"Sounds good. I'll listen to the interview and transcribe everything into the computer. Then print a copy for the file." Zimmer was more tech-savvy than Townes ever could be. He also typed faster and was more accurate, so he never minded the administrative aspects of the job. Which was a huge relief to Townes. It made their working relationship more of an unofficial partnership and both men appreciate the dynamic.

That night, back at his trailer after a long, hot shower, Ray sat on his porch looking up at the infinite stars. He's thankful to be working this case and to still be on the force. There was a time Ray thought his badge was gone forever.

Although he is on his way out the door, Townes feels there is still more he can provide to the BRPD. The conversation he had with his therapist resurfaces. Her professional opinion is that essentially his entire career is a trigger. Townes begins to look at his obligations differently. He never thought seeing so many victims' images over the years could affect him.

Ray notices the residual effects of the sleeping meds that knocked him out for an entire day. They're throwing off his schedule, causing him to remain alert and in deep thought, even though it's well after midnight. He likely won't be getting much rest tonight.

Suddenly, he hears a couple of "dings" from inside. He knows it's notifications from text messages. *Likely from Zimmer*, Ray thinks as he heads in to see what the lieutenant has to say this late.

It displays a number that isn't saved as a contact. He reads the three messages which arrived back-to-back.

'Townes, this is Gaston. I'm in town and need to speak with you. I wondered if we could meet tonight, please.'

'I have something pertinent to discuss, just the two of us. I realize it's late, but this really can't wait until the morning'.

Ray's concern and intrigue build, as he reads the third message.

'Please let me know if this is possible tonight. Could you come to the Main Stay Inn near the airport? The lounge stays open 24hrs'.

Ray racks his brain for a moment, considering how to proceed. What couldn't wait a few more hours until they get to work? It's almost one in the morning, and she wants to meet alone? He takes a minute longer to contemplate and then responds.

'Sure. Give me thirty minutes.'

Ray finds himself anxiously awaiting the next "ding," which takes only seconds.

'Perfect, meet me at the bar.'

He rushes around the trailer to find a presentable shirt that isn't too business casual. Then again, she is a colleague now, so it's not like this is a date. No need to worry about getting primped. He just needs to be presentable and get across town to put his curiosity to rest.

Ray decides on a mostly clean pair of jeans and a red and black flannel button-down with his black boots. He grabs a pack of light green mints off the counter along with his truck keys and heads out. Eager to see what this late-night meeting would entail, and why it involves him.

14

Impromptu Rendezvous

His drive to the hotel quickly becomes a battle warding off an anxiety attack. Ray is now overthinking everything. He tries to get a grasp on the situation and his nerves, while crunching on the tiny breath mints by the handful.

Ray has no reason to fear what this woman has to say, yet he's incredibly nervous. Trying to focus on the details of the case, he wonders whether Dr. Gaston might be as obsessive as he is with his work. She may want to get a head start on their investigation. He's still unsure why Lt Zimmer wasn't included though.

It suddenly registers, that Ray has no idea how Gaston got his personal cell number in the first place. His nerves shift to anger and uncertainty, wondering if this was a smart idea to meet her out here. His instincts have failed him before, so Ray begins to rack his brain about what he could be getting into. As he enters the parking lot Ray's guard is fully raised, and he prepares for the worst.

Ray Townes is on edge walking through the hotel lobby. He scans the atmosphere before being greeted by the staff. Ray says he's meeting someone and is ushered into the lounge by the young hostess. Approaching the dimly lit area, he sees a slim woman with long brown hair leaning forward onto the bar. Her feet dangle while she points to a shelf holding the specific bottle of tequila being requested. Townes grabs a seat at a nearby empty booth. Waiting patiently for the bartender to finish the transaction, so Ray can get a better look at the woman's face without being intrusive.

Ray realizes Dr. Gaston told him nothing about her appearance or what she would be wearing. This is like a terrible blind date. How was he going to identify her? Or was she supposed to recognize him? Finally, the woman at the bar grabs her drink and swirls around on a stool in Ray's direction.

"Holy shit." He says aloud, as he finally gets a clear view of her.

His heart sinks to his feet and he feels the entire room standstill. She catches his gaze, and his body floods with nervous energy. A warmth of sensations begins to scorch him from the inside. Ray swallows the lump in his throat and pushes off the booth behind him. His trembling legs hold him steady while he looks down at her. The woman before Ray, to his astonishment, is Ele Miles, his former lover.

What is happening? Ray thinks to himself as she approaches. He's confused and in utter disbelief that *she* is walking towards him.

"Surprise!" Gaston says nervously, as she throws back her double tequila shot. Then gulps down half of the margarita chaser in her other hand as she approaches Ray. "Sorry, cheers." She jokes as she holds the rest of her glass in the air.

"Cheers, I don't drink. What the fuck is this? What are you doing here?" Ray asks her sternly. Unamused by this bombshell.

Ray's brash nature catches her off guard. Gaston sits down at the booth he raised from, and Ray follows while rolling his eyes. "You stopped drinking? That's great, Ray! Look, I know you have a lot of emotions going on. And probably a million questions right now. I'll answer every single one if you let me. I must thank you for coming first and apologize that this is happening like *this*. I knew I couldn't show up tomorrow and throw this all on you, there in front of everyone. I felt I owe you an explanation and I wish we had more time, but this case started to move like a lit fuse on dynamite. I had to make a choice and it was now or never, so I came to consult. But I'm also here for you, Ray."

His irritation with her increases as she justifies this trickery. Ray's taken completely off guard and feels so powerless. Blindsided by her alter ego and deception, Ray needs answers. "So, who are you?"

His confusion causes Gaston to smile before trying to clarify the truth. "I'm everything you think I am, Ray. I'm Dr. Gaston, the same woman who has been consulting with you and Zimmer. Everything your lieutenant told you about me and my credentials, is true. I go by Gaston now, which is my maiden name. I changed it after my divorce in '91, before I went back to school."

She gives Ray a minute to process. "But he called you 'Evie,' did you change your first name too?"

"Oh, no, he was saying 'E.V.' as in my initials, Eleanor Virginia. I chose to use them as a more ambiguous professional name. I got the idea from a professor in Grad school. Tired of prejudice as a woman, not merely on her experience, skills, or merit." She states proudly.

"So, you're a feminist now?" Ray questions sarcastically, after some brief contemplation.

"There he is," Gaston says with a more playful tone. "And you say 'feminist' like it's a bad thing." She tries to lighten the mood before continuing to explain.

"I assure you I didn't plan this, though. Zimmer did reach out arbitrarily. I had no idea you were still in Beau Ridge, let alone at the 31st working on a task force like the Special Crimes Team. I've kept some tabs and knew that none of our old brass or hardly anyone I worked with is still there or even in Louisiana. Zimmer was raving about his veteran detective and how you theorized about this serial predator long before anyone else. I was impressed and wanted to help your team. Then when I realized it was you, I almost backed out.

"However, I knew you were onto something, so I thought it might be okay only doing the remote consulting. Everything changed when I had to be here in person. I thought there was a reason though, as cheesy as it sounds. Like a sign? I thought it was worth returning to Louisiana and reuniting with you, Raymond. Even if just for the remainder of this case. So, here I am." Gaston concludes with shy smile.

Townes feels her attempt to ease his discomfort. He knows that she is a psychologist and there isn't much he can hide from her. Ray wonders how well Ele remembers him and their relationship. *Does she think about me often? During sex with other men?*

He gives her body a once over as she heads back to the bar for another margarita. He notices her long, toned legs in her short black skirt. Ray watches her confidently strut around, *still sexy, even at almost 50*. She has been taking care of herself, now more than fifteen years later he can't believe Ele is here. Ray considers her words. *Could this be a sign? Is she supposed to be here?* Ray wants to play it cool and take this reunion slowly. Gaston appears nervous too. The way she is throwing back the drinks reminds him of Zimmer's need for liquid courage to tell his secret.

Ray needs to know more about what the woman of his dreams and *nightmares* has been up to in her absence. They continue to get reacquainted. "So, a divorce, huh? What happened with Stew? I gotta know." Ray asks when Ele returns to their table with a fresh drink.

Licking the salt from the rim of the large glass, Ele sneers and shakes her head. "Stewart Miles, Jesus, I haven't discussed him in some time. But for you, Raymond, I will oblige."

Ray lends a smirk as Ele takes a big drink before explaining the demise of her marriage. "Well, as I told you before I left town, he did find out about us. Although I didn't confirm the affair until a few years later." She had Ray's attention. "Stewart and I left Louisiana in 1988 for Bilbrey, Texas. He painted this beautiful picture of our 'fresh start.' His family was established out there and his dad wanted him to enter the local government and get a feel for politics to see if it was a good fit. His parents adored me at first. They thought we were going to relocate and make them grandbabies right away." Ele rolls her eyes while taking a big gulp.

"I hated everything about Texas. It took months for me even to be considered for a lieutenant's position, but I was repeatedly denied. As difficult as it was to gain acceptance in Louisiana, I had at least earned *some* respect out here. Yet, I was just Mrs. Miles, the lieutenant's wife over there.

"After a few months, I noticed a change in Stewart. The move brought us closer initially. I thought being open about how the affair got started with you in the first place, would be helpful. I tried to explain to Stewart that I was still unsatisfied sexually. I admitted things got a little carried away with you and I, though I didn't offer too many details." They share eye contact, and she lends a quick smirk. Ray now knows that she still thinks about their explicit and intimate time together.

Gaston continues, "So, I asked Stewart bluntly if he had an issue with me, or if he needed *more*? I tried to be as open and considerate as possible with the man I re-committed my life to. As it turns out, he did have some things he was holding back and a few secrets of his own. Finally, after some probing and reassurance that I wouldn't freak out, he came clean. Stewart admitted that while in college, he concluded for the first time in his life that he is gay. He came out to me, right there in our living room."

She gives Ray a second to understand the gravity of that news. Taking a few more sips of her frosty drink before he chimes in. "Wow, you must have been... well, how did you take that? You guys were married since like 1976, right? That's a long time to hide something that heavy." Ray realizes Zimmer only recently came out and considers how many others on the force might be hiding the same silent truth.

Ele sets down her frosty margarita and responds. "Yes, in April of '76, we eloped just six months after we met. And I was shocked at first, given a confession like that. Fourteen years of cover-ups and hidden truths is huge. But I took myself out of the equation and thought only about him. I realized he was only a shell of a man standing before me. Stewart Miles was lying to his entire family, his whole life, and even to himself for a while. I considered how lonely he must've been. Hiding his true interests and passion all the time, never being himself. Could you imagine how exhausting that would be?" Ele asks with an empathetic tone.

Ray nods his head in consensus before asking, "So, this was all in like, 1990 then?"

Ele nods and continues, "Yes, just before winter. We weren't sure what was happening with our marriage. I assured Stewart that I would maintain semblance throughout the engagements. I observed them all during the holiday parties and gatherings. A very traditional family. They weren't overly religious but felt that the bible was the word of God, and they were adamant about following the Christian doctrine. Or at least the convenient parts." Ele concludes with an eyeroll and another sip, before she proceeds.

"It was a New Year's Eve party going into 1991, when I drank a little too much and had a candid conversation with Stewart's mom, Opal. I asked if she was familiar with Jesus' philosophy of love and not passing judgment. I needed to understand how capable she was of thinking for herself. Opal was receptive and willing to talk at first, but she started to see where I was going. She told me, 'If a person keeps a somber secret in their hearts, it's for a reason. Knowing they have shamed God and are defying his word,' the cherry on top was, 'All sins are equal in the eyes of God.'

"I knew what Stewart had been dealing with his entire life. Not standing up for him or speaking my mind was difficult. The entire situation was disheartening, and it became increasingly harder to manage that new life. We had become more like roommates. Going through the motions each day without any real conviction." Ele takes a few more big gulps of her waning margarita.

"Valentine's Day of '91, we were out having dinner. I watched Stewart at the bar, talking to a gentleman a few years older than us. There was some obvious flirting and a clear familiarity. He eventually gestured to me at the table and casually tried to play it off. They both waved, but when Stewart returned to the table, he was a different man momentarily. Then it hit me, that was the first time I'd seen him truly aroused. I let him relish the moment for a bit, before I asked any questions. They were former coworkers. Stewart made a point to tell me that the man was 'happily married as well,' and was also there with his wife. She was beautiful and presumably blind or with horrible gaydar. But who am I to judge?" Ele winks.

They share a laugh and Ray realizes that his gaydar isn't too accurate either. Ele tosses back the remainder of her margarita, "I took the rest of that night to watch the other couple. While the words 'as well' hung there like a fucking billboard on display in my mind. He couldn't have been more obvious, and I finally saw it all clearly. Stewart was begging for a way out but desperately backed into a wall.

"So, that evening, I told Stewart a series of lies—smeared with enough truth to stick together until he bought it. With the help of a slightly coerced Mrs. Opal Miles, I had a way out of their entire family for good. We finalized our divorce a month later, and parted ways.

Ray nods with approval, before asking, "And then?"

Gaston smiles, having missed his inquisitive nature. "And then, Mr. Townes, I got right into a graduate program at

Washington State. I started working on my Master's in Criminal Psychology. I impressed one of my professors and he made me apply for this prestigious Forensic Psychology, Ph.D. program. With his recommendation, and my grades, I had an incredible opportunity I couldn't pass up."

Ele orders water with lemon from a passing waiter, before continuing with her recap. "I became a lead research assistant within one semester. And I received full tuition for the entire doctoral program through an academic scholarship. I was swamped with work, of course. I paid for my entire education three times over, with anguish, sweat equity, and paper cuts. But it was worth every second and sacrifice. I learned so much, met some amazing people, and finally earned my doctorate, in the spring of 1999.

"I was eager to get started, but I had no idea where to go from there. I had gotten so accustomed to that academic environment and all the demands; I didn't know how to *not* perform in that way. I was obsessed with my studies and always found something new to research or delve into. I had no time to think about my failed marriage, being a liar, a cheater, or anyone I had left in the wake of my bad choices.

"I eventually began an internship with this private firm, known as unofficial headhunters for the federal government. They facilitated meetings with the FBI and CIA, for their most promising recruits. I was regarded as a candidate but made it clear that I needed more time. They understood I was in a different lane—one of the few women to make it through the program. None of the others had an entire career before grad school as I did, having been a cop. A few of them thought I was a spy, which I found amusing and flattering."

Townes is captivated by Ele and still finds her so intriguing. He watches her tongue trace the edge of the lemon wedge as her face squints from the acidic tang. Ray recalls one of their escapades in vivid detail. The first time she went down on him, her mouth all over his body, exploring every inch of him with her tongue. He adjusts his pants and breaks through the trance she unknowingly places over him.

Ray clears his throat and chimes in. "Zimmer filled me in on some of your consulting experience with local units in Washington. Then you did the Anchorage case and worked to identify and capture a female serial killer. Is that right?"

"Yes. I found a passion for profiling and was formally approached by the FBI after that case in Alaska. I guess I still am considering, I just don't know about the structured environment. I like my freedom and have gotten accustomed to being a little nomadic. Taking opportunities as they come, all over the Country. I got the email from Zimmer and the timing was perfect. So, I stuck with the remote consulting to see where it might take me, and here we are. Together again, after fifteen years." Ele concludes with quick eyebrow raise.

Her smile is invigorating, but Ray doesn't want to get too excited. She is here for the case, and they must work together again starting in a few hours. Suddenly, Ray realizes that Ele's had years to reach out after her divorce. Even though she was busy with school, Ele made the choice every day, for over a decade, to stay away and keep Ray in her cloudy past. This was beginning to feel like heartbreak all over again.

Ray decides it's time to establish a more professional vibe, before she gets too comfortable, and confuses his kindness for weakness. "Well thank you for the recap. I have to say, you've been using your time a lot wiser than I have. It's getting early though, so I should let you go get ready for work. Hopefully, we can find another chance to chat soon. I will tell you about my many failures to match your amazing feats. It will be fun." Townes concludes with a smirk before exiting the booth.

Ele isn't quite ready for their rendezvous to end so abruptly. Yet, realizes this isn't the time or place to air every detail of the last fifteen years. "Right, yes. I'm sorry this was so one-sided. I would love another opportunity to catch up! And I look forward to it."

They walk out to the lobby of her hotel, and she thanks Ray again for coming on such short notice. And, for not bolting when he saw it was her. Ele mentions needing some coffee and a hot shower and that she hopes he will be okay to work after being up all night.

"I'll manage. The SCT trailer is the faded blue one behind the precinct. It's adjacent to the old city hall building." Ray leans in for a kiss on the cheek, while Ele Gaston awaits the elevator. His kiss is slow, and he lingers close to her, taking in her scent. It's sweet and still somewhat familiar. Hearing her inhale softly, Ray knows he can still read her cues.

"See you soon, Ele." He says softly, while she selects the floor. As the elevator doors hedge between them, Ray gets a glimpse of Ele biting her bottom lip. He smirks and turns away.

Ray heads to his trailer to change clothes and burn some time. There's about an hour until Daylight Donuts opens for his favorite, fresh coffee. He reflects on the magnitude of Ele's presence here, and what it means for his addiction and impulses. He feels a plethora of emotions when it comes to this woman. Most of which are comfort, excitement, and happiness. But there are still some reservations too. Ray knows he must tread lightly moving forward.

15

New Team, Old Triggers

When Ray arrived at the SCT trailer it was almost seven. Zimmer was already there, prepping for their meeting with Dr. Gaston. He's thrilled to see Townes in early and informs him that Gaston arrived late last night and is due in any minute.

Townes has been replaying their encounter in his mind on a loop. Seeing her face and thinking about her body being so close to his. Ray couldn't embrace her like he thought he would after all these years.

Before the men could get much small talk in, Ele Gaston enters the trailer. A black briefcase in one hand and a large coffee cup in the other. Gaston struggles to close the thin door caught in the wind. She fumbles her briefcase at Ray's feet, short of the conference table. Ray leaned down to help her, grabbing the handle as Ele reached for it. While bent over, their faces are so close they brush cheeks. Ray looks into her hazel eyes, and she bashfully breaks the focus with a quick head turn.

An eager Lieutenant Zimmer wastes little time welcoming their guest. Gaston shuffles through her briefcase, appearing somewhat flustered. "Dr. Gaston, thank you so much for making this trip. It's great to meet you in person. We look forward to learning something new and figuring out where to take this case from here."

"Gentlemen, good morning, and thank you for having me. As you know, we're already behind schedule, so let's get started." She says with a pat on the table and then a quick wink to Townes while Zimmer turns to grab his legal pad.

Dr. Gaston begins with a quick disclaimer. "While you've caught many murderers over the years, working with serial offenders is much more complex. The success of crime-specific consultations relies on many factors. Constructing a profile to identify a suspect is still a new methodology, and we're working to standardize the field. It's a fluid process—like many sciences it changes with new information."

Gaston remains seated but commands their attention while proceeding. "The difficulty with this case is having little evidence to direct us. I'll assist in any way possible. But you both must prepare, as I've instructed your superiors moments ago, for the likely outcome here. We don't know how much time we'll have before our subject takes Maddison's life, but that *is* his end goal."

Zimmer and Townes make eye contact and share a mutual acceptance of the grisly future this case has in store. Gaston continues, "Chief Diehl now understands that having my insight was the only way your team could have strung these cases together. I want us to move forward without reservations on responsibility. I've convinced them that you both have done as much as you could, until now."

Zimmer offers a half-smile to Townes, and they share a nod in accord, as this relieves some pressure.

Gaston says, "I also made sure that they know more victims will soon be linked to this culprit. They're preparing for that. The local news sources have yet to cover Maddison's disappearance—at the family's demand for privacy. Your brass wants to honor that choice moving forward. Now, let's go over the timeline of her disappearance. I need the statements and any reports you've obtained. Get me up to speed on everything we currently know." Dr. Gaston completes her introduction, impressing her new team with her assertiveness and competence.

Townes and Zimmer fill her in on the statement from Joey Turner, Maddison's husband. They all agree that Maddison was likely taken from the park in Glendale Forest, on her way home. Once Gaston is aware of everything they have on the Broussard-Turner case, the trio discuss the other crimes associated with this unknown perpetrator.

The possible linked victims are Tina Richard, Roxy Williams, Justine Nichols and Michaela Hardy. Townes slides the Natalie Ruiz case file into Gaston's briefcase while she and Zimmer were at the dry-erase board writing their subject's proposed timeline. Gaston agrees with Zimmer on the case of Tina Richard having some inconsistencies. Pointing out that she was not strangled in the same manner as the others, due to her differing injuries. Insinuating that she could have been suffocated or smothered. Which would stray from their subject's signature methods. Dr. Gaston explains their culprit was likely looking at the other women face to face. Strangling them from above with his hands around their necks placed higher up under their chins. That would cause the hyoid fractures and bruising they all shared. Tina Richard's killing doesn't quite fit based on the evidence. Gaston adds that Tina could still be in his count. Even without her though, they all agree there is little doubt. Beau Ridge does have an active serial killer at large.

The confirmation nearly sends Zimmer into a tailspin. Dr. Gaston explains how many active serial killers are currently spreading their destruction across the United States. Assuring the team that she isn't used to hearing about them from working in such proximity. Rather a frightening number have and will earn that title.

Zimmer calms down and tries to focus. He remembers the disc dropped off from their tech team earlier. It's a copy of the surveillance footage from the drugstore Maddison was last seen alive in. They gather around Zimmer's computer and watch Mrs. Broussard-Turner's last few moments of freedom, before her abduction. They observe her power-walk thru the entrance of Walden's and straight to the photo counter. Maddison retrieved the pictures that had been developed the previous day. You see a new angle of her inside, strolling away from the counter. Maddison skimmed through the pictures while heading towards a particular aisle. A quick look around, then she selects a certain item. The Special Crimes Team can't see exactly what Maddison picked up, but that it was in a small box.

They watch her grab some gum and a bottle of water, then head to the checkout counter. Maddison then takes the bag with her purchases and walks casually to the back of the store. Maddison is seen gulping down the water as she heads into the bathroom. They skip the video forward about four minutes until they see her exit the restroom. Maddison slides the pictures and gum into her small backpack, then throws away her plastic bag before walking out the sliding doors of Walden's Pharmacy and Photo.

The team discusses what they saw—Gaston's perspective was a little more informed than her male counterpart's. "I think I know what she bought. I believe she was on the women's hygiene aisle. She took her purchases into the restroom and exited without the box."

The men assume Maddison bought menstrual products that she needed to use before leaving for her run home.

Gaston clarifies, "No, I don't think she was on her period guys. In fact, I don't think she was going to be getting one for some time."

Townes instantly picks up on what Gaston is referring to, but it takes Zimmer a bit longer. Ray chimes in, "So, you're saying you think Maddison was pregnant? That she bought a test, and went to take it right then and there?"

Zimmer understands now and agrees, "That makes perfect sense. She drank the water, it takes a few minutes for the results, so she must've waited in there to see what it said."

"Right, about three minutes I believe," Gaston replies. "And that would explain why she couldn't sleep with the uncertainty. Also, you mentioned her friend Brynn said that Maddison was unwell and left early, right? Could have been another reason for her shortened celebration on New Year's Eve. Unfortunately, if that was the case then Maddison could have likely seen a positive result on that test—just before she left."

Zimmer realizes what this means and in a depressing tone confirms it. "She found out she was pregnant, and then got abducted by a serial rapist and murderer. My God. This poor woman. She can't end up like the others, Dr. Gaston. Please, help us find her!" the lieutenant pleads.

Gaston mentions them needing fuel for their work. Attempting to distract him, she requests that Zimmer goes to pick them up some pizza for lunch, her treat. They send Lt Zimmer out the door with Gaston's credit card and the team's order. Gaston then informs Townes that she needs to check in with some colleagues on another case. Townes explains the crappy cell reception and she agrees to take the call in her car. Dr. Gaston remains outside until Zimmer returns with their food about 40 minutes later.

The team spends the rest of the afternoon canvassing the park in Glendale Forest. Looking for anything they could've missed or something new that stands out. Townes suggests they go over 911 calls later, to verify if anything was reported the morning of Maddison's disappearance. The team notices the area is remote and there aren't many facilities where a city worker would be assigned. They consider if their guy has a ruse that he pulls. Pretending to be an injured runner or having a disability that could render him unsuspecting.

Lt Zimmer gets a call from their captain about another case going to trial next week. His presence is requested back at the precinct. Zimmer asks Dr. Gaston if she can give Townes a ride back when they finish up—since the men rode together out there. Gaston agrees and is now alone with Townes after the lieutenant heads out. Ray attempts to fill the silence by commending Ele on the way she is handling the case so far.

Then asks why she was out the whole time when Zimmer went to grab lunch. She shoots him a confused look as they follow the path through the pine trees.

"Ray, I told you that I need to focus. I must resist the urge to wink and make eye contact. And I shouldn't watch you lick your lips and pretend like I'm not thinking about your—" Gaston sneers. "I'm sorry. See, it happens so quickly. I need to remain professional, and this woman is relying on us to bring her home. Please don't take it personally or make it a thing."

Ray teases, "Ugh, totally not making it a *thing*. You're right. In fact, I won't even mention it again, because I'm just as committed to the outcome of this case as you are. We are both professionals!"

Gaston snickers while shaking her head as they make their way toward her rental car. On their way back Ele makes a wrong turn in the park, ending up on a small road that takes them into a deeply wooded area. After turning around, she stops before realigning her vehicle on the dirt path. "You knew that was the wrong way, didn't you? Are you trying to get me alone out here like some teenager looking for a make-out session?" She's awaiting an answer, still not moving the car in the right direction.

"Dr. G. if you want to kiss me, we can make that happen. I guess I wasn't paying attention to your directions. Or maybe I *did* want you alone out here. Is that what you want to hear?" Ray toys with her.

Gaston admits that she apparently doesn't know what she wants and is sorry for sending mixed signals. She grabs the gear shifter about to move into drive. Ray places his hand on hers. "Don't be sorry. And don't be scared." He looks into Ele's eyes and watches her take a deep breath before looking away.

"I'm not scared, I'm just… Sorry. I know exactly what I want Ray, and I'm sure you do too. But I don't want it to be at anyone else's expense. Not again." She confirms solemnly.

Ray can see Ele has confusion and deep sentiment wrapped up inside. Exactly as Ray endures when thinking about the two of them together. He also knows that this is the woman he has desired for almost twenty years. Ray has considered every position he can put her in. How he can get her to climax and how wet he can make her within a few touches. He wants to take the time to show her everything she's been missing. Ele shudders when he gets close, so he knows she's in need of attention. Ray wants to make her feel safe and comfortable. He grabs Ele's hand away from the gear shifter, bringing it close to his face.

He whispers, "I know, and I'm right here. Whenever you're ready. I'll take care of you. I promise." Ray kisses her hand softly, and she lets out a single tear as her eyes close tightly.

Ele wipes the tear from her cheek and takes off down the road. They drive in silence, aside from the Beethoven she finds on the radio. Ray usually dislikes classical music, but he allows it to resonate in the moment. As his tension subsides, he's reminded of how relaxed she makes him. Ray can only hope he is doing the same for her, yet he is still concerned with what upset her. These two have a ton to figure out and might not ever get to any of it.

Arriving back at the precinct, Ele flashes a quick frown. Explaining she must make a run somewhere, and they can catch up later. Ray asks if she's okay, and sure she doesn't need any help. Gaston assures him that she will be fine but needs some time.

Townes waits inside alone for a few more hours. He's been reviewing the case files and comparing victim notes, hoping to wait Gaston out.

Zimmer pops in just before dusk. "Hey, there you are. Sorry, I've been at headquarters all afternoon. I spoke with Dr. Gaston; she was rather fatigued and is calling it a night to get a fresh start in the morning. Also, I confirmed with dispatch there were no emergency 911 calls near the park around the abduction time. Only a report of a dead animal found in the parking lot, off the main trail. The city said that an animal control officer might have been by to collect it. That was the only employee who would have been dispatched to the park that morning."

Townes was curious if that could be their connection. The men decide to await Gaston's return in the morning and go from there. Ray is unsure why she left so abruptly and hates thinking he did something wrong. Or worse, that he should have done more and wasted an opportunity. A discouraged Townes agrees they all need some rest.

Ray found it challenging to get comfortable and clear his mind that evening at home. He called his therapist's after-hours line. Informed by the operator that the provider was currently out with the flu. They were to reschedule any calls and appointments for next week. When she suggested he 'Call 911, if this is an emergency,' Ray laughed at her and promptly hung up. *What a fucking joke,* he thinks to himself, his mind racing in various directions. Ray's unable to focus on anything but Ele. He contemplates going straight to her hotel but is unsure which room she's in. Working up the courage, he calls her cell. Getting no answer, he hangs up before her voicemail finishes the recording. Feeling foolish, Ray waits a few more minutes and then decides he will send one text message.

'Ele, I want to talk. I can come to you. I just need to know what room #'

Ray reluctantly presses send and then anxiously awaits a response. Fifteen more minutes pass. No reply is leaving him irritable and feeling rejected. Getting impatient and hungry, Townes checks the kitchen for options.

A mostly empty fridge leads him to search the freezer for anything with substance. He shuffles through a couple of frozen dinner boxes with ice built up around the edges. Pushing them aside, he reveals a half-empty bottle of whisky staring back at him. Unable to muster any willpower, Ray grabs the bottle and heads to his recliner.

He gives Ele one more chance. *If she is ready and we're supposed to take advantage of this time, she will answer*, he convinces himself. The frosty whisky bottle sits on the end table. Ray dials each digit with painstaking reluctance. He brings the phone close and discovers he got sent straight to voicemail. "That bitch is ignoring me now?" Ray grumbles aloud. Growing angry, he gulps down the cold liquor before he has a second to think about it. He tosses the empty bottle into the trash and heads out the door for the bar.

Ray is idling in the parking lot of the Treetop Tavern after arriving moments ago. He desperately wants Ele to pull him back in. Watching his cell do nothing only enrages him more. Intrusive thoughts lead Ray to believe Ele might have found someone at the hotel bar to give her what she needs.

Convinced he shouldn't spend another second waiting for Ele Gaston, Ray walks into the Tavern to drink away her memory for tonight.

16

Blackout Date

Ray wakes to a splitting headache and a woman shaking him. She says that his phone has been buzzing from his pants on the floor. She asks if he needs to be at work? He realizes he has no idea who this woman is.

Looking around cautiously, Ray confirms they are in his trailer. Several beer cans and a new bottle of whisky complete their empty collection on the floor. With no memory and a pounding head, he knows he overdid it. Ray asks if he owes her anything and the woman giggles. Explaining they had a deal worked out and that she has already been taken care of. She asked if it was still okay to use his shower, which he allows.

"But make it quick." Ray adds as she shuts the bathroom door.

While the unfamiliar woman gets cleaned up, Ray checks his phone and sees '7 *missed calls*' displayed. Five were from Zimmer since about 06:00 and two from Gaston. One she placed after midnight, and the other at 07:15 this morning. It's now almost eight and Ray begins to scurry around his place getting dressed. Gathering his belongings for work, he returns Zimmer's call to see what's up.

Zimmer informs Ray that a body was discovered early this morning. Moments ago, it was viewed by Mr. Broussard in the morgue. There, it was positively identified as Maddison Broussard-Turner. Townes assures his boss that he is on his way in, and they will handle this together.

Townes gets his lady friend back to the Treetop Tavern as she explains was their agreement. Although he still has no recollections of their night. Before he pulls off to head towards work, Ray knows she can help, so he tries to fill in some blanks.

"Hey, so, because I'm a little fuzzy here, what exactly was our, uh, *arrangement?*" Ray asks, timidly.

The woman was polite and explains what they discussed a few hours ago. "It's a little more awkward now that we're both sober." She laughs nervously. "But I had you promise you weren't a murderer, and that I would arrive back here at the Treetop in one piece. I made you for po'lice pretty quick. You admitted that you shouldn't be fraternizing with a 'working girl.' But added that if you didn't pay me, it's technically not a transaction. I told you that my safety was more important. You said that you would prove how safe you are by giving me an orgasm with only your mouth. And that you wouldn't touch me unless I asked for it," the woman ends sheepishly.

"Oh, okay. And I take it that you are, uh, *satisfied*...with the deal?"

They both dawn a flirty smile, then she nods quickly before exiting the truck. On her way-out Ray grabs her wrist and asks her for one more question. She looks concerned and hops off the bench seat. She waits wide-eyed for his next prompt before shutting the door.

"Sorry, but did we uh? Did we have, intercourse?" Ray questions.

The woman lets her guard down with a soft giggle. "You are such a cop. No, we didn't have sex. You kept your word and even though I was ready for more, you told me you needed a minute and then passed out. I laid right there with you all night and let myself sleep. Which I normally don't do. And I could have totally robbed you, but I didn't. I guess I needed the rest more than your money. So, it looks like it worked out for both of us, huh?" The woman pops a bubble with her gum. "Anything else, officer?" she asks in a playful tone before closing his truck door.

Ray shakes his head no. She tells him through the open window with a wink, "You know where to find me if you need another sleepover."

Ray drives away with a smirk, wondering how he gets himself into shit like this.

Entering the SCT trailer, Townes is greeted by Zimmer and Gaston. They're accompanied by Cpt Thompson, Chief Diehl, and Mr. Broussard. Ray is caught off guard by the small crowd and hates having so many unexpected eyes on him. Townes stands behind the group at the conference table and observes.

They're all discussing how Maddison was found and what could've happened to her. A bakery worker discovered her body before dawn. The delivery truck was parked in front of the dumpster where her discarded remains laid. She was to be disposed of with the trash that morning around 07:00. Maddison would have ended up in the city dump, where they might not have ever found her. The baker was preparing their van for the day's deliveries when he discovered her and called it in. Maddison's corpse went straight to the morgue and Mr. B. got the first call. The mortuary staff was almost expecting her. Mr. Broussard informs the team that he's awaiting an update "as soon as they complete her autopsy!" which is currently underway.

The retired judge explained how devastated his wife was with this entire situation. Jack Broussard again pleaded for them to keep this quiet and not give his family or the public any details! Townes doesn't like Mr. Broussard's tone or his demands. As if he has any place within this department or investigation. Becoming territorial and combative, Ray bites his tongue.

Mr. B. asks the team if they're sure his "schmuck of a son-in-law isn't responsible in any way?" Chief Diehl does his best to explain the profile of their culprit, and the likelihood that he was a repeat offender. Mr. B. was no stranger to violent crimes and even serial killers. Still, Jack Broussard was eager to blame someone, and it's clear he intends to get answers for his daughter.

Jack reiterates that his wife won't be able to process the entirety of this crime. Instead of the actual events, he concocts a story to tell her. He'll claim, "Maddison was robbed and killed for money she took from the ATM at the drug store, before continuing her run that morning. No details will be leaked to any media sources. Only the personnel in this trailer and the medical examiner, Dr. Cox will know what happened to my daughter."

Ele Gaston boldly chimes in, "And the killer, Mr. Broussard. He also knows the truth. And he has a version of the story that may come to light *eventually*. You should prepare for that, sir." Townes admires Ele's moxie.

"Right, well, let's make sure this team does its job here. And that we don't give that asshole the time of day. Understood?" Mr. Broussard mandates.

His pleas are becoming harder for the team to digest. Chief Diehl feels the momentum shift in the room. He tells Jack they can talk more in his office while they await the autopsy. The two men along with Cpt Thompson exit the Special Crimes trailer—taking the stringent energy with them.

Townes wastes little time sharing that he doesn't trust Mr. Broussard. And that he's unsure why the man is being allowed so much access to this case. Zimmer agrees and directs Townes to the morgue to get the autopsy results straight from the coroner, before they go to Mr. Broussard. Ensuring they cover all their bases with this case. Zimmer indicates that the pair likely have a relationship; the M.E. might have some loyalty to Mr. Broussard. Zimmer advises Ray to act as though they are all on the same team and trying to advance the investigation.

Gaston volunteers to assist, catching Ray off guard. She indicates that seeing the body is helpful and information from the exam will be useful to her profile. Perhaps to understand why their suspect's timeline was expedited. She adds that the Medical Examiner is married to an old friend of hers and they have a history.

Zimmer agrees it can't hurt and says that he must make a call to the District Attorney, regarding the Arturo Ruiz appeal. They all agree to meet back at the Special Crimes trailer as soon as they know more.

17

The Morgue & The Match

O n their way to the morgue, the first few minutes are spent in silence. Townes isn't sure how to approach the miscommunication from last night. Gaston is busy trying to navigate, as she's unsure which building the medical examiner was currently operating out of. She apologizes for missing Ray's call and not responding for so long.

Ele claims to have been asleep after taking a long drive to reminisce. Admitting that she went by her former home shared with her ex-husband, Stewart Miles. Then, "spent hours traveling around the city checking out all the changes that have occurred over the decade-plus since I've been gone." Claiming she woke to her phone dead later that night. After getting up to charge it for her morning alarm, she saw Ray's message. She then tried to call him back with no answer.

Ray believes her but still feels some rejection. "It's fine, I can't even remember what I needed to discuss anyway, so it must not have been too important. Huh?" He attempts to downplay his night, pointing at the street ahead. "It's gonna be a right up there by the bank and then that brick building on the left is the new morgue."

"Well, I think I know what it was about." Gaston retorts. She's caught Ray's attention. He begins to worry that she might have seen him and the mystery woman he shared his evening with.

"Uh, do you now? Well please, enlighten me." He tries to play it cool, but she can sense his discomfort and some awkwardness.

"It was about Natalie, right? Mrs. Ruiz. I saw her file in my briefcase and I assume you were the one who slipped it in there."

Relieved and eager to move along, Townes agrees. "Yes, that was it. You're right, I remember now, that's exactly what it was about. Look at it when you get a chance and let me know if you think she was another vic. of our psychopath, or if it was her husband after all."

Gaston knows that Townes is deflecting, but they don't have time to hash out personal issues. They must continue with business as usual. The pair enter the cold, sterile building and walk down a bright hallway. Gaston remarks that it has the same smell and familiar ambiance, despite being in a new location.

Townes checks in with the lab tech running the front desk. After a brief wait, they receive scrub gowns and gloves that they each slip on. Then they're escorted to the examination room, where they wait on the other side of a large window. Watching thru the glass as the doctor closes Maddison's large "Y" incision. Dr. Cox records inaudible notes into a microphone held near him by an assistant. When he finishes a few minutes later, he waves the two of them back into the room. They brush past the assistant's white coat, as he exits with the tape recorder and a clipboard in hand.

"Morning folks, I assume you two are with the Special Crimes Team, from the 31st? Wanting an update on Mrs. Broussard-Turner here?" The medical examiner says, with his large grey mustache hiding his top lip.

Dr. Gaston and Townes give their introductions while the examiner moves the shiny steel table holding Maddison's body. He slides her into the square slot of her refrigerated resting place. Gaston asks Dr. Cox, if his wife Brenda is doing well, and he realizes who she is. They catch up briefly and discuss the changes to BRPD over the last decade and a half.

Getting back on track, Dr. Cox explains that they're awaiting toxicology analysis. He did confirm that Maddison was about six to eight weeks pregnant with a viable fetus. Dr. Cox mentions concern about sharing that detail with Maddison's father but knows the Broussard family deserves the whole truth. This confirms their theory that Maddison was buying a pregnancy test and took it in the store's bathroom. But it certainly doesn't make their case any easier.

Dr. Cox describes, "Sexual and physical assaults over a few days. Maddison has fractures around both eyes. She was manually strangulated with enough force to cause severe laryngotracheal injuries. Her cricoid fracture would have caused breathing issues and possible suffocation. Although further analysis is needed, I intend to rule her death a homicide, via strangulation."

As with other victims, there was little physical evidence available. The suspect attempted to clean Maddison's fingernails, but a small sample was taken from under her toenails. She presumably fought back and scratched the perpetrator with her feet. The examiners also recovered a 4-inch piece of duct tape tangled in Maddison's long blonde hair. They're working with their forensic team to get any viable prints from it.

If they recover any DNA from her samples, it will go through the Combined DNA Index System (CODIS). As well as the National DNA Index System (NDIS) for a possible match. The M.E. reiterates that everything is being pushed through the state crime lab in a rapid manner. Due to the "VIP status," this case is branded with. Gaston has a more scientific discussion with Dr. Cox, and they exchange ideas and theories for a few minutes longer.

They thank the M.E. for his time and give a direct number for him to reach Dr. Gaston in the future. The pair leave with the smallest amount of hope since this investigation began.

On the way back, Gaston and Townes discuss the likelihood of gaining a print from the tape. Townes notes that their guy has left almost no physical evidence behind for years. Believing the culprit is rattled and finally making mistakes, which is a break for their team. While he knows that it's a long shot, Ray chooses to remain optimistic. They might finally get somewhere with this modest opportunity.

Ele agrees with his assessment and decides that finding a print is their most promising option for now. They profiled a possible city employee or someone with police or military experience. There should be other victims, and if one of those women did a rape kit when reporting it could provide another link. There is a good chance their suspect has a profile within a federal or state database, Gaston reminds Townes.

Back at the trailer, the pair enjoy a minute alone, with something positive ruminating. Hours later, Zimmer returns from several meetings. He explains that the duct tape analysis is complete, and they found one viable impression in the adhesive. It is currently being run through statewide databases.

The team can't believe it and don't want to get too excited. They all sat there awaiting the call from Chief Diehl who was going to receive the news first. Almost two more hours pass while they read various reports and meticulously examine details of their case.

Suddenly, Zimmer's phone buzzes on the table in front of them. He looks closer at the screen. "This is it. It's the chief." He states, before grabbing the phone and heading to the front steps.

Gaston and Townes eagerly wait inside for an update and the only break this case has had. After a few minutes, Zimmer walks back in, with wide eyes and a look of awe on his face.

"They got a hit. One latent print and it has a match." Zimmer says in disbelief, before continuing. "The print went through a database shared with the Louisiana National Guard, and the US Army Criminal Investigation laboratories. That finally provided our connection. The guy is a 29-year-old Army veteran, living in Beau Ridge since his court-martial separation, presumably. He has been working for Beau Ridge animal control for the last six years. We have an address, and I'm going to get started on the warrant. We have identified our suspect as

Mr. Steven Franklin Landry. Get ready guys, this is it." Lt Zimmer concludes with confidence.

The enamored lieutenant heads to his cubicle to get started typing the warrant. Gaston and Townes stare at each other. Ray reaches out and gives Ele's hand a squeeze as they both take in this monumental discovery. An hour later the team is instructed to "go rest, eat, and be ready to move." They already have a judge lined up to sign off. They also made arrangements with SWAT to assist in the arrest. Not knowing what they'll be walking into, the 31st must be as prepared as possible for this interaction to go smoothly. The team is to reconvene at 04:00 and plan to serve their warrant just before sunrise.

Townes can't nap or rest at all, he's anxiously pacing around his trailer for what felt like hours. He contemplates years of police work about to come to an end. Raymond Townes's has been unknowingly chasing this suspect for so long and was finally going to put a face to the crimes. He thought about Steven Landry raping and torturing so many unsuspecting women. Abducting them and holding them against their will. How frightened they must've been—alone and without any help. Ray can't believe that his team is going to be apprehending such an ominous character.

Ray suppresses his urge to drink, which begins to feel unbearable. He must find another way to calm his nerves and anxiety before they execute this mission. He doesn't even think to call Ele, forgetting that she was an option momentarily. Unable to hold back with his urges intensifying, Ray gets in the shower to masturbate and collect himself. He earns minimal relief before getting ready for the mission.

Townes is going to grab coffees for the team at a 24-hour donut shop on the other side of town. This should burn some time and keep him occupied until they're ready to move on Steven Landry.

18

Apprehending A Psychopath

The team gathers at the 31st precinct in the chilly darkness of winter. They brief the assigned task force, with the plan to apprehend a suspect in a kidnapping and murder case. They're to serve the warrant at the suspects' grandparent's home in Beau Ridge. They distribute maps and the last DMV photo of Steven Landry amongst the tactical team. Wasting little time, the entire convoy begins its journey towards the target's location.

A thick layer of fog makes visibility limited, but they arrive on the scene without issues. SWAT disburses around the home's perimeter, disappearing into the cloudy mist. They carefully approach the property, as the sunlight peeks in on the very edge of the horizon. Townes locks eyes with Dr. Gaston, who shoots him a wink. He leaves her in the vehicle, where she will await the suspect in custody before entering the home.

This bust is bittersweet for Detective Townes. He surveys the property, analyzing the small brick home surrounded by an unkempt yard. Years of trash, debris, and various rusted objects were piled up all over. Townes considers the neighbors who must pass this place daily, unaware of the horrors that went on inside over the years.

Upon entering the home, the tactical team announced they had Landry in custody rather quickly. Det Townes stood by the doorway as they brought him past, staring at Landry's face as he is escorted outside. In his mind, Townes sees the monster who committed these crimes. Yet, as Gaston explained, Steven Landry was a very average-looking resident. Unsuspecting and blending into the norms of society on a regular basis.

Once Landry was outside and placed in a squad car the team entered the home cautiously. Lt Zimmer had already informed the masses about clearing the home for any unknown victims. The search of the main home went swiftly; there are three bedrooms to inspect. Two rooms, when entered, have piles of family belongings nearly touching the low ceilings. Old furniture, clothes, boxes, and totes filled with various household items were packed in tightly. One room had shelves of nick-knacks displaying tiny, glass cherub children. This collection, despite being buried in dust, appears intact. These memories were locked away and appeared untouched for years.

The entire home has almost no furniture or personal items in sight. Large cracks were on full display, as no family pictures or artwork hung on the walls. The paint is chipping from all angles, and a stale cigarette smell lingers in the air.

The team enters the third bedroom at the end of the hall. It's nearly empty, aside from a twin mattress resting on an old metal bed frame. Inside the closet they find a single cardboard box on the floor. After careful review the box is opened to expose three notebooks hidden inside. A quick flip through the pages reveals them to be handwritten journals or logbooks. Dr. Gaston takes an immediate interest knowing this could be a significant find. She ensures each book is adequately packaged and labeled for inspection later.

Townes and Zimmer agree that Landry has his abode assembled more like a military dorm or prison cell. This wasn't the house of horrors they had been expecting. Admitting they predicted more of a challenge and believed they'd uncover something genuinely vile.

Suddenly, they hear a call over the radio from SWAT. While securing the perimeter, they entered an outside garage and claimed the SCT needed to see it right away. Townes, Zimmer, and Gaston move outside to inspect this new location.

Upon entry, the place appears to have been made into an apartment. However, just a few steps further supplied the shock value the team had initially anticipated. This garage apartment was further altered into a torture chamber. It's undoubtedly where (at least a few of) Landry's victims succumbed to his insufferable fetishes and likely took their last breath. A putrid stench of burnt flesh and singed hair drifted past, which made two officers run outside to vomit.

Gaston immediately calls for their crime scene investigation team to seal off the converted garage. "Take pictures of everything exactly where it lay before any evidence is touched!" she snaps at a CSI photographer strolling in. "There could be links to unidentified victims somewhere in this garage. Everything is important." Gaston emphasizes.

Zimmer adds, "Everyone must adhere to all protocols and take the utmost caution. We can't give Steven Landry a single way out of this, especially not from our error."

The investigators take the next couple of hours to scrutinize every square inch of this chamber. Many boxes of evidence were loaded into a van for transport. This case could put the state crime lab to work for the rest of the year. Townes points to the chains and cables dangling from the ceiling. He asks his team if they thought Landry attempted to suspend the women.

Gaston agrees, "Quite possible, especially if you recall Justine Nichols' leg injuries. If she was strung up there and fell from that height, it certainly could have caused the severe fractures she endured." Gaston continues as they stroll through the room, "It was likely an accident that Landry used to his advantage. Being curious about pain and wanting to inflict as much as possible. He was gaining more organization and skill with his crimes. If you didn't already have a grasp on this case, Mr. Landry may have gone undetected for many more years." she admits to the team.

Yellow tape flapped in the wind and twisted around large oak trees, creating a bright border around the entire property. Steven Landry was secured and preparing to head to the jail. Gaston requests that they wait to do any interviews or explain the charges beyond Maddison's murder. Until they have time to process the evidence and fully understand his crimes.

The team gives instructions for transport to the officer who is managing Landry. Before the car could pull away, they hear a loud commotion that catches their attention. They discover Jack Broussard has arrived on the scene and made his way through the barricade down the block. Special Crimes didn't share the details of this arrest with anyone. Gaston indicates that it's a liability for him to be here.

Jack Broussard was pounding on top of the squad car asking if this was the man. Demanding to see his face and for them to remove Landry from the vehicle so he could, "just get a word in." Townes and Zimmer help to get a handle on the situation. Zimmer takes Mr. Broussard aside, explaining that he should know better than to be here. Adding that his interference could provide Landry an advantage to use against them. Which could inevitably hinder his daughter from getting the due process she deserves.

Townes got Landry's escort away from the scene, while Zimmer walked Mr. B. towards his sportscar. The young lieutenant assures the ret. judge that they're doing everything by the book. Adding that he will have a chance to speak to this man, as soon as they can allow. Zimmer made the mistake of saying *"all"* of Landry's victims deserve justice." And that if anything jeopardizes that, they could be risking more women's lives. Jack Broussard boldly claims that he doesn't care how many women Landry was responsible for hurting. Announcing that he only needed justice for his daughter, Maddison. And insists that he will do everything in his power, to ensure Landry pays for her death. The enraged Mr. Broussard finally leaves the scene, squealing his tires while speeding away.

The Special Crimes Team has a lot of work to do, and this man isn't going to make it any easier. Lieutenant Zimmer decides to escort the evidence to the crime lab. Dr. Gaston insists the three notebooks can't risk mishandling, so she takes the box with her to the trailer. Townes follows her back to the office to assist. They must begin to make sense of what has finally been uncovered from this harrowing scene.

19

Chronicled Correlations

Moments later, Dr. Gaston and Det Townes arrive back at the SCT trailer and get set up to read through the three journals they discovered at the Landy house. The mature detective with decades of investigative experience, and a criminologist who has acquired several degrees and years of her own expertise, appeared to have adequate credentials. Yet the duo was still unprepared to read the gruesome details they found on Landry's journal pages.

They skim through the books to get an overview of the material. Gaston annotates a few dates, which they use to provide a chronology and begin to form a timeline. The books are a combination of log-style inputs and detailed catalogs. There are locations described, which likely correspond to where Landry was hunting for future victims. Landry chronicled their hair color and physiques, what they wore, and if the women were alone. He wrote down whether they were drinking alcohol and how intoxicated they appeared. He was seemingly patrolling many bars and areas near Beau Ridge University, where Dr. Gaston is sure they will find early rape victims of Landry's.

They begin to see the progression of Steven Landry's crimes unfold through the meticulous annotations. Hearing the details read aloud, one crime stands out to Townes and captures his attention. "I think I know who that is. The woman he is describing. Any dates or timeframe references?" Ray asks, almost excitedly.

They can only identify the timeframe as the late 1990s, after Landry returned from the Army. Townes had an inkling early on, that the case he recalled from his past might somehow relate to their suspect. Yet he was careful not to make any premature assumptions. Not wanting to dredge up any false hope or negative reminders for the family. He sat on the theory until now, but Townes is finally convinced after hearing the description of the experience recorded in the journal.

Landry wrote about losing control and savagely beating the woman before leaving her for dead. Only to learn she narrowly survived his attack, when the local news informed the public that the woman was discovered clinging to life by the dumpsters near the bar.

Ray affirms, "That's Poppy Sanderson he's talking about, I'm certain. I worked that case; it was 1998 and I still remember it vividly. She was a 22-year-old student from BRU, taken from a bar while out drinking with friends. They all said she was highly intoxicated and became combative with people until she was eventually thrown out by the bouncer. Her friends claimed they made it outside about twenty minutes later after squaring the tabs. By then, Poppy was nowhere to be found. They assumed she had hailed a cab or gotten a ride back to campus from another student. It wasn't until the next day when Poppy's desecrated body was found, her friend's realized how wrong they were."

Ray continues, "Poppy was ruthlessly assaulted and suffered a brutal head injury which caused significant blood loss. The EMTs said she barely had a pulse when they arrived. They administered CPR to keep her heart pumping and bagged her in the rig. Despite their efforts and getting her to Mercy General within minutes, Poppy Sanderson never regained consciousness. Her mother was livid and demanded information from us. Mrs. Sanderson blamed everyone at the school and made several news appearances, right from the bedside of her incapacitated daughter. Poppy lay there motionless, kept alive only by machines. Their chirps and alarms echoed around Mrs. Sanderson, as she pleaded with the public for answers or help of any kind.

"The doctors diagnosed Poppy as having a severe brain bleed, with no signs of function in her scans. Claiming she would never regain any viability. Mrs. Sanderson continued to fight for her daughter, despite the prognosis. She even moved Poppy to a nursing home where she remained on life support for almost two years." Ray recalls grimly.

Gaston chimes in empathetically, "My goodness, how terrible. That poor mother, having to watch her daughter like that. What a tragedy."

This was somewhat comforting to Townes, who has marinated with the agony of that case for years. Ray presses on, "We continued to work the case but had next to nothing. There were no cameras, no witnesses, and we had no idea where Poppy was assaulted or when she was dumped back at the bar. It was a tragic mess, and the entire family was torn apart by the ordeal. Her parents divorced a few months after Poppy was moved to the nursing home. They ended up having a court battle for guardianship of their lifeless daughter. I had never seen anything like it. Her father wanted to allow Poppy to die peacefully. But Mrs. Sanderson would not let up. She hired a legal team who seemed set on making a name for themselves. They did an exclusive interview with a local news station. During which Mrs. Sanderson gave some extraordinary details about their situation. Ones that I don't think the public and especially Mr. Sanderson were prepared for.

"She claimed that Poppy's menstrual cycle had returned while she was in hospice. Which she announced was 'a sign from God,' that her daughter 'is still in there.' Mrs. Sanderson went on to explain that Poppy could still bear their grandchild. Claiming that if *she* was granted rights over her daughter, she would consider artificial insemination from a sperm donor. Adding that it was medically possible to deliver the baby via cesarian. Can you believe that? This woman wanted to impregnate her own daughter, who was lying brain dead in a hospital bed. It's one of the craziest cases I've ever worked, and I wasn't sure how it would end up."

Ray continues as Gaston listens ardently. "It was the father's final testimony, which seemed to have gotten through to the judge. Mr. Sanderson pleaded for his daughter's rights. He claimed his ex-wife was determined to benefit from the tragedy. He begged the court to grant him guardianship so that he could pull the plug and finally lay their daughter to rest. The judge required mandatory grief counseling for both parents and told a sobbing Mrs. Sanderson that 'it's time to let go'.

"In the spring of 2000, Mr. Sanderson went straight to the nursing home, with a court order in hand, to remove Poppy from life support. I was told the mother went to a psychiatric clinic following a breakdown in court and remained there for an extended stay. When Mrs. Sanderson was finally released, I heard she moved out of state. Not sure how I'll explain this to the family. I can only hope it doesn't resurface too many difficult feelings." Ray confirms solemnly.

Gaston admits it's a terrible situation, but she's hopeful that the family will find some peace in knowing the man responsible was finally caught and must answer for his crimes. Ray only hopes they can link more crimes to Landry and bring closure to as many of his victims as possible.

Zimmer calls the SCT conference room phone for an update on the journals. He's informed of the extensive information and details recorded, through which they must sift. The lieutenant explains he's sending over two young detectives they were assigned today. They can aid in uncovering some earlier victims and work to make sense of the notebooks.

20

Unveiling Victims

Hours later, notebooks and documents were scattered around the table in the Special Crimes trailer. There is now a timeline on the dry erase board and the team is working diligently to fill in as much as possible.

These journals began after a recommendation from a mental health specialist during active duty. Steven Landry found comfort in the privacy when he realized no one else would be reading his thoughts. He began sharing memories and accounts from his childhood—often involving abuse and violence. Dr. Gaston identifies several precursors to psychopathy, along with Landry's complicated relationship with his grandparents, who raised him.

Steven Landry recorded minimal details of his first assault, which occurred while he was still in the Army. The team distinguished when Landry separated from the military and how soon his second and third victims were chosen after he moved back to Beau Ridge. Each woman appeared to have been abducted and raped but not beaten. Landry described being nervous and getting performance anxiety on his first attempt. Dr. Gaston indicates that the nerves could have prevented Landry from arousal or maintaining an erection. Because of this, Steven Landry was likely unable to follow through with his plan, causing him to rape again the very next evening. The team sent the new investigators to sift through unsolved assault cases and reports on file, to attempt identification of either of these local women. They know the crimes occurred in 1997. At this point, the victims may not even be in Louisiana, so making contact could prove difficult.

Later that evening, after a quick dinner break, the team reconvenes in the SCT trailer to determine the day's progress. They've found two possible rape victims who fit their case. Rachel Klein is being identified as victim 'number 2' of Landry's. He appears to have numbered each woman. Ms. Klein's statement was in their system as unsolved from 1997. There's a note that a university counselor urged Rachel Klein to come forward and formally report her assault.

Tracing Rachel's contacts and family information, the new investigators receive a phone number to reach her. They're informed she has been living in New York state, since graduating from BRU in 1998.

The call was brief, Rachel Klein is thankful the man was in custody but discouraged at the number of years it has taken. Rachel said that while he did not "fully penetrate" her, Landry did have her "captive in his truck, for what felt like hours." Ms. Klein claims to have been more traumatized by the abduction than the sexual assault itself. Rachel said the school made a huge deal of her attack, pushing student safety, especially when drinking. She admits BRU being so vocal allowed the news to spread fast. Before she even understood the damage it caused or the repercussions of reporting. "Everyone had an opinion and not one of them hesitated to share it," Rachel explained through gritted teeth.

Ms. Klein is grateful that Steven Landry is off the streets, but makes it clear she wants nothing more to do with the case or a trial. Rachel has put the entire situation behind her and "moved on." That was all they got out of her before she asked them never to call back and promptly hung up.

The third victim of Landry's, the team believed to be an African American woman named Claire Leroux. She was also a BRU student but didn't report her crime to the school, based on her statement. It was on file with the BRPD when she went to the police, a few weeks after the incident. The delayed report is partly why there wasn't a connection drawn to the Rachel Klein case at the time. The details Claire did share were limited, with no evidence to corroborate her accusation.

They discovered Claire Leroux is still a Louisiana resident and living in a nearby parish. Gaston says she wants to make an appearance in person. Lt Zimmer admits that although it is getting late, going now makes sense. He also understands the importance of sharing news like this in person. He grants permission for Townes to escort Dr. Gaston to the residence.

The pair take the twenty-minute drive through the bayou, discussing what they've read in the journals and how this case was unfolding. Dr. Gaston is eager to inform Claire Leroux of their investigative efforts. And hopeful that it will finally provide the woman some closure. "Especially after all this time, and with so many unanswered questions," Gaston adds.

Pulling into the quaint suburban neighborhood where Ms. Leroux was living, they find her house and prepare to make contact. Answering the door in scrubs, Claire appeared confused by their arrival so late in the evening. Ms. Leroux invites the pair into her home after they explain they're here to discuss a crime she was a victim of years ago.

Claire pours a large glass of wine. She politely asks the team if they would like one too. They respectfully decline.

Ms. Leroux starts after a couple of big gulps from her glass. "I know why you're here. I think. I mean, aside from my car getting broken into last summer, there is only *one* other reason you could be here. So, is that it, am I right? You finally know who did that to me?" Claire asks with skepticism.

Dr. Gaston responds with a sympathetic tone, "Yes ma'am, we do believe we have found the man who attacked you seven years ago. He hurt many other women too. We have him in custody now and we wanted to inform you in person."

They give Ms. Leroux a few minutes to process, letting this unfold on her timeline. Gripping her wine glass, Claire gulps down the rest of her ruby red drink before she's ready. With a long exhale Claire shakes her head and then stares off towards a wall in her living room in deep recollection.

"Wow, I haven't thought about that incident in so long. I guess a part of me thought it was buried for life, along with a piece of my soul that I never regained after that night. I wanted to crawl into bed and die. I fell into such a deep depression and totally let myself go. I would've taken my own life if it weren't for my mother. She came over after a university guidance counselor called my parent's house, to report my absences and missing mid-term exams. I was on the verge of failing my sophomore year at BRU. I was going to lose my academic scholarship and was ready to give it all up at that moment."

Claire closes her eyes for a moment and then grabs a blanket from the back of her couch. Wrapping it around herself, she takes another deep breath before continuing. "I had a bath drawn and a razor blade sitting next to the tub. I had gone over the plan hundreds of times. I knew which direction to cut and how hard I needed to press. I was certain bleeding out into the comforting warm water would be pure bliss, compared to the torment I had been experiencing since that monster violated me."

Claire takes a second to catch herself before going any further. "Sorry, is this all, too much? I haven't shared this with anyone *ever*." Before Gaston could comfort and reassure Claire, to her surprise, Ray beat her to it.

"Don't be sorry, we can handle it, I assure you. We're professionals and deal with survivors like yourself all the time. You are courageous and we commend you for speaking with us at all. Please go on, we're here to listen to your story, Ms. Leroux. We only wish we could've been here sooner." he concludes empathetically.

Gaston agrees. Only adding that they use any information shared, to further their investigation, and hold their suspect accountable. "Thank you, for listening and for not calling me a victim. No one ever says 'survivor,' but I guess I am." Claire states with growing confidence.

Townes and Gaston nod in approval. Then patiently wait for her to continue. Claire has kept this inside for the last seven years and feels ready to finally release it. "My mother is the reason I'm a survivor though. She happened to call just before I got into the tub that night. I told her I was running a bath and couldn't talk. I wouldn't have even answered if I knew it was her. My caller ID was broken, and it displayed everyone as an 'unknown caller.' A small part of me thought it might be a sign. Which my therapist says was a 'cry for help.' My mother could sense something was wrong. But her concern and questions only angered me more, which is strange.

"I didn't understand why they couldn't see it sooner, even though I was hiding away. I assumed they would criticize me for being so careless. For drinking excessively when they lectured me so many times not to. I hung up the phone and paced around my bathroom while the tub finished filling up. Then I drained all the water and sat there contemplating that choice of death—its repercussions and what my next steps should be. I remember I was mesmerized by the little cyclone swirling into the drain. Watching all the water waste away, I felt just as empty.

"So, I laid there naked and cold, curled up against the porcelain tub. Trying to work up the courage to slice myself open and end that misery." Claire wipes away a couple of rogue tears. "Before I knew it, my mom was there, in my bathroom. She got into the tub and wrapped her arms around me. I let the tears stream down my face as she held me. I told her I was 'sorry,' and she hushed me right there. Not a single word was spoken until we left. My mom refilled the tub and bathed me with a sponge, not leaving my side for a second. She helped me get dressed and drove me straight to the police station.

"We sat in the car for almost ten straight minutes in silence, until she finally spoke. She told me that I was stronger and braver than I knew. That my soul was, 'blessed by our ancestors' and she knew I was powerful from the moment I came out of her. She's always said my eyes were wide open at birth. Claiming she stared into them and knew 'we had a connection right from the start.' She named me Claire, after my grandmother, who was a civil rights leader and freedom fighter. She also said there was a nod to Mrs. Huxtable because she was obsessed with the Cosby's."

The three of them share a smile and a brief reprieve from the devastation they've dredged up.

Claire says, "I guess I finally felt that love and support I had been needing from my family, and I was ready. My mom asked if I needed her to come in and I said no because I wanted to spare her the details. But everything that happened with that man was in my statement. I was way too drunk, and I lost consciousness. But when I could finally open my eyes, he was already inside me. I felt so frozen with fear and shock. I had a panic attack and started hyperventilating. He kept telling me to 'calm down or I'll shut you up for good.' I was terrified. I remember he put his hands around my throat and started choking me. I tried to hold my breath for some reason and lost consciousness again." Claire shakes her head.

"The cops kept asking me to describe him or anything I could remember. The man had a hat on, like a baseball cap. It was dark but I knew we were in the cab of his truck, right on the front bench seat. I didn't have anything useful according to the officer. I couldn't recall the make or even the color of the truck. There were so many people at the bar that night. I couldn't remember if I had seen the man earlier that evening. I know I was drinking with a study group; we were trying to blow off some steam before midterms. I got carried away and it was the first time I ever drank like that. I didn't know how to handle it or what to expect. I suppose my guard was down and I got, sloppy. I stumbled outside because it was so hot in there. I remember becoming nauseous, so I started walking to the side of the building and that was it.

"There were no surveillance cameras, and that alley was unlit. 'No witnesses and no evidence,' they said, 'basically no crime.' I couldn't believe the officer's words, I was furious. A superior overheard me getting upset and tried to calm me down but only made things worse. He kept talking about a 'rape kit' and I felt like he was shouting the words. I could see the eyes looking in our direction and judging the entire encounter. They discussed the timeframe amongst themselves and discovered it had been a couple of weeks. They all agreed that the first asshole was right.

"So, I signed my statement and walked out. I never expected to hear about it again. Up until you two showed up tonight, I haven't discussed this with anyone other than my therapist. I didn't think I would ever have to talk about any of this again. I won't, right? Uh, need to testify? Do I have to tell this story all over again?"

Claire's growing concern was quickly de-escalated by Dr. Gaston. Explaining that they have enough evidence to put this Landry away for life. Adding they will likely not even see a trial if he pleads out, which is probable. Claire Leroux thanks the pair for listening and taking the time to drive out to tell her the outcome of her case. Admitting that it was "much more comforting than hearing it over the phone."

As Gaston and Townes return to Special Crimes to wrap up for the night, some tension lifts. They both seem a little more at ease, having finally given some well-received *good news* for a change. Townes claims that he hadn't considered Landry pleading out and there not being a trial. Although the Broussard family would probably prefer it that way he admits.

Townes gets a call on his cell from Lt Zimmer. Gaston hears only one side of the conversation from her passenger seat. "Sir, we just finished up with Ms. Leroux and we're on our way back."

Gaston hears the muffled voice of Zimmer but can't make out his words. If Townes was better with technology, he could put the call on speaker. Gaston listens to Ray's responses, her curiosity intensifying as she awaits an update. "No shit, wow. That is certainly, *interesting*. Okay, roger that sir."

Gaston doesn't wait for him to close his cell before she asks impatiently, "What's up?"

"You're not going to believe this. Well, you might because you study these sickos. But they dug up some records on our boy Landry. And get this, the man is married. The psychopath has a wife!" Townes can hardly contain his emphatic intrigue.

Gaston is less stunned, having seen it before. Although she didn't expect Landry's type to hold down a functional relationship long. They discuss the wife leaving and how much she may know about her husband's crimes. Getting her side of the story is imperative.

At the 31st precinct, Det Townes and Dr. Gaston get preliminary information on Amy Daniels, the estranged wife of Steven Landry. They've made initial contact thru DMV records, determining she is still living in Louisiana, but now a few hours from Beau Ridge. Zimmer informs them that "arrangements have been made and you two will be meeting Ms. Daniels at the Landry home tomorrow."

Gaston and Townes head out for the night, to prepare for their meet-up and interview with Ms. Daniels. Her information will lend a new perspective on their psychopath. Fueled by their passion for this investigation and excited to be working together again after all these years, they both eagerly anticipate their return.

21

Estranged Anecdotes

The next morning, Ray and Ele meet at the SCT around eight. They share some pastries and coffee during a morning briefing from Zimmer. The pair exit a couple of hours later and Gaston drives them to the Landry home to meet Amy Daniels. They're anxious to know more about the woman who married a serial rapist and murderer. Whether she was aware of his nefarious lifestyle, which was presumably conducted from their own home.

After a stop for gas and fresh coffee, they arrive at the Landry home ten minutes before Amy Daniels pulls into the driveway. It's almost noon and the clear January sky fully displays the large sun beaming above them.

Amy slowly gets out of her old dinted and scratched-up SUV. She appears upset from seeing the crime scene tape draped around her former home. She's petite, with long, light brown hair and brown eyes which were already teary when she approached. The pair were waiting for Amy on an old, iron bench under the large oak tree in the front yard. Dr. Gaston introduces herself and Det Townes, then asks Ms. Daniels what she currently knows.

Amy speaks up with a strong southern twang, "Not much, I spoke to a police lieutenant, and he told me there was an *incident* at our home. And that Steven was in police custody. I was asked to come here this morning, alone, and that I would be filled in by y'all. I'm sorry I couldn't get here sooner, I had to stop for gas, and I live about three hours away now."

"Okay, that's fine, no worries. Ms. Daniels, when is the last time you were at this house or saw your husband, Steven Landry?" Townes asks.

"Well, I left him in 2001 and I haven't been back since. I don't know what Steven did, but it has to be real bad. There's so much that went on in that marriage that I am not proud of. But I never thought I'd be getting a call and coming back to see the house like *this*. What happened in the garage? There seems to be a lot more tape over there." Amy makes a sudden connection, "My goodness, y'all, did he... hurt someone?" Growing more impatient and fearful of her assumption, Amy's shaking hand covers her mouth. She knows their silence likely confirms her suspicions. Townes and Gaston explain to Ms. Daniels that the man she married is being charged with murder. In addition to the sexual assault of a woman he captured and tortured in the garage.

Amy explains through tears with a shaky voice, that the garage used to be a converted apartment for Steven's father, Frank Landry. She says Steven used to come out there often and liked his privacy, so she rarely entered the building. Detective Townes explains that it has been further converted into a torture chamber. Adding that boxes of evidence were collected and are still being analyzed. The results could bring more charges in the future and identify additional victims.

They ask Amy what she can share about Steven Landry and the life they used to have. This is the first audience aware of her husband's somber side. She is willing to share her experiences. Amy sits down on the bench in the spot Townes rises from, after he gestures for her to take a seat.

After taking a deep breath and long exhale, Amy begins. "I met Steven Landry when I was sixteen years old. I used to work at my parent's store back then. In the summer of 1992, he got his license and started driving his grandpa's old truck into town. After that, he came in often to get things for his grandma, usually. Miss Norma was always sick with a bad cough. Steven and I dated off and on for months. We even lost our virginity to each other."

Amy looks down timidly before continuing. "He left for the Army right after graduation, in 1993. I stayed here doing college prep courses at our church, 'cause I didn't have the grades to get accepted into BRU right away. I thought I might never see him again after he joined the military. And knowing what I do now, I wish I didn't! But I was young, and I didn't know what I wanted.

"Steven was a complicated man. He seemed honest with me though. I guess I thought you had to work that hard, to get information and affection from a man. He was hard to talk to. He'd shut down often, and rarely shared much from his past. I know he never trusted or understood women very much. We broke up after graduation when he joined the Army. And like I said, I thought he was gonna be gone for good."

Amy shuffles her feet while staring down at the ground. She frees a small rock from the matted leaves and kicks it out in front of them while conjuring more flashbacks. "To my surprise though, he returned home in 1997. I didn't even know he was back until his granddaddy, Mr. Clint Landry died. I went to the funeral in June of '97 to pay my respects. I saw Steven there at the funeral and we reconnected a bit. He told me he was discharged from the Army and would be staying home to take care of his grandma, Norma Rae, since Mr. Clint was gone. Steven seemed changed, like a new man almost. I thought his time in the service affected him. Or burying his granddaddy and being home, was harder for him than he was letting on?

"I guess I was more attracted to him when he got home. He had filled out and was bigger, like with muscles, you know? I started flirting but Steven made it clear he wasn't looking for a relationship. I musta seen that as a challenge. Ugh, I'm not proud of this, okay? So please don't judge me. I just know y'all think the worst right now."

Amy takes a second to collect herself. Fending off an emotional breakdown with some deep breaths. Slowly blowing out the air, she shakes her head and reaches into her purse, digging around for a second. Amy lights a cigarette with a trembling hand. Dr. Gaston calms Amy with supportive encouragement that she is doing the right thing. Her insight into Steven and what led to his decisions is paramount for investigators. She is helping in ways she can't understand. Amy proceeds with her tumultuous relationship recap.

"Well like I said, I saw him as more of a challenge and for some reason, I didn't let up. I should have listened to my parents, dear lord." Amy shakes her head and scoffs, then takes a few more drags of her cigarette. "Well, I kept seeing him at church with Miss Norma, around Christmas. I eventually worked up the courage to approach Steven again. I invited him out for New Year's Eve, to bring in the year 1998 together. He didn't want to go anywhere public, so we went to my parent's house, where we were alone. We both tried some champagne, but he hated it. So, I drank almost the whole bottle myself. Of course, I was very tipsy before I knew it. I started to flirt again and for the first time since we were teenagers, we ended up *hooking up*. It was just that one night and Steven freaked out a bit at first, saying it wasn't right and wouldn't be what I wanted. He basically told me to leave him alone. So, I did. I was embarrassed I guess, he made me feel like something was wrong with me for even *wanting* him."

Getting teary-eyed, Amy sighs and then continues after a long pull on her cigarette. "Well, I stayed away for a few months until I realized… I was pregnant. I prayed about it for weeks and when my belly started to grow, I knew I couldn't hide it or wait much longer. It was April of 1998, just before Easter Sunday. The only thing he said was that I was so stupid and just ruined my life. I broke down crying in his driveway, right there." She points towards their parked cars a few feet away. "I was a mess and couldn't keep it together. He asked me why I waited so long because by then I 'couldn't have an abortion,' and I lost it.

"I stayed with my parents throughout my pregnancy. But I was dying to get out and wanted so badly to have my own little family. I guess I was delusional, fantasizing about the best-case scenario. My daddy wanted us to get married. Surprisingly, Steven eventually agreed to it. I thought that was another sign, that he really did want me."

Amy sneers while tossing her cigarette butt towards her feet. "I had his baby, our baby, my son Matthew Steven, on

October 4th, 1998. Then it was about a week later that he agreed to the marriage.

"I moved in with Steven out here after we got married. Norma Rae had us in her and Clint's bedroom, which was the biggest in the house. Since Mr. Clint had passed, she wanted us to have the space for the baby. Norma Rae convinced Steven it was okay and that she would take the spare bedroom he grew up in. The change was rough on Steven—he didn't adjust well to becoming a daddy. He hated hearing the cries and never changed a single diaper or gave Matthew even one bath. If it wasn't for Norma Rae helping me, I would have gone back to my momma way sooner. I guess I wanted to prove to my parents I could do it all alone. I was determined to make my family work. What a mistake."

Amy takes out a nearly full pack of cigarettes from her purse. She lights another one up, taking a long, slow drag and blows out a small cloud before proceeding. "I haven't even smoked a cigarette in almost two years, I just knew I would need one today," Amy admits with a smirk before continuing.

"Norma Rae loved having baby Matthew here. She was always singing hymns and would rock him till he fell asleep. Norma told me that she took care of Steven as a baby too. His momma left him at just six months and didn't return until Steven was five years old. Can you believe that? Norma said that Steven's momma, Angie, 'wasn't meant to be a mother, and she did more damage than good to Steven.' I'll never forget those words. Our son won't ever know his grandparents or any of his daddy's family. Now I see that might be the best thing for him."

Amy takes a few more quick drags of the cigarette. "Matthew is a good boy—he isn't sick and twisted like his daddy or their deranged family. I'm raising him right and I will shelter him from all this nonsense, *forever* if I can!" Amy states definitively.

"When he was about a year old though, I stopped breastfeeding Matthew, and shortly after that my cycle started back. Steven rarely wanted sex, but there were a couple of times that it happened. I ended up getting pregnant, again. I told Steven right away because I could tell that my body was changing, almost instantly. Of course, he freaked out. We got into a huge fight, and Steven slept in the garage apartment. Which was his daddy, Frank's old place. The Landry's had converted it into an apartment back when Frank turned 18, I believe."

Amy looks away, reflecting on the details while her cigarette ash creeps towards her fingers. "Anyway, Steven came into the main house the next day and asked Norma to watch Matthew. He told me we had to go somewhere, and it would take a while. I knew what he wanted, but I didn't think he was going to *force* me. We drove across the Texas border, straight to an abortion clinic. I don't even know how he knew about the place. He pulled up outside and told me to, 'Go take care of it. Don't get back in this truck with a baby inside you.' Oh God, I remember him looking right into my eyes while saying it. I felt like he had no soul. His eyes were just these dark, empty holes. No sympathy, no emotions at all—no one to reason with. I just had to accept it… and I did."

Amy wipes away a tear from her cheek after flicking her half-smoked cigarette butt into the yard. "I went inside alone, waited for about two hours, explaining that I couldn't leave without having it done. The nurse must have felt the fear inside me. Shortly after that, they came out and got me. After getting undressed I sat there alone and cold in the stiff gown, just shaking. I got all hooked up to the machines and then finally got the procedure done. I was released about an hour after when my vitals were stable, they said. I waddled back to his truck with a few painkillers and some pamphlets on birth control options.

"When I got to him, I couldn't believe my eyes. Y'all, he was sleeping! Just taking a little nap, feet kicked up across the bench seat, not a care in the world. I was livid and felt terrified for me and Matthew's future. We drove straight back, and I didn't say a word the entire time. He seemed to favor the silence and it was easier than trying to talk about what happened.

"Everything changed after that day, it was like he got some new power or something, I don't know. But Steven became bolder and angrier. He was way more controlling, always on edge and anxious. I felt like I was walking on eggshells and couldn't do anything right. I was refraining from sex all the time. He said I could get on birth control and 'wouldn't have to worry about another slip.' He read through every damn paper I brought home from the clinic. Rattling off different methods and telling me that I should start the pill right away. That was scary too though. I kept thinking I would miss a pill one day and end up... having to kill another baby. I knew I couldn't handle it."

Tears stream down Amy's face, and she lets them fall to the cold, brown, matted foliage on the ground below. "I was depressed after that. I wasn't eating, lost a ton of weight, and felt like I was sleeping with one eye open. Always on edge and smoking like a damn chimney, thanks to his grandma rubbing off, I guess. Steven hated that habit almost as much as drinking.

Same as his Grandaddy Clint, from what Norma used to tell me."

Amy pauses there for a second with a slight smile. Savoring a few decent memories she's summoned from her time with Norma Rae. Wiping the remaining tears from under her eyes, Amy Daniels continues after a long sigh. "Steven was still staying in the garage apartment every night and seemed to prefer it. I did too, honestly. Things were almost peaceful in the house at times. I thought I could handle it if we could keep that balance."

Amy stands up to stretch her legs. Townes contorts himself against the oak tree to crack his back, before he walks towards the house. The ladies follow him to the front porch steps which are in full sun. Amy looks up with closed eyes and lets the comforting afternoon rays shine down onto her face. Amy takes a few seconds longer to soak up the warmth before resuming. "Everything took another turn on me when Norma Rae passed away before Christmas of 2000. Steven was different after that. It changed him completely. Any light he had before, was gone. Steven became so angry after her death, and I knew things would never get any better. I was almost *jealous*, that Norma Rae had such an effect on him. Ugh, that probably sounds bad, I know. And it was bad, *all* of it. I realize that now.

"I started planning for Matthew and me to move in with my parents after the new year. Then by the spring of 2001, we were gone. I haven't been back to this place since. And I'm sorry! You know, maybe if I had come back, I don't know... I'm... just so sorry." Amy wipes away a few tears and steps up to the house to peer through the windows which are unobstructed by blinds or drapes. Gaston and Townes give her time to look around. Waiting for Amy to take in all the emotions and memories which have resurfaced over the last couple of hours during this interview.

Several silent minutes pass as Amy walked the perimeter. She returns to the team in the front yard, deciding not to go into her former home. Amy takes another second before pointing in the other direction and asking, "Can I see it? The garage. I want to know what he did. Please?"

Townes informs Ms. Daniels that it's a difficult sight since it's still an active crime scene. "It's still intact, basically just the way he left it." His words give Amy goosebumps and stimulate her curiosity. Townes states, "We can if, you're *sure*."

Amy Daniels takes out another cigarette, offering them each one, which they decline. She lights it up and takes a few long drags. She glances around the property and after a few more minutes she tosses the barely smoked butt to the ground. Amy says, "I'm sure," explaining to the pair, "I *need* to see it."

Gaston signals to Townes in approval and they all set off in the direction of the garage. They walk with Amy over the threshold of her estranged husband's dungeon of torment. The team prepares her before they all enter completely, for the many alterations soon to be revealed. Amy shuffles around the unfamiliar space. Taking in all the noticeable changes and devices he's installed. She sees bloodstains on the walls and floor, shaking her head with disbelief at every turn. Amy spots the cables hanging from the ceiling above them and bursts into tears. "My God, what did he do y'all? How many women were brought here? And… when?" Amy asks with a trembling voice weighted by sorrow and concern.

Townes informs her, "We're still working through all the details and analyzing evidence, as I said earlier. But at least three women that we know of were brought and likely killed here.

That didn't start happening until August of 2003, so rest assured it was long after you were gone. Steven likely started this conversion the spring that you left. It would've taken some time to complete all this. We don't have any victims connected to him from April 2001 through August 2003."

Amy asks with a remorseful tone, "So, right after we left, he started this?"

Dr. Gaston chimes in, "Amy, you should know that Steven Landry has victims of rape and assault tracing back to at least June of 1997. And even an unidentified first victim, while Steven was still on active duty. We found journals, with detailed accounts of his violent acts over the years. We're still working through them to identify each victim and their corresponding catalyst in Steven's life. But you shouldn't focus on those details, as none of this was your fault. I assure you that you and your son can move past this and live a happy, full life. There are excellent family therapists who can help you move forward in the healthiest way." Gaston concludes.

"Journals? Steven wrote things down. Like feelings?" Amy questions, while caught off guard by the notion.

Dr. Gaston tries her best to explain, "Well not exactly. There are explicit details of his crimes and victims. We believe they would have acted as his *souvenirs*. It'll take more time for us to dissect it all, but again, you shouldn't worry about that. You didn't know and couldn't change the outcome. Steven Landry is a psychopathic sexual sadist. With genetic and environmental influences. So again, don't take this personally or feel responsible."

Dr. Gaston takes the time to go into more detail on Steven Landry's psychopathy. Explaining some of the genetic characteristics that could have been passed on to their son so

Amy can spot the early warning signs if they arise. "Yes ma'am, thank you for that." Amy responds, now more confident with her knowledge and understanding.

The three of them exit the garage and walk back to their vehicles in the driveway. The sun now lowering in the sky around them. Their interview has taken more time than expected. Leaning against her SUV Amy adds, "I know it's not an excuse, but Steven did have a rough life. I don't know much, but I can tell you that he was raised by his grandparents. Well, by Norma Rae most of the time. He had a real bad relationship with both his grandpa, Clint, and his daddy, Mr. Frank. I think it was right before Steven joined the Army and our high school graduation that Mr. Frank died on the road—in an accident with his 18-wheeler. In fact, most everyone died on Steven.

"His momma, Miss Angie, all I know is that she was a crazy woman. An alcoholic who died when Steven was about ten years old. As I said earlier, she was missing for years, leaving him behind when Steven was just a baby. Apparently, when Angie finally got back, all she did was drink herself to death for the next five years. Steven didn't talk about them much, but you know he used to mention a man who knew his momma real well. He was a bar owner for a place she worked at. What was it… Joe something?"

Amy ponders to herself for a moment, racking her mind for details. "It's near the docks, over the bridge… oh yes, JoJo. That's right, 'JoJo's Poker Club' is the place." Amy announces.

Townes perks up and says, "I know exactly where you're talking about. JoJo's has been there for years! I've been once or twice. Not in a while though, but I think it's still open!"

Amy retorts, "Well, if it is, that man can probably tell you a lot more about Miss Angie than me or anyone else can. If it's helpful, maybe check him out. Sorry, I wish I knew more for y'all."

Townes and Gaston agree they'll investigate it. Amy Daniels climbs into her faded black SUV and Gaston gives her a card for a trauma therapist in a parish not too far from Amy's current home. Gaston then tells Amy to take care of herself and Matthew.

Amy Daniels appreciates their concern and empathy. She mentions them being so understanding and easy to talk to. She feels some relief after finally discussing the truth about her marriage. Amy is ready for closure from the Landry family, once and for all. Before pulling off, she jokingly asks the team while leaning through her open window. "Don't suppose you have a good divorce attorney to recommend along with that shrink?"

Ray and Ele share a quick chuckle and tell her that they'll let her know. Amy asks nervously, "He should be easy to find when the papers are ready, I suppose. Cause he will stay there, right? Uh, behind bars I mean?"

Ele reaches out and grabs Amy's arm which was resting on her door through the open window and gives it a soft squeeze. "Ms. Daniels, I will personally ensure that you're on the contact list, to be alerted if Mr. Landry is ever let out of jail. But rest assured, Detective Townes and I will do everything we can to guarantee that never happens."

A sense of comfort comes over Amy's face. With a smile, she says, "I can't thank y'all enough. Y'all have a great night, okay?!" As she pulls out of the driveway Amy lends a wave out the window before her long brown hair follows suit. Blowing freely in the crisp evening breeze, as Amy Daniels rolls away from her disturbing past.

Back in the rental car, Ray gets excited about this new turn of events. "Ele that was great, you were amazing with her. You have a way with the victims, er uh, survivors. They all open to you so quickly! Christ, most women barely get a few sentences out through clenched teeth. But you're here, and they're all spilling their guts. Extremely helpful I tell you! If I had *you* as a partner, we could have solved so many more cases I bet. I don't know why you ever quit being a cop!"

Ray quickly stops talking. Ele's squinted glares occasionally drift from the road over to her passenger seat. They travel in this uncomfortable silence for about three traffic lights before Ele retorts. Her tone was more playful than he expected. "Thanks. But it wasn't my choice exactly. I would've loved nothing more than to stay here and help you solve crimes, Raymond. Although, I was your boss, if I recall."

Ray laughs and nods his head, "You're right. As usual." He shoots her a wink before Ele glances back to the green light prompting them forward. "Now let's go to JoJo's!" Ray snaps.

"What? Now? I thought we were going back to brief Zimmer?" Gaston asks with confusion.

"And what, come back in the morning to interview JoJo? He's a bar owner Ele, if you want to talk to him, we need to do it tonight. I'll call LT and get him up to speed. Take this right. Right here!"

"Okay, Jesus Raymond. Do you want to drive?" Ele snaps. Townes puts a finger up to his lips to hush her, then points to the phone at his ear while smirking. Ele rolls her eyes as Townes gestures to the street she should turn onto. Gaston is eager for the next piece of this puzzle and enjoys Ray's take-charge attitude. She works to hide her excitement and growing adoration as they progress to JoJo's upon her *partner's* request.

22

A Blast from the Past

Pulling into JoJo's Poker Club, a vibe begins to erupt between Ele and Ray. Sexual tension and some underlying excitement effortlessly grows stronger as their time together continues. When they enter the smoky bar, the stench of boiled peanuts and decades of bad decisions greet them. There are no longer any poker tables or much of what Ray remembers from years before.

"Smells the same, looks different." Townes notes as they stop to take in their new atmosphere and orient themselves. "The guy used to sit at the end of the bar, I think he might be blind. He always wore these dark glasses inside," Ray explains as they round the corner of the establishment.

Once in view, they see an older Black man sitting on the last stool, wearing thick-rimmed sunglasses, just as Ray predicted. The man was smoking a cigarette with a small foam cup of black coffee in front of him. They pegged him at about 70 years old. "That's him, exactly as I remember. Let's go see what he can share." Townes states, as he grabs Ele's hand and guides her forward.

They approach the old man at the bar and Townes takes the lead. "Good evening, Mr. uh, JoJo?" Ray asks customarily, confirming they have the right person.

"It's Phillips. Mr. Joseph Dewayne Phillips. But 'JoJo' to most, you got me..." he confirms, waiting for Townes to continue.

"Yes sir, well, I'm Detective Townes of Beau Ridge PD. Sent here by a young lady who says you might have some information. We're doing an investigation into Steven Landry."

JoJo turns his head away from the TV behind the bar, which he's been fixed on since they walked in. JoJo looks in their direction after hearing the 'Landry' name. They all remain in silence for a moment before Ray proceeds. "Uh, you might not recall, as it was some time ago, sir, but the Landry family was said to—"

JoJo cuts him off, "I remember the family just fine. I was waiting for you to introduce your partner. Or is she here for a drink?" The old man laughs to himself while putting his cigarette out. Then turns his barstool to face the pair completely.

"My partner, right, sorry. This is Dr. Eleanor Gaston, she's a criminologist here to consult on the Landry case. And... I'm sorry, I can't help but notice, you knew she was a woman. So, you *can* see?" Townes blurted out before he had a second to think about keeping that thought inside.

"Of course, I can see! I'm old, but not blind. Damn, a Black man can't wear sunglasses inside without being Stevie fucking

Wonder. I get headaches and the shades help. That's all. And I don't play the piano either detective, sorry to disappoint you."

Ray smirks at Mr. Phillips' humorous side. Then continues trying to salvage the interview. "My apologies sir, I guess that was an old rumor I must have heard years ago. Always bad information in circulation out here."

"Yeah well, don't believe everything you hear, detective. Now, what is this all about? What did that boy do? Must have been bad if you have a criminal doctor here for it." JoJo asks while shaking his head before lighting another cigarette.

Det Townes responds, "Well, Mr. Phillips, Steven Landry is charged with the murder of a local young woman. We have reason to believe that he left a lot more destruction in his wake over the years. We've spoken to his estranged wife, Amy Daniels, and she sent us to you. She said it might be worth our while to speak with you, as you apparently knew Steven's mother better than anyone else. That's why we're here I suppose. So, what can you tell us about Steven Landry's mom, Ms. Angie, sir?"

JoJo takes a long drag of his cigarette before asking his barkeep Shay to top off his coffee. When she finishes pouring, he waits for her to walk away, then continues. "Wife huh? Well, I don't know much about her boy or his wife, but I suppose I was a decent friend to Angie. I always knew someone would likely show up askin' questions about that woman. She was trouble from the start, so it figures it's the po'lice askin'."

JoJo continues in a softer tone, his voice still gravely, "I saw right through her tough side. Deep down Angie was a gentle soul. But getting through to her wasn't easy. And not just 'cause she was hardheaded. It was more for her not trusting anyone. Angie was always mistreated, her whole life. Poor thing; bless her heart. I remember the day I first saw her—curled up behind the dumpster out back, must have been about 1972. I didn't say a word to her for three days straight. She kept coming back though. I'd see her trying to sleep out there and rummaging through the dumpster for anything useful.

"Finally, on the third day, I brought out a plate of food and a bottle of water. She was hungrier than scared by then, it seemed. She scarfed that food down so quick. A few minutes later she thanked me and asked what I wanted in return. I told her I just needed her to leave. Angie said she had nowhere to go and wouldn't be any trouble. I didn't want to force her out to the streets. Women were dying every day and getting caught up in sex work out there. I asked her if she wanted a place to stay, in exchange for work around the bar. Nothing sexual, I made sure she knew that! She thought I was crazy at first, and I guess I don't blame her. But we warmed up to each other and I realized she needed me."

JoJo sips on his coffee and Gaston adds to further the conversation. "That's amazing for you to offer something like that, Mr. Phillips. To a stranger especially. Very brave. How did she handle working for you? And where was she staying—the office up there?" Ele asks while pointing to a small staircase in the corner of the building that leads up to a single door.

"It's an office now, but it was an apartment. I was almost done renovating it when Angie appeared. I was scared at first, this young white girl shows up, all strung out. Looking to me for help and I'm already struggling as a black bar owner, trying to keep this place open. I guess I tried to keep her a secret, or at least that she was staying here quiet from people. I didn't know who might come looking for her. She was a 20-year-old runaway, headed to New Orleans. She'd been hitchhiking all the way from Ohio, with truckers mostly. Working her way down here as soon as she was released from the state's system up there. I don't know all the details; Angie didn't talk much about it. But she was carrying some demons around with her.

"Angie loved to travel and always wanted to see new things. It was her only relief, I guess. Aside from alcohol or drugs numbing her up, making her forget for a bit. Said she had always wanted to get in the car and just drive away. Angie never learned to drive growing up though, so she was scared to be behind the wheel. She just had to get right—you know? She needed some money and rest. She wanted to buy a bus ticket this time when she was ready. I thought she was on the right track too. Seemed to be finding her way and settling down a bit. Until… she met Frank."

JoJo pauses for a moment. He shakes his head and sighs loudly. "Just talking about Frank Landry makes me want to drink. But I ain't gonna go back on twenty years of sobriety for that asshole," JoJo declares.

He takes a long drag of his cigarette and a moment later JoJo proceeds with his story. "Angie changed after they started dating. She was happy at first, said Frank was treating her okay and that had never happened before I guess. It didn't take long for him to be head over heels for the girl. All the while Angie was more concerned with getting out of here and not trying to get too attached. Plus, she was always flirting and accepting attention from any man who was willing to show it. I think she felt like she had missed out on a lot in life and wanted to, make up for lost time or something?"

JoJo wafts the cloud of smoke away from his listeners. "Angie thought she was more grown than she was. Got herself into some trouble a few times. Showing up needing an advance on her paycheck that she was barely owed by then. It was always something with that girl. I was watching my back and worried about getting caught up in her messes.

"But it was when she found out she was pregnant with Frank's baby, that everything took a turn."

Gaston and Townes each grab a stool and continue to listen attentively. JoJo proceeds after a few more drags from his dwindling cigarette. "Frank wanted a little family and had some ideas of what his woman should be doing, I guess. Angie was having a hard time *adjusting*. Frank hated her working here and blamed it on all her issues. Not knowing shit about the girl or what was really going on with her. Eventually, Frank got Angie to quit working and move in with him, over at his folk's place. I didn't see her for a bit and thought they were getting things worked out. Until she came to me late one night pounding on the back door, distraught from some experience over there. She was askin' about going to get an abortion, insisting I help her. Angie kept saying she couldn't have the baby and that she needed it out of her. I told her it was too late, she musta' been almost five or six months by then, already had a big ole bump, ya know? She went to pounding on her belly with clenched fists, screaming to 'get it out' and that she 'didn't want it.'

"I thought Angie was going to kill the damn baby before she even had it. She broke down crying, completely hysterical. I could see how frightened she was, poor thing. Thankfully it was after hours. I brought Angie upstairs and got her cleaned up. Let her rest for the night and I slept on one of those benches to make sure she was okay 'til mornin'." JoJo points to the empty booth tables behind them.

"Angie went back to Frank the next day and I didn't see her much after that until the baby was born. She was right back in here, just a couple weeks after she gave birth, in the spring of '75. Drinking on anyone's tab who'd let her. Angie would stay the night upstairs when they got into it. Or when she claimed she couldn't 'handle the baby crying.' Then one day, around September of that year. Just as quietly as she showed up, without any warning, Angie disappeared.

"A few days went by, and Frank was going crazy. In here every day questioning people or sitting out in the parking lot waiting for her. I thought Angie was gone for good. Or maybe even dead. Until I got a postcard. It was from New Orleans, and all it said was:

'I made it. —A'

"I knew it was from her. She sent more over the years too. Every few months I'd get one from wherever Angie ended up. She went all the way to California, and I think as far north as Montana. Seemed to stay on the west coast region, probably sticking with truckers as she did before."

JoJo takes another sip of his coffee and crushes his cigarette into the ashtray in front of them. Gaston chimes in, "You must have been her only semblance of family—Angie trusted you. She left her baby and significant other here and only contacted you, over a five-year period?"

JoJo scratches his stubbly grey chin hairs and responds, "Yeah, I guess that's right. The boy was about five years old when Angie got back in 1980, and she wasn't any better. Worse, in fact. Doing any drugs she could get her hands on. Angie drank herself to death, but it was quick, once it finally happened. It was a bad accident back in 1985. She was in Frank's white pickup truck which she had barely learned to drive. Angie took off and ended up wrapping it around a tree a few miles away from the Landry home. The accident separated the entire bed from the cab of the pickup. It was quite a scene from what I heard. Angie went through the windshield and died on impact. I think it was a suicide, really. Them talking about how fast she musta been going and all the alcohol in her system." JoJo shakes his head.

JoJo shakes his head before concluding, "But anyway, that's all I know about Miss Angie, okay? If you want to know more, you will have to read through her own words and figure it out for yourselves." JoJo concludes while gesturing for Shay to come over their way.

Gaston and Townes look at each other puzzled as JoJo asks his barkeep to grab a box from his office upstairs. "Right on top of the filing cabinet, you'll see it," JoJo hollers, as Shay disappears up the stairs. JoJo explains that he kept each of the postcards Angie sent him over the years. Along with the one picture he has of Frank and Angie together. Which used to hang behind the bar—like many other patrons' photos who have visited JoJo's over the years are displayed.

Shay returns a minute later with a small dusty box folded closed at the top. JoJo opens it, revealing a time capsule from Angie's short life preserved since 1985 inside this small cardboard cube. JoJo reaches in and pulls out a few different notebooks. "I also have these, her uh, diaries? Angie wrote in them over the years on the road. Maybe her whole life before she made it here. I don't know. Every time she returned to the bar, Angie was up there scribbling some thoughts down. I think it helped her make sense of things. Not sure what's in them, 'cause I never read a single page. Not my business and I don't want any more of that crazy in my head than Angie already left me with."

JoJo puts the contents back inside and slides the box across the bar top towards the pair. "But you guys should take this, hell maybe there is something in here that her boy should know? I'm sure he has a lot of questions. Sounds like his upbringing has taken its toll. What a shame. You know he came in here once, years ago. He was all grown up and I didn't recognize him at first until he saw their picture back there hanging up. The one in the box of Frank and Angie. He walked right behind the bar and grabbed it off the wall. I knew right then it was Angie's boy. I was thinking about giving him all this stuff at the time, but our meeting didn't go too good. Steven got upset that I knew his momma so well and was asking a bunch of questions. He claimed I knew her better than his daddy did and kept calling her a 'waste case.' The boy was troubled, that was clear. He left here in a rage and I haven't seen him since. You guys should take it all. I don't need any of it back, trust me." JoJo seems troubled by digging up Angie's memories and the Landry family's history.

Gaston and Townes thank Mr. Phillips for his time and the information he provided. They give him a card for Lt Zimmer and ask JoJo to contact the Special Crimes Team directly if he thinks of anything else.

"I promise you—this is it! I haven't seen a member of the Landry family since that night Steven left here, and that's fine with me. I don't know how he will feel about me having Angie's stuff all this time either… so maybe don't tell him where you got it? Okay?" The team assures JoJo that Steven Landry will likely never be released from prison. And even if they tell him about these items, he won't get a chance to see them. JoJo shakes their hands and walks the pair to the door.

Leaving with the box in hand, Ele asks Ray to drive them back to the SCT trailer, so that she can begin looking through Angie's items along the way. "This is incredible! Two generations of traumatic events and chaos, all documented for us to analyze. My goodness Ray, this is going to make for amazing research opportunities! I can't wait to get some answers about the mother who influenced a psychopathic serial killer." Ray laughs at her enthusiasm and can't help but feel his adrenaline rushing too. Gaston's passion for this work was infectious and Ray loves being a part of this moment with her.

Townes reflects on some of JoJo's insights. "I remember that accident she was in. Angie, the one that killed her. I was there on the scene that night, it was just as horrific as he said. The pickup truck she was driving really did separate. The two sections were laying a few feet apart in a field. With Frank's tools and debris from the bed scattered around the smashed-up remnants. It looked like a small plane crash. Do you remember me telling you about it when you read the report the next day? You asked if I was okay and that was one of the first personal conversations we had." Ray recalls.

Ele takes a second to think back and remembers exactly what he is referring to. "I do remember that, yes. See, I told you it was a traumatic scene. You were still a new patrol officer, and I wasn't sure you could handle it. I was wrong I suppose, but glad I called you in the office for a private chat that day."

Ray notices her smile and believes Ele's reflection on their past is also fondly remembered. Before they arrive at the precinct, Townes gets a call from Lt Zimmer. Informing the pair that he is heading out for the night and has an early meeting tomorrow with the District Attorney, to discuss the Arturo Ruiz appeal. Townes tells Zimmer that they had a good meeting with JoJo and had some personal items given to them. Explaining they needed to be inventoried when they return and will be further examined in the morning.

Arriving back at work, Ele is too eager to know what these pages hold. She plans to stay a bit longer and look things over, before heading out for the night. Ray understands and agrees to stay with her. They inventory the items and make a brief chronology of the four different notebooks, so Gaston knows exactly where to start tomorrow. When they wrap up about an hour later, Townes locks up the office and the pair walk out to the parking lot together.

The sky is now black and displays a bright moon hanging overhead. Ele jokes about years ago during their affair. How they couldn't have shared an office alone, at night, without being all over each other. Ray confesses that he thought about it too. And would love nothing more than to recreate a special moment they once shared.

Ele wasn't expecting such an obvious suggestion but appreciates the honesty. Not wanting to make things awkward, Dr. Gaston cuts it short, leaning in for a quick kiss on Ray's cheek. "Get home safe, I can't wait to see you in the morning and continue uncovering new information. This has been quite a memorable investigation so far, Raymond." With a wink, Ele turns away to get into her car. Leaving Ray wanting more but settling for a wave before hopping into his truck to head home, alone.

23

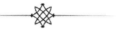

Macabre Memoirs

The next morning, Townes arrives to work thinking he's early. Yet Gaston was let in an hour prior by Lt Zimmer, who just left to meet with the D.A. Gaston's reading through the journals and smiles big when she sees Townes. "Good morning, Raymond. Grab my keys on the table and take me to get coffee, please. You drive, and I'll talk! I can't wait to tell you about what this woman has gone through."

Ray needs coffee anyway and the station's brew is always burnt or too weak, so he agrees. On the way to the shop, Ele Gaston explains what she has already read in Angie's first journal. "So, she was abandoned as a newborn, then adopted by a couple who happened to divorce just a year after they brought in little Angelica. That's what they named her. The mother, Kathy, was granted temporary custody during the divorce. Kathy was in jeopardy of losing Angie as a single mother with limited resources. Her ex-husband was adamant about not wanting to be financially responsible at any point, and his lawyer petitioned to exhaust his parental rights. Kathy told all this to Angie growing up. Trying to spin it like she was a good mom and worked so hard to keep Angie. Kathy met a new man and quickly married him. In hopes that it would stabilize her case with the adoption, presumably."

Dr. Gaston continues as they travel towards the coffee shop. "Although he married Kathy, he never adopted Angelica. This guy, Keith, was bad news. He was controlling and abusive. As Angie grew up and developed into her body, she writes of Keith violating her, every chance he got. It started with groping Angie's breasts and commenting on her size or that she needed to wear a bra. Ugh, this guy was such a creep." Gaston comments, seemingly disgusted.

"Angie was about thirteen years old when Keith started molesting her, based on her written accounts. A few years of dealing with that in silence took its toll on Angie. It was around age fifteen when she finally admitted some things weren't right in her home life. Angie began confiding in a male teacher at school, to whom she also developed an attraction. It appears she fantasized about this Mr. Dickson and began obsessing over him. Angie misunderstood his attempts to comfort her, as Mr. Dickson's love and affection for her. Angie had their initials with hearts scribbled all over a few pages in her journal. Now without this guy's side, I can't say for sure, but it appears Mr. Dickson handled it all professionally.

"So, I guess Angie finally had it all planned to tell him how she felt and that she wanted to be with him. Somehow believing they could make a legitimate relationship work. Of course, it didn't go well. So badly, Angie attempted suicide that evening by cutting her wrists in the shower. She later writes about how she lost consciousness and fell outside the tub. Her stepdad,

Keith, discovered Angie passed out on the bathroom floor and called 911. The EMTs managed to stop most of the bleeding before they arrived at Mercy General. Angie's wounds were severe enough to cause permanent nerve damage in her hands and several fingers. Angie was also given a psychiatric evaluation where the staff identified some red flags.

"Angie gave a social worker information about Keith's abuse and her home life. When corroborated with records from her school, they realized the extent. Thankfully, Mr. Dickson reported what Angie confided in him, and the school was working with Child Protective Services to document what they knew. They immediately called an emergency hearing to have Angie removed from Kathy's care. CPS filed a petition with the court for the state of Ohio to regain custody, and the adoption was terminated a few days later. Angie was then sent to a psychiatric facility for further evaluation and treatment. According to her record, they deemed Angelica a threat to herself and unfit for foster care at the time."

Ray pulls into the lot at the coffee shop, and Ele pauses to grab them each a hot cup of joe and donuts for the team. Ray waits in the car, considering the new information he's received. This is only mid-teen years for this woman, and Angie has already had a terrible run of events. Ray's empathy for Angie increases, along with his understanding. He sees how Angie's disturbed past could have affected her life and parenting.

Ele gets back into the car and hands Ray a tall, warm cup. That comforting java aroma steams up from the small opening in the plastic lid. Ray holds the cup up to his nose and takes in a long sniff, exhaling with a smile. Ele grins at him, "I love how much you love the smell of coffee. And I know what you're thinking! Yes, we're only sixteen years in and this is already dreadful."

Ray raises his eyebrows in agreement as he blows on his beverage to prepare for that first sip. Ele continues as he carefully pulls off, heading back towards the office. "A few days after the suicide attempt was Angie's 16th birthday. Because the only facility for juveniles apparently cut off intake at fifteen, the state placed her in Findlay Women's Reformatory. She was under the care of a psychiatrist, Dr. Zwift, who was solely responsible for Angie's treatment and evaluations. Sadly, this man may have done more damage than anyone in Angie's life."

Ray shoots Gaston a look of disbelief. His face was pressed into confusion. Ele snaps, "I know, right? He's a professional, a doctor for Christ's sake, yet he was a complete fraud. And maybe his credentials were legitimate, which is likely how he got away with it for so long. Based on Angie's annotations this asshole remained in practice. He likely would have dozens of victims before and after Angie's time there. Dr. Zwift may have never gotten caught in fact…" Ele trails off while staring out the window shaking her head in contempt.

"So, this *doctor* was 'treating' Angie with a made-up cure to fulfill his sick indulgence and sexual perversions. He started with some legitimate behavioral and cognitive therapy tactics. Earned Angie's trust with his intelligence and some coercion. Eventually, Dr. Zwift pushed Angie to start this 'sexual manipulation therapy' as he called it. Until Angie was 'ready for full penetration' as he disgustingly claimed." Ray gives her a wide-eyed, empathetic look of concern, knowing where this is likely going.

Ele nods somberly before confirming. "Yes, her therapist masterfully cultivated an environment of secret abuse. Until he was raping Angie in the comfort of his own office. And getting paid for it from the state of Ohio. Dr. Zwick told Angie that he would 'rehabilitate her sexual drive and redirect her hormones.' Along with some other ridiculous ideas which he portrayed as 'progressive medical practices.' Audaciously asserting that they were necessary for a trauma victim of sexual abuse. And this poor girl, she was buying it, completely. So much so, that Angie fell in love with this asshole too. Or so she thought, which of course is enough for a sixteen-year-old girl."

Ray shakes his head with a grimace. Angry and disgusted that this man was so brazen and illicit in his operation. Ele continues, "So this was going on for a while, as Angie is getting more comfortable and believing he's helping her. Even naïve enough to think that she's *special*. Being the predator he is, Zwift eats that shit up. He completely played off every vulnerability Angie displayed. He told her she is his only patient with this 'ground-breaking treatment.' Claiming that Angie was aiding him in 'making revolutionary medical history,' ugh." Gaston and Townes share a synchronized deep eye roll, both equally appalled by these details.

"Yeah, this piece of shit thought he had it made, and he did, for over a year, Raymond! Until a new patient starts talking during their socialization time in the dayroom. The young lady began asking the other patients about their experiences with Dr. Zwift. Angie overheard a few women sharing similar stories and discovered the truth. She goes straight to his office and confronts him. Zwift doesn't take this well, of course. He threatened to expose Angie to the state as a 'suicidal, troubled kid' who wasn't socially acceptable for foster care. Making it clear he could keep Angie locked away for life. Zwift went as far as telling Angie the story of her adoption and supplying details found in her case files from the state. He told Angie that her biological mother was a mentally challenged teen. The family overturned baby doe to the state hours after the teen gave birth to Angie. Only for her to be adopted by a couple who couldn't stay together long enough to love her. Dr. Zwift made sure to solidify Angie's abandonment issues. Killing any fraction of self-esteem conjured up throughout her depressing life." Gaston shakes her head.

"I left off right before she departed from Ohio. Angie was demanding emancipation at seventeen after learning of the option from another patient at Findlay. The state, however, continued to side with Dr. Zwift. Stringing her along until Angie aged out of the system in 1970. Just before her 18th birthday, Angie was summoned late one evening to Zwift's office. There, she had to sign several papers, which supposedly bound her from discussing any part of their treatment. Claiming that if anything did come to light, Dr. Zwift would ensure Angie ended up in a cell for life. Reminding her that he was a professional and she was the patient, asking who she thought they would believe?

"Angie ended that first notebook with a plan to hitchhike to New Orleans, as JoJo said. Of course, I already know the ending to this story, and it's imminent, but I'll press on through her journey." Ele claims confidently as they pull back into the SCT lot with their breakfast. The pair head inside to keep researching the ominous details of Angelica's life.

About an hour has passed when Townes finishes some paperwork for Zimmer. He walks over to check on Ele, reading through the second notebook. She wipes a few tears as Townes approaches, then closes the book before shooting him a half-smile.

Ray asks with genuine concern, "Hey doc. Are you okay?"

"Yes. Thank you. There's some heart-wrenching material on these pages."

"Got it, but hey," Ray leans in close, "don't think you *have* to finish these. If it's too heavy, someone else can jump in. No worries," he assures Gaston.

"Thanks. But I feel like I owe it to her, as strange as it sounds. Angie spilled her guts on these pages and deserved someone to understand her and to care. You know? I need to see this through. For Angie." Ele states compassionately.

"Okay, I understand. But I'm here to listen. Please, debrief me if it will help."

Gaston eases back into her professional role and taps the empty chair next to her for Townes to sit and listen. She clears her throat and proceeds, "Angie left Ohio to hitchhike south in 1970. She met several truckers along the thousands of miles traveled. These strangers proved to be a variety of characters—usually assholes and possibly a few sociopaths, based on her accounts. She was raped and beaten, forced to perform oral sex at gunpoint several times by one man. A former preacher seemed to help her out some. He tried to teach her about Jesus and provided a safe place for a bit.

"Continuing that journey south, was an agonizing mission that she pressed on with for two years! Eventually, Angie made it to Louisiana and held up in Beau Ridge. She was pretty strung out and beaten down from the harrowing expeditions during her travels. Angie writes about meeting JoJo and working at the bar. She stayed in Beau Ridge, even though she wasn't too far from her goal of New Orleans. Angie dreamt of living down there and finding some blues café to work in. Listening to live music and selling beignets and bourbon all night. But she ended up feeling safe with JoJo and needed to relish in that comfort for a while, as far as I can tell. Now she's about to meet Frank Landry and will soon become a mother. I didn't know how unprepared she was until I read all this. Now *I* need a drink."

Townes smirks and tells Ele it's lunchtime, so she's getting closer to happy hour. He offers to grab them some sandwiches from a nearby deli. Saying he will return for another update after she has combed through more material. Gaston thanks him and asks for a pickle spear. She then reminds Ray that she hates onions, which Ray claims he has never forgotten. Ele smiles fondly while reopening the journal and sifting to the page she left off.

On his way out, Townes recalls their first private lunch together when Ele was his lieutenant. They were approaching their first intimate encounter and full of sexual tension. Their conversation was easy, and Ray discovered Ele's sense of humor and intelligence during that lunch. Seeing her as a normal woman took away the tension of being with his superior officer. Ray solidified his adoration for Ele that afternoon in 1985. His lust grew intensely after they finally gave in to their yearnings on New Year's Eve. Despite so many adverse effects of drinking, Ray is happy to still have fragments of their happier memories.

Thirty minutes later, Townes returns carrying sandwiches, chips, and two sweet teas. He gives Gaston a few minutes to enjoy her meal. Ray watches Ele lick several fingers, and indulge in every discarded morsel on her wrapper.

Ele wipes her mouth and smiles, "That was delicious, Ray. Thanks again for lunch. I needed that!"

Townes gives her a wink as he slurps down his tea and then replies, "Of course, any time. You know I'll always take care of you." Gaston blushes, then quickly looks away while cleaning up her mess on the table. Ray changes gears, not wanting things to be uncomfortable. "So, where'd you get with Angie's thoughts? You make it past the pregnancy yet? See where she disappeared to for five years?"

"Well, I am making progress, and Angie was too it seemed. Even after she met Frank Landry. It was Frank's parents who aided in pushing Angie away. She was terrified during her pregnancy. Convinced she was unworthy of being a mother and that the baby would die inside her. When that didn't happen, Angie wrote about the night she went to JoJo begging for help with an abortion. Apparently, Frank shared some information about Angie's past with his parents. She writes about Clint Landry calling her a 'lot lizard' after learning how she arrived in Louisiana.

"Angie felt trapped and scared. She began having panic attacks from what she described in her writing. Angie was aware of the symptoms she endured, which sometimes increased her anxiety. Angie believed something was inherently wrong with her. She wrote about contemplating suicide on many occasions. Remembering what Dr. Zwift shared about her birth mom, she knew her own DNA was 'tainted.' Angie was terrified to have the baby and wrote about her fears of being unable to love Steven on top of passing along shitty genes from both sides. Admitting she and Frank were ill-equipped to be parents.

"Angie described Clint Landry as, 'a vile man.' He would grope her and ask for sexual favors, likely to garner a reaction and test her tolerance. She annotated that Frank's mom, Norma Rae, was a 'doormat' for the men and oblivious to their true nature and sinister secrets it would appear."

Gaston pushes against the metal chair to stretch her back and continues. "Clint was wheelchair-bound from a truck driving accident that left him a paraplegic when Frank was a young boy. Clint used his settlement money after suing the driver he hit, to buy their property and the home Frank, and later his son Steven, grew up in.

"By the time Frank hit puberty, Clint began to live vicariously through his adolescent son. Frank confessed several secrets to Angie when sharing stories of their pasts. Like how Clint converted that garage into an apartment when Frank turned eighteen, as we heard. But it wasn't for his privacy and independence. Angie wrote that shortly after Frank moved in, Clint began hiring hookers for his son to have sex with, and he would watch from his peephole. A small opening was cut out for Clint to see into the bedroom area from the hallway. The hole was hidden by the same calendar still hanging inside the garage when we examined it."

Townes thought for a second to recall what Gaston is describing. "The calendar? Oh, with the naked chicks? Yeah, they did look like some older women. I guess it could have been there a while. The crime scene guys noted that all the women were 'hippies' since they had 'bushes' and that's no longer in, apparently."

Ele smirks, "Right, same calendar. When removed from the wall by Frank, the peephole was revealed to Angie. She noted that it was waist-high and would have been perfect for

Clint to view his son's sexual encounters from his permanent seated position. Clint would demand that Frank choke the women and spank them harder. Saying he wanted to 'hear the smacks from the other side of the wall,' according to Frank."

Gaston shoots Townes a side eye, and he scoffs while shaking his head in astonishment, listening to her continue. "Frank got hired to drive long-haul, keeping him on the road for weeks. He eventually got into an AA program and told Norma he was sober, which was true. Although he began skipping the meetings for poker games at JoJo's, where he met Angie, and later returned to the bottle. Frank believed the baby was a blessing for their family, and naively told Angie 'it'll all be okay.' Reminding her that if they give their baby away, it could end up in a situation like she experienced and repeat the cycle.

"Angie reluctantly agreed to keep the baby. A day later, she writes about going into labor. She had significant tearing during her delivery. Angie described it as feeling like she was, 'getting split in two.' She got an infection from the botched episiotomy and was admitted for an additional week receiving intravenous antibiotics, while they monitored her wound. The baby went home with Frank and his mother Norma Rae. Angie said that Norma was able to bond with her baby and began to soothe Steven in ways Angie couldn't.

"When Angie finally got home, she wrote about Steven not knowing her face or voice. And that he would cry constantly when Angie picked him up. She was scared to handle the baby and claims that she left him in the crib unless she was changing him. Angie even propped up Steven's bottles with a pillow and blankets, so she didn't have to hold him while he ate. She explained returning to the bar and working around JoJo's club for money, but mostly to stay busy and out of the house. Angie got tired of stringing Frank along, and eventually convinced herself that Norma Rae could better handle raising Steven. It's about there that she decides to take off." Dr. Gaston lends a half smile while patting the closed notebook in front of her.

Gaston adds, "It was evident Angie suffered from post partem depression. She needed therapy and help, but instead, she ran. Angie ended this notebook by heading out on the road again. Without telling Frank or JoJo that she was leaving. She's about to walk away from her son, a mere six-month-old baby. She is leaving the only man who has ever loved her. About to embark on what we know is a five-year trip around the western part of the United States, alone. I honestly don't know if I'm prepared to read about those events quite yet. Especially knowing that JoJo said she returned worse than she left." Gaston remarks despondently, then sighs in defeat as her body slouches forward.

Ray says empathetically, "Damn, I can imagine how exhausting this must be for you. You have that caring nature, you want to help her, but we both know it's too late. Again, I just don't want you to think you have to do this alone."

"I appreciate it. But don't worry, I can handle it. You're right, I do want to help her though, and I wish I could have! But anyway, I'm going to take these and head back to my hotel. We still need to finish reading Steven Landry's last notebook. I think I need some wine for that. I guess I'm more used to working at home and not in a stenchy old police trailer," Ele admits.

While Gaston takes her briefcase to her car, Townes grabs the book she was last reading from. He quickly shuffles through the pages. Ray's eyes dart towards the door occasionally, ensuring he isn't seen. Ray finally lands on the section where

Angie illustrated her pregnancy fears and becoming a mother. He lays the notebook on the copy machine and photocopies two pages before returning the notebook to the conference room table. Just then, Gaston swings open the door and reemerges with a smile. Ray assists in taking the box of evidence to her car and sends Ele Gaston on her way.

The Lieutenant calls Townes as he's heading inside, with information. "Steven Landry has plead guilty to Maddison's murder. As a result, they've waived the death penalty and there likely won't even be a trial." Zimmer confesses that he feels the brass is trying to close this prematurely, and the SCT must be careful how they proceed. Townes is confused and angry, considering how many other victims still deserve justice.

After hanging up, Ray walks to the copy machine and looks over the journal pages. He folds them up and slides them into his back pocket. Townes doesn't understand why Landry would only confess to this one crime and decides that he needs answers. Ray locks up the office a few minutes later and heads straight to the jail for an impromptu visit with Steven Landry.

24

Spontaneous Sit-down

Townes arrives at the Beau Ridge County Jail with his badge in hand, providing him the necessary credentials for access. Landry enters the interview room about twenty minutes later. His tall stature and slim frame slink through the doorway, and he appears angrier than at his arrest. Ray hardly remembers Steven's eyes being so dark from their brief encounter.

Landry's voice rang out with a tremble at first, asking Townes, "Who are you, and what the fuck do you want?"

Sensing Landry's attempt to assert power, Ray introduces himself. "I'm Detective Townes; I work for Beau Ridge PD. 31st precinct, Special Crimes—my team brought your ass in. I wanted to have a *quick chat.*"

"What the fuck for? More intimidation tactics? Jesus, you guys are all the same, huh? I told them I have nothing to say. You got what you wanted, right? I signed the plea agreement. What more do you need from me, detective?" Landry retorts.

"Uh, well, I'm unsure what you're talking about. I came here of my own volition with a few questions. I work with a criminologist who has taken on your case. We have *information,* and new details about your mother, Angelica Hartfield."

Landry shoots Townes a look of suspicion at the thought and asks, "My mother? What do you want to know about that woman? She is a waste case who drank herself to death. End of story." Steven bleakly concludes.

"Well, that is part of her story, but it certainly isn't everything."

Steven snaps, "I don't give a shit about everything. And what *information* are you even talking about? No one in my family is alive to tell you shit about her. Not that they knew anything worth sharing in the first place." Landry looks Townes up and down slowly and squints his eyes, unsure where this is headed and becoming less amused by the second.

Townes continues with intrigue, "We'll get to that, but let's start with these intimidation tactics. My understanding is you've only been visited by your court-appointed public defender. And the District Attorney's assistant to set up your psych eval. Who else has been here Steven? Who's doing this intimidation?"

"The judge," Landry affirms while staring into Townes' eyes.

"Judge? Which one? They don't typically make jailhouse visits." Ray questions.

"Well, retired ones do. Or maybe just ones who are the daddy of a dead girl?" Steven concludes arrogantly with raised eyebrows. He sits back in his metal chair, appearing more relaxed, now. Believing Townes isn't here for the same reasons as his previous visitor.

"Mr. Broussard? Came here, to the jail? When? And what did he have to say?" Townes asks, genuinely perplexed by the accusation.

"Well, he wasn't *here* but he did send a message. I guess one of the guards is kin to him. He delivered a letter to me in my cell. Didn't say a word, just left it with my lunch tray, right under that dry-ass sandwich. It said that I could be 'reached' in here, whenever he wanted. He advised that I plead guilty to 'only her murder' and give no details about the crime, to anyone, *ever.* Landry continues, realizing Ray is fascinated by this information. "The D.A. didn't even seem to know about this little request. He made it seem like my confession was sparing me the death penalty and a trial. Which he claimed was 'a good deal, considering.' But I never planned to be sitting in here like an animal; caged and waiting for someone to take care of me all the time. Dependent on another man to give me the essentials in life, to allow me to shower and wipe my ass. At least with capital punishment, there's some dignity and a worthy ending. Because waiting around for these assholes to toy with me, isn't how I thought it would go. I guess number ten was never according to plan either, so it figures it would end like this." Landry states bitterly. He sits back into the metal chair as far as his cuffs will allow. Fully extending the chain link from the table he is bound to. Which is all that stands between the two men in this otherwise empty room.

"So, this letter, it's the only reason you plead guilty and are avoiding the death penalty? And you are certain it was from Mr. Broussard? That's an awfully bold move." Townes admits with some disbelief.

"Yeah well, I'd show it to you, but they took it. I came back that same night after a shower, and it was gone. I guess that means they're serious. I fucked up. What else can I say? I should've grabbed a less risky bitch. My bad." Townes is floored by Landry's smug attitude. This man is more communicative and intelligent than he expected. Curious if he is being played, but Ray doesn't want to push the issue. Det Townes chooses to believe Landry and makes a mental note that Mr. Broussard has more gull than Ray expected.

"I appreciate your honesty and if I'm doing the same, I'll admit I don't exactly know what the purpose of this visit was. But I assure you, I'm not working with Mr. Broussard. I guess I'm leaving here with more questions than answers now. Shit." Ray admits aloud before backpedaling. "Look, I have to... get back to this, uh, the case. Sorry to have wasted your time. But a little break from in there isn't so bad, huh?" Townes tries to divert the nervous tension away from his impulsive decision.

"Right, whatever. You guys get your shit together over there and just leave me alone, okay? I'll be here rotting away. But I won't let them break me, detective. None of you can take my sanity! They think me festering in this cell is the ultimate punishment." Landry scoffs. "I have plenty of footage to reflect on. I can escape this hell hole every night when I close my eyes." Landry declares pompously.

Townes is surprised by this display of pride and hollers for the "guards." They enter a couple of minutes later and remove the inmate. Ray watches Landry shuffle down the hall, his shackles clanking along with each tiny step. Unable to move past Landry referring to Maddison as 'number ten,' Townes suddenly feels panicked and anxious.

Raymond flees the jailhouse for his truck in the parking lot. Taking off with no destination in sight, he drives away trying to deescalate his reaction. Minutes later, Townes aimlessly parks his truck and looks up to see the Main Stays Inn hotel sign shining brightly. Realizing he arrived at Gaston's location, instant relief sets in. He gave her a quick ring to say he was nearby and needs to talk, hoping that doesn't sound too weak. Ele admits she was going to call him shortly to discuss some things in Landry's journals. She advises that Townes stop by and head up to her room, which is number 307.

Not wanting to arrive too quickly, Ray grabs the table they reunited at a few nights ago in the lounge. He stares at the empty bench where Ele sat, from his side of the booth. All the sensations that have been ruminating since her return, begin to reignite. A waiter appears, asking Ray if he was waiting for anyone or ready to place an order. Tempted, but staying strong, Ray declines, saying he's awaiting a call before heading back to his room for the night.

Proud of his refusal to drink, Ray sits back against the leather cushion and tries to gather his thoughts. His confidence doesn't linger for long realizing Gaston was already going to call him to discuss Landry's journals. Townes can't help but feel nervous and uncertain. Thinking again of Landry referring to Maddison as 'number ten,' a pit forms in his stomach. *What is happening?* He thinks to himself while trying to regain some control. Unprompted thoughts of the faceless woman from Ray's nightmares suddenly appear in glimpses. Her nude body and smoky void are displayed for the first time in his sober and conscious mind. Now more tempted to take that drink, Ray quickly makes his way closer to Ele. The experienced doctor can likely help him make sense of these invasive images and emotions.

25

Intrusive Inquisition

Walking off the elevator Ray follows signs on his way to room 307. A short stroll down the hall brings him to the other side of the threshold from his long-estranged lover. A shadowy force pours over Ray, but he's unsure where this fear comes from after having been so comfortable with Ele the last few days. Raymond takes a few more seconds to stare at the grain patterns in the wooden hotel door—while garnering courage. He finally knocks and instantly retracts. Before Ray's body allows him to pivot back towards the elevator, Ele Gaston swings the door open. She flashes her bright white teeth and ushers Ray into her room.

Ele's sweet aroma floats past as Ray enters her domain. Some nerves and fear begin to subside as her presence and familiarity put Ray at ease. His therapist doesn't even provide this much comfort and security. And yet the woman he hasn't seen in nearly two decades makes him feel like they've never skipped a beat.

Ray breaks the silence first, by thanking her for inviting him up. Gaston responds, "Oh, no problem at all. As I said, I need to discuss some things with you anyway, and in person might be best. So please, make yourself comfortable on the couch here." Ele states while pointing to the sitting area and lending that comforting smile.

Now more at ease, Ray starts by explaining his spontaneous visit to Steven Landry in jail.

Gaston asks. "Do you think Mr. Broussard really sent that threatening note?"

"Yeah. I think there is more to Jack Broussard than any of us imagined, and I plan not to underestimate the old man moving forward. What's strange is, I couldn't help but feel a connection to Landry. Maybe it's got something to do with having a tumultuous upbringing and sharing in so many unknowns the kid faced? I don't know, but I was drawn to meeting him. Then for some reason, I left doubting my ability to even do this work any longer." Ray takes a second to let that realization resonate. "Wow, I can't believe I admitted that. Holy shit, I'm losing my touch, huh? Damn, and I thought the brass would stand in the way of my career. But honestly, I'm my own worst enemy. I've self-inflicted more chaos in my life than anyone else." Ray contemplates internally for a moment. "This is not how I thought this was going to unfold," he admits.

Ray sighs and sits back on the firm burgundy hotel couch. He begins to squirm and fidget in noticeable discomfort. Ele says, "Self-reflection is important Raymond. We all have our pasts, and we have all made mistakes. Being able to identify troubling behavior, breaking patterns, and reaching out for help, is what sets you apart from a monster like Steven Landry.

Having accountability is certainly important." Gaston begins to assume a more clinical role.

Ray ponders for a moment, before concurring. "You're right, I'm not much like Landry, I guess. I fucked my own shit up anyway, especially with the bottle. I probably damaged my own development drinking the way I always have, huh?" He questions rhetorically. "Hell, I started guzzling bottles of whiskey at sixteen and never slowed down much. Even after joining the force. I hid it well at first, but it became too easy and before I knew it, it was my only coping mechanism. That didn't help much, huh, doc?" Townes asks somewhat antagonistically.

Gaston observes him rubbing his legs and can tell Ray's getting agitated and uneasy. She doesn't want to overwhelm him but needs to push a little harder to uncover the reasons for his behavior. She wants to help him with what he's been experiencing. "You're right, drinking so young and often certainly didn't help. But there were likely many factors that played into your development. Perhaps you want to use this time and my expertise to dig a little deeper? Try to discover what is causing you so much internal turmoil?"

Gaston probes a bit further. She's armed with more intel and perspective having read through Landry's journals. Ray is blindsided by the unsuspecting trajectory she takes him in. Gaston reads his confusion, ascertaining the need to aid him in connecting more dots. "Ray, I'll be honest with you, okay? Because you need this. I didn't return to my room today only to finish Angie's journals. I was awaiting some information from your records division. You know by now that Steven Landry numbered his victims. Maddison Broussard-Turner was solely referred to as 'number ten' in his journal records."

Gaston waits for Ray to nod that he understands. "Right, and we have discussed all the women connected to his dreadful reign of terror, as far as we know. There was always some confusion around Natalie Ruiz and Tina Richard though. Based on Landry's count and timeline, they cannot *both* be his victims, Ray. I read through the Ruiz file last night, as you instructed. I agree completely that Arturo is innocent. More importantly, Natalie matches one of Landry's victims completely. There is no doubt that Natalie Ruiz is in Steven Landry's count. What we weren't sure of, is how Ms. Richard fits into the puzzle. Tina Richard was found in the spring of 2001 and was believed to have been discarded the winter before. Sometime in December of 2000, correct?"

Townes agrees, trying to understand where Ele is going with this, while eagerly awaiting clarification. "Now Raymond, I want you to think back to the year 2000. After Natalie Ruiz was discovered and her case was gaining traction. I read through some personnel reports that I acquired. There were several assessments conducted by your superior officer. He identified you as 'exhibiting troubling behavior.' He made sure to annotate all your discretions. Adding that he was requesting aid and guidance for the Special Crimes Team. He was having trouble trusting your instincts Ray and they were viewing you as a liability to the force."

Townes shifts his posture and begins to get more agitated. Dr. Gaston is now dredging up an uncomfortable past that Ray tries desperately to keep hidden. Ray is terrified about what some of his blackout episodes might reveal if they were ever brought to light. "I'm sorry if this is too much for you or you need a break—" Ele trails off. Townes looks at her, realizing she is fixated on his trembling hands. She continues apprehensively. "I wouldn't normally advise this, but... do you *need* a drink?"

Ray scoffs, "No! These aren't DTs Ele, I'm actually more sober than I've been in a long time, and it's finally providing some clarity. What you're describing is a part of my life that I'm far from proud of. I only scratched the surface of these incidents with Dr. Pfeiffer. I even lie to myself most of the time. But with you, I just can't hold back." Townes realizes these deep-rooted secrets might benefit him by being released finally.

Ele replies, "Well, I'm happy to provide you with a safe place to talk. I think my professional insight may be different than Dr. Pfeiffer's." Ele is still a few steps ahead of Ray. She begins to guide Ray into recovering some deeply repressed memories from that troubling period in his past. "Raymond, when you saw the picture of Tina Richard's remains, did anything stand out to you?"

Ray works to remember her case. He tries to visualize the image, assuming he missed something that Gaston was able to piece together. His frustration intensifies as he responds, "Not that I can recall. It was mainly skeletal remains found, and from what I saw nothing specific stood out to me. I guess I'm unsure where you're going with this. What did I miss? What do *you* see?" Ray impatiently snaps at her.

"Well, you're right, seeing her postmortem, she is hard to identify. So, I called in a favor from a grad school friend, who works at Quantico. We know Tina wasn't from around here, and we only have limited information from the bars in Beau Ridge. We know Tina dyed her hair a few times and was no longer wearing glasses. But we had no updated pictures of her face and body before she died. I think it made it easy for you to forget her."

Ray shoots Ele a look of contempt, utterly appalled by her accusation. "Forget? No, I have *never* forgotten her! I can't. Not one of my cases or faces for the last nineteen years have I *forgotten* Ele, Christ. I know you haven't done police work in some time, but surely you have seen some things that are seared into your mind, right? Things that you can never unsee. How could you even say that? Forget. No!"

Ele sees this is taking a turn and attempts to reel him back in with a new approach. "Ray, my friend at the bureau has access to software that reconstructed Tina Richard's face, based on the information provided by witnesses and natural age progression. It gives us a better idea of her appearance right before her death. I have it here, and I'd like to show you. But… I need to prepare you first."

Ray interjects before she opens her laptop on the table in front of them. "Prepare me, for what?" he asks with a quiver. Raymond Townes sits up straight as Dr. Gaston pecks at the keyboard and clicks around.

Ele explains, "Based on my research, I fear that *you* may unknowingly hold another piece to this Tina Richard puzzle. You shut down during that period Ray and could have done something you never thought possible. When you get blackout drunk entire occurrences can be abandoned. Packed tightly into the crevices of your mind. Which are difficult to bring back to the surface, unless you know what you're looking for."

Ray feels entranced by her line of questioning and probing. He's unsure what Ele knows that he can't put together himself. He takes a moment to wade through the deep trenches in his disturbing memory banks. Raymond admits that in April 2000, he was in a very bad place and his drinking was out of control. He was on convalescent leave following the accident in his patrol car, then got a DUI and demoted a few weeks later. Townes had an addiction to the pornography he got from AA-Bill. He quickly realized that masturbation wasn't providing any relief at the time. He feared impotence and that he was deeply troubled. Townes was drinking excessively to drown out the intense sexual impulses, unsure where they might lead on some occasions. There were nights Ray tried to pick up hookers, yet feared getting caught. Drinking was his best option until it took over his decision-making.

Townes affirms that by the end of the year 2000, things were bleak. His return to duty without his stripes was a challenge. Ray was only a hollow version of himself and a fraction of the man he once thought he'd be. Admitting there was a severe downward spiral around the holidays. Which he tries to block out, at his therapist's insistence to 'leave the past alone and move forward.' Which Ray thought was the best course of action, up until now.

Ray puts the timeframe together, realizing December of 2000 would have been his absolute lowest point. Suddenly, he realizes he must have made a grave mistake. An error displaced in the darkness for so long, he can't bring it into focus. Still unsure what she might be referring to, Ray solicits more answers. "What did I do, Ele? Who was Tina Richard? Help me remember, *please.*" He pleads with her.

Ele turns the laptop in Ray's direction with the image blown up of the woman who they know as Tina Richard. Now in full color and with visible attributes making her easier to scrutinize. Ray takes time to study her features and think back on that period in his life. Ele sees it is starting to click for him.

Dr. Gaston persuades this unearthing of dark recollections with a recap. Reminding Raymond of the bar and location Tina may have left from that night. His hands tremble and a bead of sweat rolls down his left temple. He is on the cusp of a monumental breakthrough. Raymond Townes is finally willing to unleash some of the unsightly skeletons from his closet of despair.

26

Exposed Enigma

With sweaty palms and a bouncing leg, Ray swallows the lump in his throat. He begins to sift through the hazy details from a couple of years prior, during his rock bottom. "That's her, isn't it? Wow." Ray closes the laptop while shaking his head in disbelief.

Ele reaches out and places her hand on his. "It's okay Ray, I'm here for you. Just think back and let those reflections come to the forefront of your mind. This is your chance to release this wraith."

Ray appreciates Gaston's concern. Yet he's fearful to give in and piece together the fragments of wretched mementos. He takes a few minutes to work through the scene until it is all finally in focus. "I see it now, I see her. *She* is the woman from my nightmares. She always appears faceless—only her naked body and this grey smoky cloud where her face should be. I talked to Dr. P. about it, we always thought it was you. But we were wrong."

Ray lowers his head into his hands and distraughtly sifts through the darkness. Revisiting his last encounter with Tina Richard and her last moments of life. He takes a few minutes in silence to regain his composure. Ray suppresses the urge to hit the minibar next to them. Instead, he allows this nightmare to reconstruct in its harsh entirety, within his sober mind. After watching it all unfold, Ray's ready to proceed with the recollections of that night. Which he now sees vividly playing like an explicit movie in his mind.

Ray explains, "I was at a new bar, looking for a woman I didn't know. One who wouldn't remember me or knew who I was. She was perfect. Not a hooker or a junkie, but not stable enough to see my glaring red flags either. Tina was looking for a good time and free drinks. I told her that we could run by the liquor store and drive out to the lake. She agreed, hit the pisser while I paid the tab and met me in my truck out front. No one even saw us leaving together.

"I got us each a fifth from Taft and we split for the Lake Gerbeau. Tina wanted to go skinny-dipping, but I told her it was too cold. She didn't believe me. I remember she stripped down completely naked and walked right into the water, about waist deep. It shocked the hell out of me but turned me on too. She came darting back to the truck. She was shaking, so I pulled her into the cab, on my lap, and cranked up the heat. I held her tight and remember smelling her hair and embracing her naked body on top of me. This flood of hormones came over me. Tina chugged the last half of the second bottle to warm herself back up and I guess that put her over the edge."

Ray shifts in his spot, readjusting and trying to stay with the moment. "I remember she got very sexual after that, and things moved quickly. She said something like, 'I need to fuck, and I want you. Do you think you can handle me?' I was wasted by then—I remember slurring my words and my eyes were heavy. Whiskey was fueling my fantasies and I was ready to unleash all the pent-up sexual tension I had.

"Tina said she liked it rough and put my hands around her neck. I remember she held them there, tightly pressed against her skin. She said that I had 'big, strong hands,' and that she wanted to feel them all over her body, or something to that effect. Tina knew what she was doing. I was rock hard and ready to give her everything we both wanted. I needed it and I couldn't hold back. I'll admit, it became almost animalistic."

Ray runs his left hand through his hair a few times and stares off to the corner as he proceeds. "Tina was on top, I was choking her and letting her ride me. She was bouncing up and down and told me she was close and not to stop, so I didn't. It seemed so euphoric when she finished. I needed more! I made her bend over but couldn't get a good grip on her throat the way she wanted.

"That's when she suggested the belt. I was caught off guard and wasn't sure at first. But I was interested after seeing it in porn. I gave in completely and stopped holding back. I let out months of suppressed sexual urges and hormones on that woman. It was more than ecstasy; I was unleashing something overpowering. I almost couldn't handle it, but I couldn't stop either. She was moaning and so into it... I remember I squeezed the belt tighter. I guess it was too much. I had never done it before, so I wasn't sure how effective it was and I—"

Ray shakes his head but stays with the memory, not wanting to lose everything he's finally seeing clearly. Ray hopes Ele can handle these gruesome details as he confesses more. "She clenched up and thrashed towards me in a way that sent me over the edge. I quickly climaxed and couldn't hold back. All that energy I had expressed completely exhausted me, I guess. Plus, all the alcohol I had all day—I didn't have anything left. I passed out right there, still inside her."

Townes is deeply troubled by this admittance of guilt and takes a second to catch his breath and refocus. Ele is captivated by his recollection and patiently waits for the rest of his story to unfold. "It was maybe an hour at most that I had been out. I first thought she was asleep too, staying so still and sprawled out across the bench seat of my truck. I moved her away from my lap so I could pull my boxers up, and her body slumped down onto the floorboard. That's when her hair slipped to one side, and I could see the belt still secured around her neck."

Ray pauses while reviewing the horrific images like a digital file on display in his mind. He can visualize Tina's purple face and bloodshot eyes. The fluids pooled around her mouth. The leather seat that she was pressed into featured a similar-sized puddle of her saliva. Ray can still see it glistening in the exposed moonlight peering through the windshield. Townes continues, wanting to relinquish himself of this nefarious tragedy. "Her eyes were bloodshot and bulged out; it was a terrifying sight that is difficult to focus on. But I don't deserve the luxury of memory suppression here. I need to face this and accept what my depravity has caused. I did this, Ele. Tina Richard is *my* victim. I'm more like that monster Landry than I was willing to admit." Ray concludes in disgust.

"Ray, it was clearly an accident, and—". Dr. Gaston is interrupted as Townes dashes towards the bathroom. Tossing the door aside he slouches his 6-foot frame down, kneeling on the tile floor. Ray begins to fiercely vomit into the hotel toilet. Ele hops up to run in but stops herself in the doorway.

Clutching the porcelain rim with white knuckles, Ray violently expels years of guilt, concealment, and loneliness into the water below him. Ele Gaston wants to rush to his side and provide Ray the comfort and love she knows he deserves and needs. Yet she is bound by a strict professionalism which runs as deep as her integrity. Ele is teetering between her position as a doctor, and the urge to fall back into a role they once ignited.

Instinctively, Ele follows her heart and gives in to her ingrained loyalty to Raymond Townes. Although so far removed from their tortuous affair many moons ago. the excitement Ray once gave her and the passion he inundated Ele with still raged inside. She enters the bathroom as he's at the sink, splashing water onto his face and swishing it around his mouth. Ele soaks a washcloth in cold water, wrings it out, and drapes it across the nape of his neck. Pressing it against his skin, to bring him quick relief. He leans in close, but instead of needing intimacy, as she feared, Ray embraces her for a hug. Lifting her feet up off the floor as he stands up straight, bringing her level with him. Staring into her eyes to see if Ele shutters away and is now fearful of the man she once loved. She wraps her arms around his neck and gives in to the moment. The look on her face as they lock eyes puts Ray's soul at ease, and doubts to rest. Reaffirming in his heart that Ele is still his and reciprocates this passion. Despite his demons, her love appears unconditional.

The pair head back into the sitting area. As Ele sits down in her chair, to her surprise, Ray heads straight for the door. "Oh, are you leaving? Are you sure you don't want to gather yourself a bit longer or try to come to terms with what we just uncovered?" she asks with concerned inflection.

"No thanks. Look, I appreciate you. And what you did here tonight, this was like some voodoo shit, I can't explain it. I just know that it's kind of a lot to take in, and I... I need some time to, *process*. Holy shit look at that, you shrinks are rubbing off on me!" Ray jokes half-heartedly, trying to lighten the mood.

Ele flashes a quick smile knowing that he is mentally tougher than she gives him credit for. Remembering Ray is not her patient, yet her oldest friend, whom she intends to cherish for life. Ele opts for acceptance and gives him space. Knowing Ray must develop the emotive management and self-control to live a productive life. A life she is unsure where she fits into, if at all. Ele must give it some real contemplation now. After all this time and these incredible circumstances, she must see this through.

Nothing else is said between the two as Ele meets him at the door. Ray leans in and wraps his arm around her shoulders, pulling her into his chest. With a quick kiss on the top of her head, he exits. They part knowing how much trust they're requiring from one another. They are still the same people who fell in love so long ago. Although time and distance have certainly taken a toll on the pair.

Ele hopes Ray makes it home without stopping to buy a bottle. She also hopes that he isn't too distraught to see himself the way she has always viewed him. Perhaps her blinders give her a skewed picture of who the real Raymond Townes is. But Ele knows that he is a special man and will always have a place in her heart and life. Torn between her moral compass, professionalism, and personal feelings, Gaston goes to bed for a few short hours, to ponder her next move with a clear mind.

27

Epic Immoralities

The next morning, in the Special Crimes trailer, Chief Diehl calls for an update on the Landry case. Lt Zimmer prepares his team for the task. Within an hour they're ready to proceed. Dr. E.V. Gaston lays out the entire Steven Landry case. Putting her personal matters on hold, she illustrates the case of a serial rapist and murderer who ravaged this town for years. Right under the noses of the men who were listening to this lecture. Det Raymond Townes was in the small group. Which also included Lt Zimmer, Cpt Thompson, Chief Diehl, and D.A. Robert Lange.

A timeline will display each victim and their corresponding catalysts. The men listen intently as Dr. Gaston shares this ominous history of violence. "Gentlemen, I thank you all for being here. This sinister history is going to be difficult to hear at times. I know we're all busy, so let's get to it." Gaston hangs two pictures on the display board. One is of Landry in his military uniform, and the other is his booking photo.

Dr. Gaston says, "Steven Landry was born to Angelica Hartfield and Frank Landry, right here in Beau Ridge, in 1975. Steven's very first victim came while he was still on active duty, in the U.S. Army. The information he recorded, indicates that she was chosen after his first time out in a bar. Some guys in his unit discovered his 21st birthday was on March 15th. There was a huge St. Patrick's Day celebration downtown, in Georgia, where they were all stationed. Landry became sexually provoked by the drunk women. He describes little detail about the assault of the first woman in Georgia. Despite cross-referencing police reports in that area at the time, we have not yet identified her. We only know it occurred in March of 1996. Right after that, his behavior began to change. Landry got into trouble repeatedly, various incidents resulted in disciplinary and UCMJ action taken. Landry was eventually Court Martialed and discharged, which is why he returned to Louisiana in 1997. That unknown woman was Steven's only victim during his time in the military."

Gaston continues, "The other nine victims of Mr. Landry's have all been local to the Beau Ridge area. I will shed light on each of them briefly, to pay respect to their untimely demise. And to paint the complete picture of who you all are dealing with." Ele brings up the stack of photos she has for each corresponding victim of Landry's. Numbers two through ten respectively. Each picture was selected from friends, family, or public records, to avoid only displaying the graphic postmortem images.

"Landry's second victim was Rachel Klein. A 24-year-old Caucasian woman and Beau Ridge University student at the time. She was taken from a local bar in June of 1997. Rachel was grabbed outside, while alone and highly intoxicated. She had little memory of the abduction but knew she was kept inside Landry's pickup truck for a couple of hours. Landry's catalyst for this crime was reconnecting with his ex-girlfriend Amy Daniels, and the death of his grandfather, Clint Landry. This was shortly after he returned to Beau Ridge in 1997, following his discharge. During the attack of Rachel Klein, Landry was unable to maintain an erection. This angered him and left him feeling quite inadequate. As a result of this unfulfilled encounter, he went back out the very next night and patrolled for another victim."

Gaston closes that file and adds the next picture to their display board. "The very next evening, Steven scoured a bar not too far from where Rachel was abducted. He came across Claire Leroux outside, alone, stumbling from severe intoxication down an unlit alley. Claire awoke to being penetrated by a stranger and panicked. Steven Landry strangled Claire until she lost consciousness. He then left her partially naked, a few hours later, behind the dumpsters in that same alley from which she was taken. Ms. Leroux was ashamed and embarrassed by what happened to her. She spiraled into a deep depression after her assault. Claire refrained from reporting for a couple of weeks. Which resulted in no forensic evidence being collected. Compiled with little memory and no identifying information on her attacker, Claire's statement was difficult to use by the officers at the time. No investigation was conducted by Beau Ridge PD and Claire Leroux's statement wasn't turned over to the new Special Crimes Team. As the reporting officers felt they had nothing useful to provide the detectives."

Gaston shoots the men a look of contempt, knowing they failed this woman. "The fourth victim of Landry's was a young woman named Macey Childs. She was recently identified by our investigators who matched her report with the timeline of April 1998, after Landry's journals identified the assault details. Steven was provoked by Amy Daniels having confessed she was pregnant with his child and too far along to terminate. Landry panicked and felt out of control. He describes picking up the young Macey Childs, who voluntarily got into his vehicle, to his amazement. She was only eighteen years old and attempting to use a fake ID at a bar but was turned away. Landry says Macey was walking alongside the building alone and he offered her a ride. She propositioned him for a sexual encounter, in exchange for money or alcohol. He was disgusted with her behavior and reminded of his own mother.

"Macey Childs later reported her rape and pictures were taken of her injuries. Deep bruising surrounded her entire neck after being strangled so hard. Landry began to get more aggressive, and he evolved with this rape. This is where his desire to torture women emerged. Upon contacting Ms. Childs' estranged family, we learned that Macey committed suicide just a few months after the assault with an intentional drug overdose. The family says Macey reached out and explained the crime she endured. Informing them that she was checking into an inpatient rehab facility but needed funds. Macey's family reluctantly gave her several hundred dollars in cash. They identified her body, had a small service a week later and laid Macey to rest. They were informed by us that Macey's attacker was found and apprehended. This didn't seem to provide any solace to the family. As they are still quite distraught over the unfortunate outcome of their only daughter."

The men in attendance are beginning to show concern and anguish. Gaston knows they are only barely scraping the surface and presses on. "Steven Landry's next victim was one you all are probably more familiar with. She was Poppy Sanderson, a 22-year-old college student. It was early October 1998, and Poppy was out with friends. After becoming extremely intoxicated and combative, Ms. Sanderson was removed from the bar by security. Landry was out patrolling for his next victim. He likely discovered Poppy alone, outside, and abducted her from the parking lot. You may remember the facts of this case. She was severely beaten and left for dead, yet somehow narrowly survived the attack. Poppy Sanderson was rendered brain dead by medical staff after her arrival to intensive care. The beating Poppy sustained was ignited after Amy Daniels gave birth to Landry's son on October 4th. He was having a hard time adjusting to the changes of parenthood.

"Landry wrote about Poppy's attack, claiming to have lost control after Poppy fought back and was stronger than he anticipated. She managed to get out of the truck and Steven had to wrestle her to the ground. He had to dominate Poppy to perform the rape. He attempted to subdue her by mercilessly beating her face in and slamming her head against the ground. Landry described Poppy's eyes rolling back and her body 'going limp.' He thought he had killed her and panicked. Then promptly dumped Poppy body back at the bar.

"You all know the public outcry and media attention that case got. How vocal her mother was to get justice for her young daughter. The attention received and extensive coverage scared Steven Landry, since Poppy saw his face during their lengthy struggle, before he incapacitated her. This prompted Steven to accept a demand from Amy Daniels' father, that the two young parents get married. Steven wrote that it was a good way to 'lay low and look less suspicious.' This was a turning point for Landry, he began to get more organized and careful with his crimes. Steven appears to have decided at that moment, that he needed to kill each victim moving forward. Sadly, we know he stayed true to that commitment." All the men including Townes are shaking their heads and appear more despondent as they know where this is heading. Collectively unsure how they allowed this terror to transpire in their city for so long.

"Okay gentlemen, this next victim might be hard for some of you to accept, but I must report the facts as I know them to be true. Likewise, your department has an obligation to ensure justice is truly served." Ele Gaston takes a moment to let the men squirm and look around at each other in confusion. She feels a heaviness come over the room, as she places the next photo up on the board.

A close-up of Natalie Ruiz stares at the group. Chief Diehl shoots Cpt Thompson a look of disdain. Which has him searching for an interjection from Lt Zimmer or Det Townes. While D.A. Lange becomes flushed and places his head in his hands. The men sit in silence, smoldering. Gaston proceeds by illustrating their egregious error. "So, I'll start with the obvious, yes, we're sure. Natalie Ruiz was *not* killed by her husband Arturo, and in fact, was victim number six of Steven's. Landry's description of Natalie and the damage he inflicted matches the forensics completely.

"In April of 2000, Natalie Ruiz was abducted on her way to the neighborhood bar. Just as her husband Arturo suggested. Landry took her to an undisclosed location, where he carried out Natalie's attack in the bed of his truck. He tied her wrists and ankles to each corner, ensuring she couldn't escape like Poppy almost did. It appears, that Steven was carrying on a conversation with Natalie. He got enraged with her claims.

Unsure why a beautiful young woman would leave her children to begin with, especially for a dingy bar.

"Landry wrote that Natalie eventually admitted to being a terrible mother. Although she claimed to love her babies, she told Steven that she was never good enough. Claiming further that her marriage was failing and then to his shock, Natalie Ruiz admitted that Steven *should* kill her. Assuming it would be best for her family. Of course, Natalie couldn't have known Arturo would get blamed and subsequently convicted. And gentlemen, we can all see how quickly this spun out of control. How bad it looked for Arturo, with the initial evidence. Also, I'm sure Natalie was no more suicidal than she was deserving of her outcome. It was a desperate cry for help, which was untimely and misguided. Coupled with Landry's wife, Amy, being pregnant *again*. This time though, Steven learned the news early enough and forced his young wife to abort the fetus. Steven Landry was on edge and needed to regain dominance.

"This terrible recipe for disaster culminated in him savagely beating Natalie Ruiz. As you recall she choked on her own teeth. Her face was desecrated by Landry, while he got immense satisfaction from her murder, and his sadism fully surfaced. When Arturo was arrested, it fueled a darkened passion inside Landry, and he began to feel dangerously untouchable. His urges and sexual impulses could only be fulfilled if he inflicted more pain and damage. Which Steven knew required privacy and specific conditions."

Gaston gives the men a few minutes to gather themselves and consider what this means. Having to publicly admit to convicting an innocent man could ruin all their careers. Townes, however, knew all along that Arturo was innocent. And he's willing to take the perjury charge if needed and recant his testimony. Especially if it provides true justice and reunites Arturo with his children, Iliana and Israel.

Suddenly, Townes is stricken with intense anxiety and nervous tension, as he determined where they are in the chronology of Landry's crimes. The timeline is approaching Tina Richard's case next.

Chief Diehl told the group that he and D.A. Lange would get with Arturo Ruiz's lawyer. They will handle the outcome of the conviction and the appeal that was recently filed. Lt Zimmer tips his head to Townes in approval, but he can't find alleviation. Raymond Townes' fate and future are dependent on the next words expressed by Ele Gaston.

They all refocus and allow Dr. Gaston to complete the briefing with their full attention. "Okay, so Landry was escalating. With Amy and baby Matthew moved out, and his grandmother Norma Rae deceased, Steven was left to his own devices. Landry didn't hold back on the garage conversion and his next victim had the inaugural experience. Steven knew he wanted to keep her for a while and decided he should choose a prostitute or another homeless woman.

"It was April of 2001 when you all discovered that Landry chose Ms. Roxanne "Roxy" Williams. She was a 52-year-old former prostitute and lifelong Beau Ridge resident. Roxy had a history of medical issues from her extensive drug use in the past. Roxy was walking to a nearby store when Landry encountered her on his prowl. He kept her only about 24 hours total in the torture chamber, although it still needed work. Steven Landry hated that Roxy kept asking for a cigarette. It's a disgusting habit to him, that he blames for killing his grandmother. Norma Rae passed from lung cancer that wasn't discovered until late in stage four. Landry allowed Roxy to light a cigarette, but the smell made him nauseated. He burned Roxy with it repeatedly, then continued his torture by using a cow prod on her inner thighs after Roxy refused to open her legs. To Landry's upset, Roxy Williams suffered a heart attack and died right there in the garage.

"From there, Steven had more work to do in the garage. Allowing him more ways to perform the sadistic acts he intended to carry out. Landry also learned from his time with Roxy, that an easy target wasn't all it would take. She needed to be younger and strong enough to endure what he intended to accomplish. To satiate his nefarious appetite." Gaston closes Roxy's file and places the next photo on their board.

They have moved past the crime of Tina Richard. Ray doesn't have much time to find relief, as Gaston quickly moves on. "Steven Landry's job at Beau Ridge Animal Control took more of his time after a promotion to a supervisor role in 2002. Working so often and conducting the garage conversion, meant Landry had no other victims until late 2003. The discovery of Justine Nichols was in November, but as we know, she was abducted in September. After a late shift, leaving a bar Justine was working at, alone and on foot. Landry kept Justine Nichols in his garage for over 45 days. She was suspended on cables that he rigged up to the ceiling. To evaluate her body more completely and 'see her from all angles,' as he described. Ms. Nichols somehow came disconnected and fell onto the concrete floor, causing severe compound fractures in her legs. Steven wrote that Justine passed out for several hours after the 'reset to her main fracture.' Landry offered no pain medicine other than four aspirin and some cough syrup from inside his grandma's old medicine cabinet. When he realized Justine's wounds were becoming infected, he wanted to prolong her tenure. Landry then attempted to *treat* her infections with a rabies vaccine he had access to at work. Ms. Nichols became septic and eventually succumbed to her injuries. Steven Landry dumped her body and immediately began to look for his next victim."

Gaston has processed much of what she is explaining to these men. Yet bringing it all together is difficult for her to handle as well. "I'm sure we all need a break, but we're almost done gentlemen, so please bear with me a bit longer." Gaston pleads with her audience, who all oblige knowing the nature of their business.

"We are brought to Michaela Hardy. This is in late November of 2003, before Thanksgiving last year. Reported by her girlfriend Jazz with whom she was living in the Tent City out by the docks. The file wasn't originally drafted as a missing person's case. Despite Jazz's insistence that something happened to Michaela from the start. The officers waited to send it over to detectives, assuming that since they were young, homeless women, drugs and sex work were surely involved." Gaston refrains from scolding the men further.

Ray notices Ele biting her tongue but appreciates her tenacity as she continues. "What we know is that Michaela used a fake I.D. to buy alcohol. She was wearing a long blonde wig that matched the woman in the photo better than the short red hair she naturally adorned.

"Landry abducted Michaela Hardy and took her back to his property. There, we know she was held until her death in December of 2003. During her time with Landry, Michaela was raped repeatedly. He used foreign objects inside of her, including the same cow prod he electrocuted Roxy Williams with. Landry forced Ms. Hardy into a dress that belonged to his late grandmother. Steven wanted Michaela to also have blonde hair, but the wig was tossed around during her assaults and was matted with blood and dirt. Steven wrote about getting incredibly frustrated that the image of her in the dress wasn't satisfying him. As a result, he beat Michaela until she curled up on the floor. Steven then kicked her repeatedly with his steel-toe work boots. He unknowingly ruptured Ms. Hardy's spleen, which resulted in massive internal bleeding. While Landry was in the main house getting cleaned up, Michaela Hardy took her last breath on the cold, concrete garage floor. Alone and in agony.

"Landry describes returning and having a breakdown, crying next to her corpse on the floor. Landry was furious that he couldn't piece together this vague illusion he had only fragments of in his mind. I think he was blurring the lines between his maternal figures. More importantly, Steven was angry with himself and felt powerless because he couldn't keep these women alive long enough."

Everyone takes a second to stretch in place and understand the magnitude of this case. Dr. Gaston prepares to wrap things up while pinning the last picture at the end of the board in front of the men. "Now, we are brought to his tenth and final victim, Mrs. Maddison Broussard-Turner. She was out jogging and picked up family photos from a nearby drugstore Maddison also purchased a pregnancy test and took it before leaving the store, confirming she was pregnant with her first child. After receiving this news, Maddison departed on foot through Glendale Forest, exiting on a path that put her straight into the crosshairs of Steven Landry. He recorded only one page about Maddison, which were her last moments of life. Landry believed he had finally found the woman he was searching for all along.

Maddison had natural long blonde hair, she was athletic and beautiful. Steven came back to add to this entry, presumably later that day or the following. Claiming he almost didn't want to hurt her and that he might refrain from beating Maddison or experimenting on her. This was to keep her calm and prolong his pleasure, since his fantasy was finally coming to life. Shortly after that entry, Steven went through the backpack that Maddison was wearing on her run. Inside, Landry found some of Maddison's personal belongings, including the positive pregnancy test. Steven was devastated, adding to the entry in scribbled writing, that she's 'a liar.' Then jotting down something about her father not being a judge and never being able to find him. Steven knew at that point Maddison was too risky to keep around. Based on whatever she shared about Mr. Broussard being a Ret. Federal Judge and realizing she was pregnant, Landry knew 'they will come for number 10' as he included in the final journal entry. Before presumably ending Maddison's life via strangulation.

"That's all we have on Mr. Steven Landry, which is pertinent to his future charges. Thank you for your time, Gentlemen." Gaston concludes dismally. The men all take a moment to let this information sink in, while stretching, gathering their notes and preparing for their next step.

Chief Diehl tells the group to take the rest of the day to decompress. Adding that he has a couple of meetings to attend before he does the same. He thanks the team for their tireless work over the last few days. Everyone begins to exit the Special Crimes trailer. Townes is unsure how to approach Gaston. He overhears her explaining to Zimmer that she has another conference call and will be at her hotel to await further instructions from the team. Zimmer thanks her for her time and help with the very thorough briefing. Gaston swiftly leaves and Ray takes the hint.

Raymond Townes heads home for the evening carrying a heaviness from the last few days. The ominous discovery and news that resurfaced are still clouding his subconscious. Intense emotions and thoughts are racing through his mind. He wants nothing more than to drown out all his complicated sensations and blackout the last few days.

It takes all Ray's willpower to stay home that evening and not run to the liquor store for a bottle of whiskey. He takes only the recommended dose of sleeping medicine and manages to eventually drift off. Tossing and turning most of the night, with intrusive thoughts and nightmares plaguing his subconscious until dawn.

28

Unexpected Empathy

The next morning Townes awakes to a voicemail on his phone from an unknown number. It's Landry's public defender who simply requested Ray pay a visit to their inmate "as soon as possible." With no other information to go on, Det Townes gets dressed and heads to the jail to see what this is about.

Townes waits in the interview room for almost thirty minutes before the inmate is guided inside. Steven Landry appears even more frail and distraught now. Steven sits close to the table, waiting for the guard to exit completely before he begins speaking. "Thank you for coming detective. I didn't have anyone else to call, so I asked my attorney to reach out. I guess I needed someone to know that this might not end well for me. And I don't want that asshole to get away with taking me out." Landry concludes softly, while looking around anxiously.

Townes chimes in to clarify, "You mean Mr. B.? Has he sent another message?"

"Yes, this time he was more direct. He came here in person, late last night with a name tag on that said Frank Landry. This guy has some nerve, you know? The asshole told me that he doesn't care what my body count is or how many women I've taken. Claiming that if I try to contact any media source or share my story with another inmate, he'll find out."

Steven leans in and speaks in an almost whisper. Ensuring the group of prisoners passing by the room can't overhear. "The old bastard said that he would kill me with his bare hands if given the chance. He said I shouldn't plan to ever admit to my other crimes in court. And that he was seeing to it that I 'wouldn't have the opportunity anyway.' I don't even know what he's talking about, okay? I haven't planned to let these details out, ever. And if the D.A. doesn't want to charge me with the others, that's fine, I don't give a shit. But look, is there anything you can do, to like, get me transferred out of here or something? Please? I'll talk to your doctor, the criminologist, I'll tell her whatever she wants to know. I'll do whatever the fuck it takes to get out of here."

Townes can hear the desperation in Steven's voice and see the fear all over his face. "Look, I'm sorry to tell you this is all way out of my league. This guy clearly means business and I guess if I'm being honest, I underestimated the old bastard. But I hardly have any allies in my own precinct, let alone the reach *he* has across the city and the state. Even if you do the psych evals and they consider you unfit, I'm not sure it would help. The only facility that could house you as a criminally insane prisoner, is at capacity last I checked. Plus, he would know where you were going anyway. I mean hell, he might even have connections there too, for all we know." Townes is stricken by the wording Landry used. "You referred to the criminologist I'm working with as 'she.' How do you know it's a woman? I never mentioned that."

"That crazy asshole told me! He said that if some hot, female criminologist came in here asking questions or poking around about my family history—I wasn't to offer any details. He told me until she leaves town, I need to keep my mouth shut, and 'let the big boys work!' Or something like that." Steven concludes with a shrug.

Townes is becoming anxious and uneasy, realizing Mr. Broussard knows details about Ele and is still interfering significantly in this case. While Ray understands the position Mr. Broussard is in, he also remembers what Maddison's husband, Joey Turner said in his statement. Ray knows that this is about Jack Broussard needing something to keep busy and not about avenging his daughter's murder. It's about maintaining that control over his family and asserting his power wherever he can. Despite Steven Landry's violent history, Ray can't help but to see him as a neglected and damaged little boy.

Wanting to be useful here, Ray attempts to offer some exemption from a lifetime of questions and uncertainty. "Steven, I'll be honest, there isn't much I can do for your problem here, with the judge. But I can offer something else."

Confused and unsure what he is referring to, Landry asks Townes bluntly. "What else could you possibly be able to *help* me with in here?"

"Well, when I came here a few nights ago I mentioned that we had information on your mother, Angelica Hartfield. And before you shut me down, just take a second and listen." Landry lets out a sigh and rolls his eyes. But he awaits further explanation as requested. Townes says, "Okay, so we came across some journals that your mother wrote, during our investigation. Records she kept, with very personal details and stories. Throughout her entire life basically." Landry perks up a bit, his curiosity now piqued.

Ray continues, "I know you have an image of the woman in your mind, from what you heard growing up. Hell, I know you've seen some things coming up, that left you filled with disdain and abandonment. But you should know that your mom had a very troubled life too. Angie was mistreated and taken advantage of in every way you can imagine. Even your own grandfather made her feel uncomfortable and unwelcomed."

Steven scoffs, "Well, Clint did that to everyone, no surprise there. But I'm listening, go on."

"Right, well, I didn't have my parents growing up either. If I had some answers and information directly from them, their own thoughts and views. Even now, it might help me make sense of some of the fucked-up shit I've done." Landry offers a pursed half-smile and appreciates Townes' honesty.

"All I'm saying is that seeing her own words, from her heart and mind might… help? I don't know. Or maybe it won't. But shit, it's about all I can offer you at this point. So, take it or leave it, kid." Landry looks intrigued but confused. Townes pulls out the two journal pages he photocopied earlier, from his back pocket. He folds them up a few more times until they're less noticeable. Ray looks around to ensure no one is in sight, before passing them under the table and into Landry's hand. Steven slides them into his shoe, with the chains bound to his wrists now fully extended under the table.

Ray continues, "Give them a once-over and decide for yourself who she was. Learning something real about the woman could provide some closure. I just think you deserve to know something that isn't tainted with other people's judgment and bias." Townes concludes.

"Right. Well, thanks for coming and for, whatever that was, I guess. I gotta get out of here before one of his minions notice I'm gone. I'll see you around, detective." Landry states, before standing up and calling out for the "guards."

Townes contemplates shaking his hand but feels it would send the wrong message. He settles for a quick head nod as the inmate shuffles out the door; the loud clattering of his chains echoing off the tile floor beneath Landry as he disappears down the hall.

Raymond Townes departs the jailhouse unsure about what to do next. Still mentally exhausted with thoughts tied to this case and his past. He calls Zimmer for advice, informed that they're still awaiting guidance from the chief. Ray explains that he needs to meet with his therapist for his weekly appointment. Then he will be taking the rest of today and possibly the whole weekend off, to clear his mind. Zimmer remains empathetic and feels it's a wise choice. Advising Townes to keep his phone close for any updates but to take it easy and enjoy the weekend.

Ray's next call is to Dr. Pfeiffer's office. He updates her on the recent turn of events and how busy he is with the investigation. He claims to have a mountain of paperwork that needs to be completed by Monday. Townes assures Dr. P. that being such an integral part of this case has made his return to duty satisfying and proved a healthy distraction from his addictive traits. Dr. Pfeiffer tries to remain supportive. She reiterates that Townes can call her back if he has anything to discuss. Dr. Pfeiffer looks forward to hearing the outcome of their case and will await an update until next Friday. Ray thanks her for her time and hangs up knowing that is likely the last session they will have.

Townes feels his time slipping within the force. Dr. P.'s expertise would be better spent on patients who are more receptive to her strategies and have the longevity to utilize them. Ray is ready to carry out what he has been wanting to do since Ele returned.

He starts making his way in her direction, unsure if she will even be in her room. On the way, Ray instinctively stops at a liquor store and buys a small bottle of whiskey. Chugging it down on the drive to her hotel, Ray begins to feel the warmth take over and his inhibitions subside. The nerves and fear diminish as he gets closer to Ele.

Pulling into the parking lot Ray finishes the last shot of liquid comfort. The final boost needed to fulfill a mission several decades in the making. Unsure if Ele will be receptive to him and his liquored-up advances. Ray knows his time is dwindling with her, and if Jack Broussard gets his way, Gaston will be gone soon, and this case will close forever. Raymond can't risk letting Ele slip away again, without finally confessing what is in his soul and the truth he has known for so many years. Ray knows right now he needs to see her and feel her. The rest he decides, will be up to Ele.

29

Arousing Ardor

Ray stumbles off the elevator and a flood of hormones begins to take over. He tries to regain his composure as he approaches room 307. Ray hesitated for a few seconds before pounding twice. A rush of adrenaline comes over him like a tidal wave. As he is about to knock again, the door swings open. Ray is greeted with Ele's gaze and timeless beauty.

"Well, hello Raymond. I wondered how long it was going to take you. Come on in." she says with sultry certainty.

"You were waiting for me?" he asks, hoping that her response will be the sign he needs to proceed.

"Of course. I know we have more to discuss, and you left in a hurry. I didn't want to overwhelm you or push too hard. I thought it would be best to let you come to me. And here you are. *Finally*." She ends with a crooked smile, melting Ray at this moment.

"Ele, look, I don't want to waste any more time. I've been thinking about you since the day you left Louisiana. I've always imagined what I would do if you ever returned. If we ever got a second chance."

"Ray—" Ele attempts to interject.

He silences her with his finger to her lips. "Ele, please. Let me get this out. Okay?" he states before removing his hand.

Ele Gaston can't help but feel turned on and she needs to see what Ray has to say. She gestures for him to proceed.

"I have played our affair over in my mind almost daily, for the last fifteen years. You were all I thought about while I was married. You were who I longed for with every woman I have been with, since 1988. You are who I fantasize about and the only woman I have *ever* loved. I'm sorry if this is too much to handle or not what you wanted to hear. I know you came here to do a job and not for me. But dammit you're here now and I just—" Ray bites his lip while holding back from finishing his sentence.

After a moment Ray proceeds with his heartfelt confession. "Ele, I need you. *Please.* You're my weakness and losing you has been my deepest regret—" Before he can continue, she reaches out and grabs his hand. Pulling him close to her. Ray takes that as an invitation but confirms first. "Can I have you?"

She mutters, "Yes."

Ele closes her eyes as Raymond takes her into his arms and kisses her passionately. Ray picks her up and cradles her as he walks them over to the bed. He lays her down. Ripping open her silk button-down blouse, he looks her over with hungry eyes. Ele eases into him and starts to give in to the moment. Years of unfulfilling sex and lonely nights have brought her back to this man. When she is most deprived of attention and at her peak of sexual frustration. Ele can't think of a better person to take care of her needs and give her the liberation she has been longing for.

Ray unclips her bra and removes it along with her blouse. Tossing the garments onto the dark carpet beside their bed. Slowly licking and suckling her breasts as she begins to heat up and yearn for him. Ray takes his time, tracing his tongue around her nipples. Grabbing her with his big hands and squeezing tenderly while reacquainting himself with Ele's anatomy. He remembers every sensitive spot and finds new fine crevices and areas to caress. Time has only made Ele Gaston sexier.

Ray pushes her navy-blue skirt up towards her stomach, and rips open her tan pantyhose at the crotch. She moans softly as he kisses her inner thighs. His tongue traces its way across her soft skin. A chill comes over Ele's body. She leans into his touch and gently thrusts towards his face, wanting more. He takes off her panties while looking into her eyes. Which are now rolling back in seductive preparation for his next move. A long overdue passion takes over when he puts his mouth on her. Taking time to lubricate her thoroughly, he swirls around in circles and then vigorously vibrates his tongue up and down. He reaches up and caresses her breasts with one hand. The other pushed her legs out of the way. Spreading them open and giving himself the best angle to sensually bring her to the peak of pleasure. Ele rolls her body into his face and matches his motions with her rhythm. Ray is rock hard now hearing her moan and give into him. He loves every part of her voluptuous body in his care and delights at this moment while she erupts for him.

Ele calls out breathlessly, "I'm almost there; please don't stop."

Ray can feel her legs trembling around him. She releases into his incredibly satisfying oral performance. Pulling the pillow over her face to muffle the sounds she can't help but express. Still shaking and dripping for him, Ele slowly rocks on the bed as the sensations pass through her. Ray lays next to her to watch her reaction, allowing her satisfaction to linger a few more moments. He patiently waits for her to regain composure before placing her hand on the bulge in his pants. She looks over at him, biting her bottom lip and barely able to open her eyes. Experiencing so much euphoria now, but still wants to return the pleasure. She strips down completely naked and crawls back onto the bed over Ray. She helps to remove his shirt and unbuckles his pants while looking into his eyes.

"That was amazing." She whispers while assisting him in pulling his pants and boxers down. Ray keeps them bunched around his thighs, but Ele shakes her head and pulls them off. Leaving him fully exposed and elated, considering how long he has waited to be back in this position. She crawls back on top of him seductively. Ele licks Ray up and down, taking in every inch of him. Carefully working her tongue around his shaft as he becomes fully engorged. His reactions express that her performance is still up to par. He grabs her head and face as she bobs around his lap. The sounds turn him on of Ele slurping and sucking up saliva, so he can glide in and out. Ray thrusts his body towards her mouth in a vigorous repetition. She feels sexy and desired right now, knowing the pleasure she's bringing him is beyond an orgasm. Ele feels the intense intimacy they share while the energy transfers between them. Ray finishes and throws his head back onto the bed, enthralled by the pure gratification she brings him.

They lay together naked and holding each other, allowing themselves to be present in this blissful moment. There's no need to communicate beyond what their bodies dictate. Eventually, enough time has passed. Ele feels Ray becoming erect again and knows he's ready for round two. This time they make love, enjoying every motion and position. Their bodies remember each other and rekindle the intense ecstasy they once shared with ease.

Before Ray peaks, he whispers in her ear, "I've missed you." Ele gives in at the same time, allowing herself to climax simultaneously. They hold onto each other tight to treasure these sensations. For the next few hours, they lay there naked, laughing and smiling in pure bliss. They take turns caressing and exploring each other's body and giving in to the moments for intimacy when they arise. Once exhausted, they pass out in the bed together, each in need of some overdue rest.

Ray awakes to Ele already out of bed a few hours later. Walking into the bathroom he finds her soaking in the tub, filled with steamy water and bubbles. "Hey there good looking," she utters to him with a smile.

"Can I join you?" he asks seductively.

"I was just getting out, but you can take a shower if you want. I ordered us some food, and it should be here shortly, otherwise I would join you," she affirms with a crooked smile.

"Great, I'm starving, you took a lot out of me." They share a laugh at his unintended pun. Ray watches her climb out of the tub and hands her a towel. Then brings her close and kisses her on the forehead. Ele leans into his embrace finding security in his arms. They want to savor the lust and continue with the erotic adventures, yet some deep conversations are imminent.

Ray showers while she gets the food inside from room service. He comes out with a towel around his waist, observing Ele setting up their meal in a robe with her hair in a loose bun, looking as radiant as ever. She tosses him the other bathrobe and tells him not to worry about clothes yet. He grins and they each sit down to eat at the crowded coffee table.

"I wasn't sure what you wanted, so I got a couple of samplers and every dessert they had to offer. You know I have a sweet tooth," she explains with a wink. Ray confirms that it all looks great, and she chose well. They take time to enjoy the meal and refuel their famished bodies.

After dinner, Ele moves to the small couch he is sitting on and kicks her feet up onto his lap. He begins to rub them soothingly and Ele sighs in relief. "I spoke with Zimmer before my bath," she explains.

"Oh yeah, how did that go?"

"It was fine. I told him that my other case was gaining some traction and that I would need to stay here to work on it. I said I'd give your department the weekend to decide if they need anything further from me. Before I plan to head out."

Ray gets a little dim with the thought of her leaving so soon. He attempts to shake that sentiment and remain in this moment while they can. "Yeah, I spoke with him earlier too and told him I was taking the weekend for some personal time. He thinks I am with my therapist. Which I guess, I technically am." Ray says with a smirk. Ele snickers at the irony.

"Do you have another case right now?" Ray asks.

She shakes her head no with a sly look. Ray enjoys this side of her. "Well then, it looks like we have some free time to ourselves, finally!" Raymond proclaims.

"Would you like to stay the night?" she asks sheepishly, as if she doesn't already know his answer.

"If you thought I was leaving any time soon, you have another thing coming woman. In fact, enough talking let's go back to bed, now!" Ele lets out a little squeal as he pulls her up from the couch and guides her to the bed. The two spend the rest of the night reacquainting themselves. A couple more love-making sessions take place. Both ensures the other is fully satisfied before they drift off to sleep in each other's arms.

The two lovers awake Saturday morning with the sunrise gleaming through the eastern-facing window. They beam with residual happiness; entangled in the bedsheets and both still naked from their intense intimacy last night.

"Good morning, Mr. Townes," Ele whispers while rubbing Ray's chest, before resting her head on his stomach.

"Good morning to you, Dr. Gaston," he responds with a smile plastered on his face. This is exactly where he has wanted to be for so long, Ray almost can't believe it's finally happening. They stay that way for another hour. Soaking up each other's energy and basking in the moment. Ray strokes her long brown hair softly and she gingerly traces circles on his torso with her nails.

After brunch and a shower that they shared, which resulted in one more hot steamy sexual experience, the pair returned to the bed. Finally, having reached the apex of pleasure.

Several hours later they order dinner from room service once more. After their meal, Ele pours a large glass of wine, then offers Ray a drink, which he declines. They sit on the couch while she gulps through a few glasses. They get lost in casual conversation about their world views and current interests.

Ele picks up the bottle for a refill and realizes she finished it. Ray notices she seems bothered and might have something important to discuss. "Look I wasn't sure how to navigate back to this and I hope it doesn't ruin the mood, but I do need to thank you again. For assisting in recovering some of those memories I had buried away. I still have a lot of guilt about it all and I know it was an accident, but I guess I'm torn on how to proceed. Part of me feels like I owe it to the woman and her family, to confess. You know they deserve answers, and she should have justice. I've been racking my brain for the right solutions and how to move on from this. What do you recommend, Ele?"

"Well, first, you're welcome. I'm always here to listen. As your friend, I feel like your heart is in the right place. As your clinician and a former officer of the law, I can tell you that it won't end well. Obviously, you would be charged. Even if they believed you and went with manslaughter, they would use your career against you. But I don't see them taking your side, Ray. We both know you have a rocky history with this department. Honestly, you have one foot out the door already and I don't see the point in doing that to yourself. That may sound selfish, and perhaps it is. I know you've made your share of mistakes. But that job is challenging, and you weren't equipped to handle it for a long time. The department waited until you were a liability to them. Do you think you're the only one they've done this to? Hell, police departments all over the Country have jaded detectives and officers who are barely coping with life and the consequences of their careers. Self-medicating and over-indulging in sex and alcohol to mask the real problems. No one wants to address the root of the issues and change the way we handle stress and trauma. Then they all act stunned when people spiral out the way you did. I'm not saying every department is producing murderers and alcoholics every day. And I am not saying that's what you are. But Ray, I don't think this is *all* your fault." Gaston reaches out and grabs his hand.

"You could have been in a better place if you received treatment sooner. Not to say Tina Richard's family doesn't deserve answers. But it could do more harm than good at this point. Your guilt and anguish are significant, and you must carry that with you, forever. You can make amends in ways that could surpass anything our broken system might deem necessary. Do something beneficial for her family. That is what I recommend. And not because I love you and don't want to see you rot away in a jail cell. But because I know your remorse is genuine and you are *nothing* like Steven Landry. Or any of the monsters we lock up out here, Ray. Please remember that." Ele concludes while holding his face in her hand. She looks into Ray's eyes and supplies him with a reassuring smile to comfort his heart.

"You love me?" he asks with a head tilt.

"Of course, I do! But is that all you took away from that monologue?" Ele asks with vexed concern.

"No, I was keeping it lighthearted. I appreciate your confidence in me and your support." Ray says with genuine adoration while holding her hands close to his heart. "And you're right, I suppose. Bearing in mind how long it's been, and my history with 31st. Maybe I should try to move on and make the most of my get-out-of-jail-free card. I suppose dealing with my secrets and shame for life is a heavy burden to bear. Not the retribution to fit the crime, but I'll make the most of it. I'll think of a way to make this right. Thank you, Ele. You help me see the good I never thought existed in myself." Ray remarks with esteem.

She nods, and they share a moment of silence to reflect and sort their thoughts. After a few minutes and a deep breath, Ele looks away quickly. Ray notices she's trying to brush away some tears from her cheek. "Hey, what's going on with you? Is everything okay? Time for you to share something to me?" Raymond asks nervously.

Ele softly utters, "Yes." Looking up at him, she closes her eyes and tears stream down her face. Concern sets in as Ray begins to imagine what's bothering her. He gives her time to collect herself.

They might not have another opportunity, so Ele feels now is the best chance to get this off her chest. After another long sigh, she grudgingly starts. "I don't know how you'll take this, but it's long overdue. Ray, there's another reason I stayed so far away from Louisiana, for so long. I wanted to return many times. I wanted to reach out and see how you were. I even thought about trying to give us another chance after the divorce and Stewart sharing his *news*. There was always something that held me back. A secret I've kept inside since 1988. You might hate me when you find out. But please know that I'm sorry and I always had your best interest at heart. I thought I was doing the right thing, okay?" Ele claims through teary eyes. Ray looks at her confused, unsure where this is going he anxiously awaits an explanation.

"You remember I told you that I lied to Stewart and his mother, Opal—for them to dislike me and make the divorce easier on us all? Well, what I told them wasn't exactly a lie. In fact, it was true. But I altered some details to make it fit. I explained to his mother that when we first moved to Texas, I found out that I was pregnant with Stewart's child. I informed them that I wasn't ready to be a mother and needed to figure out my career and life. So instead of sharing the news with Stewart and his family, I made the selfish decision to terminate the pregnancy. Alone.

"Like any indoctrinated Christian, the only thing Opal Miles despises more than homosexuality is abortion. Stewart's mother was livid and refused to believe it at first. Until I proved it by showing her the ultrasound photo, I had received at a pregnancy center. It was early, only about six weeks. It was this tiny little blip on the screen, and it looked like a grain of rice in the photo. My information was on the top, so she knew it was real."

Ele expels a deep sigh before concluding, "It was selfish and unnecessary, now that I look back. But at that moment, back then, it felt like my only option. It was my choice, so I must live with it." She wipes away more tears and looks to Ray for a reaction.

"So, you were pregnant? You had an ultrasound and confirmed it?" he asks with confusion.

"Yes, I was," she affirms.

"Then I'm confused. What was the lie?" Ray asks, looking at her with a shoulder shrug. Ele stares at him with remorse in her eyes and more tears stream down her face. Suddenly, Ray is aware of the falsehood and realizes what she did. Unsure how to feel, he knows he needs to ease her pain and take away some of this burden she has borne alone for so long.

Raymond reaches out and takes her hands in his. He wipes away her tears and pulls Ele close. Ray whispers to her for confirmation, "It was mine?" Ele nods, while sobbing into his chest. He wraps her up and holds her there for several minutes until she calms down.

"I'm so sorry, Ray… I should have—" he interrupts and hushes her. He gives Ele time to get it all out and waits patiently for her to overcome this emotional breakdown.

Ray strokes her hair and calmly says, "You don't have to explain anything to me. I know you made a difficult choice; one I can't imagine. I love you, Ele, and I trust you. Don't worry about what's already done. I hold nothing against you and never will. Just breathe, baby. I got you, and I will stay here as long as you need me. I'm so sorry you had to go through that alone."

Ele Gaston is so relieved and overcome with emotion. She lets years of covert pain and unspoken suffering pour out for the next couple of hours. Ray holds on to her and sheds a few tears in silence. Thinking of the possible outcomes that could have occurred if he had been aware sooner. He acknowledges their affair created a secret love child. That, although taken away too soon, was established from the heart, much like their relationship. It was grown in a place of beauty and respect. Being able to rekindle their intimacy and bond so easily only reaffirms that Ele is special to Ray and will always have a place in his heart.

They fall asleep together about an hour later in room 307. Simply enjoying each other's company, love, and unwavering support. Appreciative of the limited time they have left to share this feeling and this bed. All that matters is that they're here, tethered by a history that will surpass any challenge in life—if they allow each other in. No amount of time, miles of separation, or daunting situation has proved too insurmountable for this pair

30

Premature Departure

On Sunday morning, the couple awoke to Ray's cellphone buzzing from the small table beside the bed. He answers it reluctantly to see what Lt Zimmer needs. Not yet ready to return to the world outside Ele's hotel room, they each hope its unimportant.

Ray abruptly sits up, in shock by the news he is hearing. A few quick responses on his end, of "Wow, okay," and "Roger that," has Ele curious about the call. Ray hangs up and looks over at her with a glum face.

"What's up?" she asks.

Ray informs her that, "Steven Landry is dead. Found in his cell last night, during midnight checks. They're calling it a suicide. Zimmer said there's more information about the case but wants me to come in to hear the rest in person."

As Townes began to locate his articles of clothing scattered across the room, Ele's phone rings from her side of the bed. As expected, it's Zimmer. She answers and acts as if she's hearing the news for the first time. She agrees to come into the office for more information.

Moments later, the two are ready to go, in the hotel parking lot, about to head out. Ele began telling Ray she would see him over there when they both noticed that his truck has a dead battery. She offers him a ride to save time.

Most of the drive was quiet, until Ray finally spoke. "It doesn't make sense—I don't get it. Landry was adamant about not breaking in there. I mean, he was rattled by Judge Broussard and felt unsafe. He even admitted the death penalty was better than rotting away in a cage. But suicide? No, I don't see it."

Unsure if the information about Landry's mother might have pushed him over the edge, Ray suddenly harbors guilt. He was Steven's last chance for aide and now feels he should've done more to ensure his safety. Townes never imagined being so sympathetic to a serial rapist and murderer. Especially one he apprehended.

Ele tries to reassure Ray that there wasn't much he could've done or seen coming. "We know Steven Landry didn't have adequate coping mechanisms. He had deep-rooted abandonment issues and was backed into a corner, Ray. You can't always predict how a psychopath will react to stimuli or circumstances. Although, his state of mind and what he shared with you are interesting. I didn't expect this would happen so soon." Ele finishes while staring ahead in deep thought.

Arriving at the Special Crimes lot a few minutes later, the two are stunned by what they see. Several cars and a white van with Federal Bureau of Investigation logos are displayed. Federal agents in navy blue jackets are walking out of the trailer with evidence boxes in hand.

Townes and Gaston watch in awe from the parking lot as the past few weeks of extensive investigation are removed by strangers. Years of police work that Townes has spent countless hours pouring himself into are being carted off. Ele can see the anger and frustration mounting inside of Ray.

Zimmer notices the pair approaching, so he walks over to greet them and explain. "Hey guys, glad you both made it. So, all we know is that Landry was found hanged in his cell during midnight checks last night. From what I'm told, they're ruling it a suicide. There was no note found, so we're unsure of the reasoning. We're still waiting on an official report from the jail. It seems that Landry's body has already gone to a private funeral home to undergo cremation."

Ray glares at his lieutenant, dumbfounded by the words he heard. Zimmer attempts to reason with him, "I know! I was as blindsided as you are, Townes."

"How is that even possible? Nothing in the system moves this fast. It's a goddamn Sunday after all; what the fuck is happening here, sir?" Townes demands answers with increasing contempt.

"It appears some favors were called in. From what I have gathered, an 'anonymous private donor' is involved, and has covered the cost of having Landry's remains taken care of. At this point, everything is way past my pay grade and out of our hands. I'm sorry it's ending like this, though. Truly." Zimmer states with empathy.

Ray looks around the crowd gathered and those moving throughout the trailer. His eyes fix on some men across the lot. He realizes it's Jack Broussard shaking hands with Chief Diehl. Jack appears to be introducing the chief to an FBI agent. Ray shakes his head in disbelief and tells Gaston and Zimmer that he understands what is going on now, adding that they "should've seen this coming."

Just then, Gaston is tapped on the shoulder by an old colleague whom she hasn't seen in years. She excuses herself from the two men and walks away to catch up with her friend. Raymond Townes is at a breaking point with this case and the entire Beau Ridge Police Department.

"Look, sir, I admire all your work here. And I appreciate you going to bat for me and getting my badge back. I wasn't sure how this would end up, but *this* isn't right. I can't sit back and pretend to be capable of keeping up with the never-ending bureaucratic bullshit here. I'm just not cut out for this anymore. I can't bite my tongue or hold back any longer. I'm sorry, but I'm out. I can feel it in my bones."

Zimmer looks at him with uncertainty and asks, "Townes, are you sure about this?" The lieutenant understands he is serious when Ray hands over his badge and gun.

"Do me a solid and contact Joey Turner, Maddison's husband. He deserves some answers and an honest update. I know that asshole isn't going to share the truth." Ray states while gesturing towards Mr. Broussard with a scowling glare.

Zimmer nods his head in agreement before Ray continues. "Send me the paperwork, sir. I'll sign whatever I need to. If I lose my pension, so be it. I'm sorry, but this is how it needs to be. Good luck to you, Zimm. Don't let them break you, man. And hey, that offer on the *Cayenne Cruiser* still stands. You know how to reach me, whenever you're ready." Ray concludes while reaching out to shake hands with his superior officer and friend.

Just like that, Raymond Townes walks away from nearly two decades of a career that has consumed most of his life. While he's contemplated retirement for years, this decision was spontaneous. Ray realizes that if he remains on active duty, he will soon do something irrevocable. Townes waits for Ele against her rental car, staring at the scene while shaking his head.

On their drive back, Ele wasn't expecting to hear that Ray impulsively relinquished his badge and gun. Townes explains that too often he sees how negatively this job has affected him and how little patience he has left for it. Unsure what more he has to offer and how it could help him in any way to remain on the force, Townes feels now is the best time to part ways. He adds, "Plus, they can't threaten me anymore. Or hold my retirement over my head. I walked away on my terms, and something about it feels liberating!"

"Well, I can understand that. And I'm proud of you, Ray!" Gaston confirms.

Ray agrees that it's a big choice but is confident he's finally capable of moving on from this precinct and his rocky career.

"That's good. But I hope seeing the FBI take away those boxes of evidence didn't sway you. We both know that Tina Richard's case wasn't included in those files. Even if your department wanted the bureau's take on it, I assure you there'd be no way for them to link you to her death." Ele claims.

Ray nods, "Yeah, but that wasn't why I did this. Honestly, I'm at peace with this decision and my past indiscretions. I'm no more worried about them solving her crime than I am confessing if given the opportunity. I'm going to keep pressing forward and try to figure out my next step. But thank you, and I'm sure you're right."

Back at the hotel, the pair remain in her car for a while longer, discussing their next steps. They contemplate what the future might look like and how they should each move on from this. Ray is ready to relinquish some control and see how things unfold naturally. Knowing that if he attempts to hold onto Ele too tightly, he may get pushed away again. Possibly never getting another chance to find his way back into her life. Ele Gaston has her own big decisions to make, so Ray allows her to work through some thoughts and ideas.

Ele states, "I've been thinking about what you told me after our interview with Amy Daniels. You mentioned that if I ever stopped chasing the bad guys, I could have a role with the victims."

"Survivors." Ray corrects her with a smirk.

"Right, of course. My mistake. Survivors they are! I love forensic psychology, but these cases I've worked on since being out of school are becoming harder to process. I've always been able to find a healthy separation from my work. Yet you must delve deep into the minds of these criminals to be good at this work. Going to those dark places so frequently takes its toll. I'm willing to see what it looks like to walk away for a while. To try a different route myself." Ele admits.

"Well, look at us, advancing and making moves over here. Who says we can't evolve with the changing times?" Ray states lightheartedly. Then he asks, "So, how will that work for you? What do you think the first move is?"

Ele ponders for a moment. "I have a colleague who has a therapy practice in Florida. I've been thinking a change of scenery would be a good start. I love Seattle, but Washington is gloomy, and it affects my mood and motivation. I could sublet my apartment for a few months. Make a move to Florida and do some networking. See which opportunities present themselves in a clinical role. I want to do some good and help trauma survivors move forward. To live healthier, more productive lives. I want to ease them into the survivor mentality and show them what's possible with the right resources." She determines with confidence.

"Right on. That sounds like a great idea Dr. Gaston. I know you'll do awesome at that. I wish you all the best."

"Thank you, Raymond. I appreciate that. And I truly appreciate our time here. Having this opportunity to work with you once more was amazing. I didn't expect to watch you walk away from almost twenty years of police work under my watch. But I'm thankful I was by your side while you ended this case and this chapter in your life. Getting to share this weekend with you was memorable. And the most satisfied I have been in decades!"

They laugh together and reflect fondly on the last couple of nights. Not wanting to prolong the inevitable, Ray makes a move towards departure. He uses some jumper cables from his truck and juices his battery up. Standing next to his pickup, Ray takes Ele into his arms once more. Ele rests on his chest for a minute before he pulls away and looks down at her face. He sees a few tears fall from her eyes.

"Hey, it's okay. Don't start that now; you know this isn't goodbye. It's, 'I'll see you later,' okay?"

Ele slowly nods, clenching his arms in her hands, not ready to let go. "I'm sorry, you know I'm terrible at goodbyes," she admits through sniffles.

"Yes, I remember. But again, this isn't one. We had a great time, for the most part. I'm so glad you came back here for this opportunity. I'm happy that we got to share so much and had another chance to be together. Our bond is special. You are special. This isn't over, Ele. I love you and won't let you go so easily again." Ray states with certainty.

Ele hugs him tightly, and they share one more extended kiss. "I'm not sure where we can go from here, but I always want you to be a part of my life moving forward. I'm sorry it took me so long to find my way back to you, Ray. I love you too, and I won't stay gone for long this time, I promise." Ele states with an ache in her voice.

He kisses her forehead and tells her to call him when she arrives home after her flight. "You know where to find me." Ray chimes in with a wink as he gets into his truck. She blows him one more kiss and smiles as he pulls away. With a slow wave, Ele watches until Raymond Townes fades down the road in the distance.

Epilogue

A month later, Raymond Townes is heading out for a day of fishing on the lake. He pulls into a gas station not too far from home and begins to fill up his truck and the *Cayenne Cruiser*. Waiting next to the pump, watching it slowly tick away, Ray sees a man approaching his direction. With a large straw hat and sunglasses, Ray can't make out his face until he gets closer.

Suddenly he realizes it's Mr. Jack Broussard, and Ray is taken aback. Unsure what he would be doing at *this* gas station, so far from home. As he approaches, walking with a purpose, Ray determines that this is an intentional encounter. He gives Jack a once over, trying to gauge the nature of this visit, and notices Jack has something in his hands.

"Hello, detective, nice to see you out finally. Looks like you picked a good day for fishing, huh?" Jack Broussard says to Ray after glancing up at the clear sky above them.

Jack hands Ray a large manilla envelope that is sealed shut. "This is for you. I must thank you for that extra piece of the puzzle. It really helped the bureau take interest in our case and move as quickly as they did."

Ray grabs the envelope and before he can conjure any intelligent response, Mr. Broussard continues. "I wanted to let you know it was a wise choice to walk away from the department. I appreciate you and your girlfriend making this easier on me by departing so quietly too. I wasn't sure what you were doing at that hotel Saturday night, but when you two showed up together, it made sense." Jack concludes with a smirk.

He continues while Ray tries to keep his jaw from dropping. "I know you don't have much to live for, and might not understand fighting for what you believe in. My family name and legacy are dependent on my values. I couldn't let some sick punk get away with taking something so precious from me. I refused to let my daughter be the last victim of some sensationalized serial killer. Perhaps you will understand one day. Until then, you should continue to stay out of the way and let the big boys get the work done, okay? Just know I'm always around. If you keep your head down and your mouth shut, you'll be fine." Jack concludes with a wink.

Ray stares at him in silence. Uneasy with this interaction and in awe of this man's audacity—Ray's rendered speechless. Jack Broussard grins and bows his head while tapping the brim of his straw hat. "Thanks for your time. Enjoy your day, Raymond"

Without a reaction or a single word uttered, Ray watches Mr. Broussard walk away casually. Once the sportscar was out of sight, Ray opens the envelope to see what the contents are. He pulls out two papers that he quickly realized were Angie's journal entries. The exact ones he photocopied and left with Landry before he was found dead in his cell a day later.

"This fucking guy," Ray says aloud, growing enraged. Townes considers his words and suddenly determines that this confirms the theory he's had for weeks. Mr. Broussard *is* responsible for Landry's death. Shaken and irritable, realizing he's unsure what exactly this old man has in store for the future. Ray decides he's ready to make some moves. He rings Ele Gaston on the phone, and she answers as she's embarking on the next step in her career.

"Hey Ray, how are you? I'm boarding now and will be in Orlando in a few hours. Should I call you back when I land?"

"Yeah, do that, please," he utters, shakier than he expected.

"Okay, I will. Is everything alright?"

Now trying to sound more upbeat, Ray continues as if this is a casual call. "Yep, everything is fine. I just can't wait for you to get there so I can come to visit and see what Florida fishing is like. After my trip to the west coast for our Valentine's Day festivities, I can't wait to travel again, and of course, to see you."

"Well, you can make arrangements as soon as you're ready. I can't wait to see you again either. I'll call you back when I arrive in the Sunshine State!!" she retorts with excitement.

"Sounds good. Later Ele. Safe travels."

"Bye Ray, talk to you soon love."

Ray feels a calm come over him again. He takes off in the direction of Lake Gerbeau. Ready to cast a line and cruise out on his little bass boat. Trying to forget that he has people who still have eyes on him.

A trip to Florida is feeling like a good move right now. Heavy decisions for his future are looming and Townes knows this excursion will provide the best environment to make these plans. A smile effortlessly slides across Ray's face as he sees the lake water glistening in the afternoon sun.

Back to his peace, finally.

-THE END-

Thank you so much for reading my first novel!
Please consider leaving a **review on Amazon** and
recommending this story to others.

Below are the **mental health and veteran resources** as
promised.
If you or someone you know is struggling, please reach
out, find help, or offer guidance. No one should suffer
alone or in silence.

Veteran's Crisis Line:
1-800-279-8255; press 1 or text 838255
https://www.veteranscrisisline.net
Stop Soldier Suicide:
844-889-5610
Lifeline for VETS:
888-777-4443
https://nvf.org/veteran-resources/

National Suicide Prevention Lifeline:
1-800-273-8255 or text TALK to 741741
https://suicidepreventionlifeline.org/
**Substance Abuse & Mental Health Services
Administration (SAMHSA):**
1-800-662-HELP (4357) https://www.samhsa.gov/find-
help/national-helpline
BetterHelp: (Online Therapy and Counseling Services)
betterhelp.com

Acknowledgments

This book and my entire life as a writer wouldn't be possible right now, if not for my husband, Jarrod. Babe, you are the absolute best support system, and partner to share this beautiful world with. You have believed in me and my potential before I even found my deepest passions. I don't know how you deal with our beautiful chaos, but you handle it valiantly. I can't thank you enough for always dreaming big with me and holding me accountable every step of the way. I love you!

My very helpful beta audience had the first look at my words and provided my initial validation and confirmed that I was on to something. Thank you all so much for finding the time to read through my rough drafts and for your feedback. Joanie, Briseida, Swayla, E.M., Sara, Courtney, Nicole, Erica, Dree, and Tracie. You all were so excited for me and jumped on the opportunity to aid in many ways. I appreciate your contributions and support.

To Nate, my battle and friend, bro I have the utmost appreciation for your time, and in-depth constructive feedback. You became a full critique partner and really stepped up when I needed that extra pair of eyes and perspective for my story. Thank you so much for everything. I hope you enjoy the final version.

Nik, my cousin, and cover creator thank you so much for helping me out with this project, I appreciate your time and expertise so much!

To my beautiful girls, my *forever* inspiration, but especially when I write. They can't read this story yet, but they know what this book means to me. Olivia, Pen, Kam, and Mireya, I will always strive to make you proud. Love, Mama.

About the Author

 This debut novel from indie writer Amanda Purser comes after a long journey to being published. She served in the Army until 2012 and has been raising her daughters and continuing her education while researching her next path. She writes from a perspective of a woman-combat-veteran and brings personal experiences of childhood trauma and PTSD to her work.

Amanda and her husband Jarrod started Queensbriar Press publishing company, in December of 2021, to get her stories out, on their timeline. They are excited for their aspirations to bloom, as their future entrepreneurial plans unfold. Amanda is working on Book 2 in the Cost Series and looks forward to sharing details about that and all her future projects soon.

Be sure to follow her journey in indie publishing and writing. She supports fellow veterans, especially disabled-women-veterans. She is passionate about mental health awareness, veteran resources, and therapy options.

Private FB Group: Imperial Indie Writer
www.facebook.com/groups/imperialindiewriter/

Sign up for our emails and get more info:

www.queensbriarpress.com

Made in the USA
Coppell, TX
16 December 2022